CANDLELIGHT
Supreme

"WHAT IF I PROPOSED TO YOU, MAX?"

He took his time answering. "I thought you liked being single, Angel."

"Don't you ever get lonely?" she asked him.

"I didn't take a vow of celibacy after my divorce, Angel, just a vow of detachment." He studied her carefully. "Up until now, I haven't had any trouble keeping that vow."

Angel's hand moved to his chest. "I made the same vow when Lou and I split up."

Max felt a shiver of delight at her tantalizing caress. "How are you doing now?"

"Lousy," she confessed, her hand moving down his body . . .

169 NIGHT OF THE MATADOR,
Lee Magner

170 CAPTURED BY A COWBOY,
Becky Barker

171 A SECRET ARRANGEMENT,
Linda Vail

172 DANGEROUS HIDEAWAY,
Kit Daley

173 A PERILOUS AFFAIR,
Linda Randall Wisdom

174 DOUBLE MASQUERADE,
Alison Tyler

175 CALLAHAN'S GOLD,
Tate McKenna

176 SUMMER OF PROMISES,
Barbara Andrews

177 BEDROOM MAGIC,
Alice Morgan

178 SAPPHIRE HEART,
Hayton Monteith

179 LOVING CHARADE,
Linda Vail

180 THE MERMAID'S TOUCH,
Lynn Patrick

181 ORCHIDS OF PASSION,
Kit Daley

182 FOR THE LOVE OF JADE,
Erin Dana

183 RECKLESS ENCOUNTER,
Eleanor Woods

184 ISLAND OF SECRETS,
Tate McKenna

TEMPTING ANGEL

Alison Tyler

A CANDLELIGHT SUPREME

Published by
Dell Publishing Co., Inc.
1 Dag Hammarskjold Plaza
New York, New York 10017

Dell ® TM 681510, Dell Publishing Co., Inc.

Candlelight Supreme is a trademark
of Dell Publishing Co., Inc.

Candlelight Ecstasy Romance®, 1,203,540, is a registered
trademark of Dell Publishing Co., Inc., New York, New York.

ISBN: 0-440-18638-2

Printed in the United States of America

September 1987

10 9 8 7 6 5 4 3 2 1

WFH

To Our Readers:

As of September 1987, Candlelight Romances will cease publication of Candlelight Ecstasies and Supremes. The editors of Candlelight would like to thank our readers for 20 years of loyalty and support. Providing quality romances has been a wonderful experience for us and one we will cherish. Again, from everyone at Candlelight, thank you!

Sincerely,

The Editors

TEMPTING
ANGEL

CHAPTER ONE

Angela Welles spelled trouble with a capital T. At least that was the way Max Gallagher saw it. He made that assessment within moments of first laying eyes on her. Some women were just too damn beautiful. Angela Welles was one of them. In fact, Max put her right to the head of the class. She had the kind of looks that drove men to distraction—flawless ivory skin, night-black hair that fell halfway down her back in careless, lustrous waves, full, curved lips with a soft, moist sheen of toffee-candy-colored lipstick. What man in his right mind wouldn't want to sample that variety of confection? With all that going for her, Angela Welles's body only added to the picture of luscious perfection with long, creamy legs, wonderfully curved hips, small waist, and lovely full, high breasts.

But it was her eyes that were the real red-letter warning sign for Max. Those deep blue-violet eyes, the color of a lapis lazuli gemstone, positively glinted with a siren's allure. They had such magnetic appeal that it took every ounce of Max Gallagher's willpower to keep himself from falling instantly prey to them. At that, he wasn't very successful.

Their first encounter took place in the rickety elevator of a stately if somewhat crumbling apartment building in Boston's Back Bay. Up until the moment she appeared, Max had been contentedly contemplating his plans for the summer. Forty minutes earlier, at precisely three o'clock that afternoon, he'd bid his final farewell to his last someday-to-be-famous seventeen-year-old football player at the St. Thomas Aquinas School in Milton, Massachusetts. Then he hopped into his beat-up '79 Camaro and headed home, luxuriating in the prospect of nearly three glorious months off, three months of not hearing a single broad-shouldered, acned teen calling him Coach, three months to let his beard grow, walk around in shorts or even *au naturel* if he so chose, three months to do absolutely nothing but loll around, read, take a trip down to the Cape for a few weeks to swim, bask in the sun and watch the Red Sox hopefully bring home the pennant.

All those pleasant, idle thoughts immediately ceased just as the elevator doors were sliding to a close.

"Hold it. Hold the elevator." The voice was breathy and very feminine.

Max gallantly stuck his hand against one of the doors and they automatically slid open again. As soon as he saw her, he forgot all about swimming, boating, basking in the sun, even his precious Red Sox.

"Thanks. You're a lifesaver." Her voice had a

touch of vibrato in it, an earthy sound that sent little shivers across the air waves. "Hey, can you lend me a hand, neighbor?"

"Neighbor?" His own voice sounded decidedly inane. It took him several seconds to digest the meaning of the word, several more to realize her arms were loaded down with boxes.

She didn't wait for an offer, merely taking his dazed stare as acceptance. Unceremoniously, she toppled the boxes in his direction, giving Max only a second to extend his hands out in time to catch them.

Without the packages blocking his view of her, Max continued to be at a loss for words. She was wearing one of those halter top dresses that could easily pass for a sexy item of lingerie. The bodice was low and lacy, and the cut did not lend itself to the wearing of a bra. Max found himself staring through the pale peach cotton material at the shadowy outline of two of the sweetest breasts he'd glimpsed in a long time.

"The rest of my stuff is out in the car. If you don't mind holding on to these things for a minute, I'll just dash out and get a few more boxes. What a day for moving. I'm in a positive sweat." She dug out a tissue from her shoulder purse and dabbed at her glistening golden skin just above the lacy bodice of her dress. Max was working up a sweat of his own, but it had nothing to do with the weather.

She turned away, thus depriving Max of a splendid sight. Then again, the back view wasn't half bad either. Just as his eyes were drifting slowly

11

down her calves, she spun around again. "Oh, by the way, the name's Angela Welles. I'm moving into apartment 3B."

"3B?" Max began to worry that he'd be stuck for the rest of his life echoing pointless monosyllabic sentences.

Angela Welles smiled. If she was less than impressed with Max Gallagher's repartee, the smile didn't show it. What it did show was perfect, shiny white teeth. "Friends . . . and neighbors . . . call me Angel."

At least he didn't mutter, "Angel?" He even managed what passed for a smile. "I can see why."

This time she laughed. Her laugh went nicely with the rest of her. It was low, throaty, and incredibly sexy.

Angel ran out to unload a few more boxes from her car. Max shifted his weight. The boxes she'd dumped in his arms were surprisingly heavy. The luscious Angel was stronger than she looked.

She returned a minute later with another armload and stepped inside the elevator. "Thanks a lot."

"No problem." He paused. "I'm in 3A. We're not only neighbors, we're next-door neighbors. The name's Max. Max Gallagher."

"Very nice to meet you, Max Gallagher." They couldn't shake hands considering the boxes they were both carrying, but Angel stepped closer and rubbed her shoulder lightly and briefly against his. It was a friendly, innocent gesture, but Max experienced a physical response to her touch that was distinctly less innocent. Their eyes met for an instant and then Angel stepped a few inches in front of him. Max's gaze fell on a slight trickle of sweat running down her bare back. He had the craziest urge to reach out and run his finger along the glistening line. Fortunately his hands were full or he just might have done it.

That was when the caution light in his head flashed on. Watch out, it spelled out in furiously blinking light bulbs. Max Gallagher had a past history that included too many reckless, impulsive moves. And every one of them had added up to grief. As a kid, he'd had more than his share of minor run-ins with the law. When he got older, he had more than his share of run-ins with beautiful women. He'd even been reckless enough to marry one of them. That was when he was flying high, having just been signed on to his first contract with a major league football team, the Cincinnati Bengals. For a few glorious months, it looked as if his natural aggressiveness, his hot temper, and even that reckless streak were going to finally pay off.

They paid off, all right. In one too many injuries caused by some daredevil punt returns that got him axed from professional ball, and one too many marital battles that landed him in the divorce court. Laura, his stunning bride of less than six months, stood before the judge and proceeded to call her soon-to-be ex-husband a string of colorful names that nearly got her cited for contempt. However, she still managed to get a large chunk of his possessions and half of his bank account. What with paying his medical bills and settling with his divorce lawyer, Max was left with little in the way of assets. But what he got in exchange for losing most of his worldly goods, not to mention his pride, was a chance to reassess the rocky road he was traveling.

It takes some people a long time to learn a lesson. It probably took Max longer than most. But for the past four years he'd kept his nose clean, got himself a nice, steady job as the football coach in an elite private school and, most crucial, he'd stayed away from women who in any way sparked that old restless, dangerous streak in him. As he rode up the elevator with Angela Welles, he had to work fast and furious at remembering those hard-won lessons.

Angel caused more than sparks for Max. If he gave her half the chance she'd set off fireworks to outsparkle the ones set off on the Fourth of July at the Boston bandshell. So, instead of letting his eyes linger on Angela Welles's multitudinous assets and gallantly offering to help her get comfortably settled in, Max stepped back in the elevator, grit his teeth, and kept his mouth shut.

Angela Welles's mind was running on a surprisingly similar track to Max's. Max Gallagher made a striking first impression, setting off some fiery sparks of his own. First, there was that sunbleached California hair, decidedly out of place in Boston, Massachusetts, which only made it more eye-catching. Angel liked the way he wore it, carelessly long with a mere hint of a part and a few wayward strands falling sexily over a thick brow, a shade darker than his hair. He was a large man; Angel estimated he was at least six two. He carried

14

the height well with his broad shoulders, tapered hips, strong, muscular legs.

Max wasn't classically handsome. His nose was too broad, his features too craggy. But what he lacked in elegance, he made up for in pure rugged appeal and masculine presence. And he had the most fascinating shade of blue eyes she'd ever seen. Brooding, seductive, dangerous eyes. Angela Welles was very aware of the fact that those eyes were taking in every inch of her anatomy. But she picked up on his wariness as well as his attraction.

Angel had always been a sucker for men like Max Gallagher. In fact the moment she set eyes on him, she flashed back to Lou Chapman. Lou, her husband of two years, ex of three, had the same kind of rough sensual appeal. Lou's hair was a few shades darker, his face was slightly more battered and his eyes were a warm brown instead of a dazzling blue, but there was that same blend of caution and hunger behind them. She knew her ex-husband, Lou, rarely trusted anyone and she sensed that her new neighbor was of an equally distrusting nature.

Angel found the mixed messages in Max Gallagher's eyes all too familiar. So was her reaction to him. She knew, the moment after she'd touched his shoulder, that it had been a reckless move. Instantly, a rush of disturbing sensations bombarded her body. Fierce, electric attraction mingled with nervous tension. Passion, recklessly ignited, had gotten Angel in trouble in the past. And she was not looking for any more trouble. So, while Max's mind was running through his litany of past mistakes,

Angel was diligently reminding herself of her failed marriage and her firm resolve to stay clear of men that reminded her of her ex-husband, men who radiated too much fiery heat for their own good . . . and hers.

After that brief but tumultuous experience in the elevator, Angel and Max barely caught sight of each other during the next two weeks. Angel decided that her new neighbor was the most elusive man she'd ever encountered. She found herself wondering if he was intentionally avoiding her. She also found herself wondering if she wasn't doing much the same thing.

It was seven forty P.M. on a hot, muggy July evening, just two weeks after their first encounter, when their paths crossed again. Max was coming in from a day's sail on the Charles River. He spotted Angela as he approached the large glass entry door. She was standing in profile at the mailboxes, absorbed in reading a letter. He hesitated at the door. She hadn't spotted him and he had a sudden desire to duck away and avoid another disturbing encounter. But then he felt ridiculous for actually contemplating escape. So she was a beautiful woman. So she set off some sparks. So she'd played a lead role in a few daydreams the past two weeks. He wasn't about to let any of those facts push him around. He knew how to play it cool. Hadn't he been in training for the past four years?

She didn't seem to hear him when he opened the door and stepped into the marble-floored lobby. He noted the few pieces of mail scattered about her feet and then his eyes rested on her face. At first he thought it was perspiration causing her cheeks to glisten. But then he heard her sniffle and realized the moistness was tears not sweat.

He hesitated. *Mind your own business,* he told himself. *You don't need to supply a shoulder for her to cry on. A woman like Angel has to have any number of available shoulders just itching to be dampened. Just say a polite, cool hello and go your merry way.*

She looked up, her expression offering just the barest hint of surprise at finding Max standing there.

She bit her lip and Max thought she was going to break down in earnest. Max's palms started to sweat. He never liked seeing a woman cry and he especially didn't want to see Angel Welles in that state.

Her eyes glistened but she got control of herself, although her hands that clutched a sheet of white stationery were trembling so much that the paper rustled against the envelope that was behind it.

Max took a step toward the inside door, giving Angel a mildly sympathetic nod of no consequence.

Those dark lapis lazuli eyes stared at him with a soft hurt. For a moment a wave of guilt swept over him. How could he be such a cad as to walk off and leave her like that?

"Is . . . something wrong?" *That's it, Gallagher, ask her something real intelligent to redeem yourself,* he chastised silently.

She nodded, her lower lip trembling now along

with her hands. "He's dead," she said, her hands, letter and all, moving up to her face. Max realized then that the hurt in her eyes had nothing to do with his lack of neighborly concern. It had to do with the loss of someone Angel Welles obviously thought a great deal of. Father, uncle, friend, lover? Max, all at once, felt a strong desire to make it through the inner door, up the stairs and into his apartment without learning the particulars.

But she took her hands away from her face then and looked back at him. "You remind me of Lou," she said in a strangled voice, her lips curving ever so slightly.

Max knew when to throw in the towel. Those mesmerizing eyes and that withering smile melted all of his reserve. There was no chance of winning this bout with himself. So he gave a small, reluctant shrug and muttered, "How about coming up to my place for a drink or something? You shouldn't be alone at a . . ."

"Thanks." She smiled more brightly through her tears. "I thought you'd never ask."

He bent down and retrieved the stray pieces of mail that must have fallen from her hands as she'd read the bad news. He still didn't know who had died, but it was now inevitable that he would soon find out.

He found out before the ancient elevator even creaked down to the lobby. "Lou was my husband."

"Your husband?"

"My ex-husband," she amended. Her voice was calmer and more subdued. "According to this letter he died in a fishing accident off the coast of the Florida Keys." She shook her head slowly.

"I'm sorry," Max said softly.

"I can't believe it," she said in a whisper. "These things never . . ."

"Lou was a whiz when it came to fishing. Next to nosing around people's private affairs, it was his biggest love."

Max found himself wondering if that made Angel first or third in Lou's list of loves. That wasn't the question he asked, however. "What do you mean, nosing around people's affairs?"

"Lou was a private eye. He loved his work. A case wasn't just a case with Lou. It became his life until he solved it." Her eyes drifted down to the letter. "I wonder if he was on an assignment in the Keys." She paused. "Or if it was a . . . pleasure cruise." She paused again. When she spoke this time, her voice was wry. "Or maybe he was combining the two."

Max couldn't help wondering if Angel's newly deceased ex-husband combined business with pleasure during their marriage.

She smiled, her eyes meeting his. "I know what you're thinking." She gave him a measured look. "You're right. Lou never could resist a damsel in distress. Especially not a pretty one. And if they were rich, that was even better. Not that Lou didn't earn every cent. He was a top-notch detective. He had a lot of talents," she added, more slowly. "We never should have gotten married in the first place." Her smile was a touch wistful. Once upon a time she'd felt the pain of that conclusion. But three years was a long time. When she and Lou parted, she'd gone off and mended her broken heart with what she hoped was indestructible crazy glue.

She tucked the letter in her purse as the elevator doors slid open. "Neither of us was cut out for marriage," she said philosophically, stepping inside. "Neither of us could handle such a heavy commitment. Lou just coped with the problem differently." Her eyes met Max's as he followed her in. "Not that he didn't love me. In our own way, we loved each other very much. I'll always have a soft spot in my heart for Lou." Tears glistened in her eyes. "I still can't believe he'd go and get himself drowned off a fishing boat."

"Even the best fishermen can run into trouble, I guess," Max said.

"Do you fish?" she asked.

Max smiled. "No."

She merely nodded and stepped out of the elevator when it opened at three, leading the way to Max's apartment. When they got there, his hand moved over hers as she absently reached for the knob.

"Hold on," he said, his voice husky. "I do keep it locked."

"I guess I'm not thinking too clearly." Her eyes drifted to his hand still covering hers. She found his touch comforting and disturbing at the same time. He released his hold reluctantly and Angel dropped her hand to her side, wondering as she did if having that drink with Max Gallagher was a wise move.

With the shock of Lou's untimely demise, she was feeling particularly vulnerable. She wiped away a few tears from her cheeks.

Max dug into his pocket for his apartment key. He was disconcerted to note that the large ring of keys was not the only bulge his hand encountered. Max felt ashamed of the fact that Angel Welles's grief only added a new sensual dimension to her appeal, a dimension his body responded to with callous lust, even as his mind registered a blend of sympathy and nervous tension. She hadn't even stepped into his apartment yet and he was already regretting his invitation. For two weeks he'd managed to keep a safe distance from Angel and now, here he was, again rubbing shoulders with this incredibly attractive woman as he fit the key into the lock. *This is a big mistake,* he told himself ruefully as he watched her swing open the door.

He was a step behind her, partly because he had not yet managed to fully tame that lust of his, partly because Angel didn't wait to be escorted into his apartment. But as she got to the end of the hall, she sensed his hesitation and glanced at him over her shoulder. "If this is a bad time . . ."

"No . . . not at all. It's just I haven't got a great bar selection. I'm strictly a beer man, myself, but I probably have a bottle of gin and maybe a bottle of . . ."

"I like beer." She stepped inside the living room and gave an approving smile as she scanned the small but tidy room with its dark gray carpet, comfortable pale gray velour tuxedo couch and armchair, soothing landscape prints on the off-white painted walls. It was a masculine room. There was the hint of a slightly pungent tobacco scent in the air.

"It's nice," she said softly, pleased to see Max smile, his stance more relaxed. She'd felt his tension like a taut wire stretched across her path. "I'm still living out of boxes. Every time I start unpacking, I find something better to do."

"Like?"

She grinned. "Like going around the corner for a pizza. Or catching an old Clark Gable movie on TV. Or finishing an article I'd started reading the day before in *Time* magazine. Or going through the want ads in the *Globe.*"

"No job?"

Angel was silent for a minute. She removed the letter from her purse and glanced at it again. "Maybe I won't have to find one for a while after all."

"How come?"

"According to Lou's attorney, John Metcalf, the man who wrote me this letter, it seems Lou left me all his worldly possessions in his will."

"You don't sound all that surprised. How long have you been divorced?"

"Three years. But I guess I'm not really surprised. Lou knew a lot of . . . people . . . casually, but he didn't trust many of them. In his line of work, it was just as well. Lou always used to say I was the one person in this world he could trust. Apparently three years apart didn't change that."

Angel's eyes sparkled. "I'm not counting on a hefty inheritance, though. Lou never was good with money. He spent it as fast as he made it. I doubt that's changed either in the past three years. I guess it depends on what his situation was when he was . . . out there on that boat." Her voice faltered and her eyes dropped.

"I'll get you that beer," Max said hastily.

He brought back one for her and one for himself. As he handed her the bottle, he stopped. "Where's my manners? Just a sec and I'll get you a glass."

"I prefer it from the bottle," she said, reaching out and taking it from his grasp.

He released his hold reluctantly. "I've got plenty of glasses . . ."

"Relax, Gallagher. I'm the one who's supposed to be all wound up. Sit down and drink your beer."

He managed a rueful smile. "I'm not great at this kind of thing. You know, being a comfort in time of loss. I usually avoid those scenes."

Angel found his smile more than comforting. "I think you're better at it than you realize."

The air was suddenly charged with electricity again and for the next few silent minutes neither Angel nor Max was thinking about the untimely demise of Angel's ex-husband.

Angel set her half-finished beer on the glass coffee table. She gave Max a sidelong glance at the same moment he was giving her a furtive look. Laughter bubbled in her throat.

"We're quite a pair," she said. "I know what I'm

23

on edge about, Gallagher. But, tell me, what's making you so nervous?"

Careful, he warned himself as he breathed in deeply. "That shouldn't be so hard for you to figure out." His eyes traveled over her face, his hand absently swiping at his tousled hair. A day of sailing had given it a windblown look.

Angel felt the urge to help him with the snarls, but instead she reached back for her beer. "I'm not so good at figuring things out."

"I bet you're better than you think you are."

This time they both laughed.

"How about some pizza to go with that beer?"

She tilted her chin. "You always offer to feed a woman when you want to avoid her questions?"

He grinned. "I've got a fair stock of maneuvers, but I thought this one might work with you."

"You're right. I'm starved."

"Shall we go around the corner to the pizza parlor . . . or order in?"

Angel paused. "Not that I'm the grieving widow exactly . . . I mean Lou and I have been divorced for the past three years and I've probably seen him a total of twice in all that time. Still, I was in love with him once and I will always feel a certain fondness for the guy." She sighed. "What I'm trying to say in a most awkward fashion is that I find you disturbingly attractive, Max Gallagher. And you do remind me an awful lot of Lou Chapman. And, as I'm sure you've already figured out, that relationship didn't turn out very well. I'm in a rather vulnerable state right now. And it would take more willpower than I possess at the moment to turn down any . . . comfort you were to offer. So, to make a long story short"—she smiled winsomely— "we better go out for pizza."

For all his cautionary zeal, Max experienced a stinging disappointment at her choice. But he nodded agreement valiantly, telling himself it was a good thing he'd left the decision up to her. Right now his own ability to make safe, rational decisions was at an all-time low.

Twenty minutes later, they were sitting across from each other at a black Formica-topped table in the back of the pizza parlor. A thick aroma of garlic, pepperoni, and marinara sauce wafted up from the large pizza cooling off between them.

On their way over, Angel had asked Max a little about himself and had found out he was an ex-pro-football player who now coached football at a private school. He had the whole summer off and was planning to spend a few weeks at the Cape. He was just the kind of man she needed . . . .

"Aren't you hungry, after all?" Max asked gently, noticing that she hadn't taken a bite yet.

Angel gave Max a lingering look. It was the kind of look that would make strong men melt, even men as strong as Max. "Ever been to Miami?" she asked, ignoring his question.

Max slowly shook his head. Their eyes remained locked.

"Lou's funeral is on Saturday. In Miami." Her eyes started to glisten again.

Max wanted to look away. Those warning lights in his mind were flashing again stronger than ever. But he was unable to tear his gaze away from those captivating eyes.

"I'm kind of apprehensive about . . . going down there alone," she said softly.

"Isn't there anyone who can go along with you, or be with you when you get down there?"

She shook her head slowly.

"You don't have to go, do you? I mean, after all, you and Lou have been divorced for years."

"I couldn't miss Lou's funeral. He didn't have any family to speak of. I was . . . all he had. He'd want me there." Angel wet her dry lips with the tip of her tongue. It was a tantalizing gesture, and a flash of arousal blew that fuse in his head.

His hand reached across the table and took hold of hers. She could have pulled away, but she didn't. "You shouldn't be alone . . . at a time like that," he heard himself saying. "You ought to have someone with you." He could see by the look in her eyes that she really didn't want to make the trip alone. He could also see that this wasn't a seductive maneuver on her part. Angel Welles looked genuinely scared.

She could feel her hand trembling in his. Angel knew she was setting a match to a stick of dynamite. But she felt very lonely and afraid right now, more afraid than she wanted Max to know. She had a sick feeling that Lou's "accidental" drowning had a decidedly fishy scent, and that the trip down to Miami was not going to be an uncomplicated one.

So, she smiled one of her superbly enigmatic smiles and murmured, "I was thinking the very same thought."

CHAPTER TWO

Angel's doorbell rang at seven forty-five the next morning. She groped sleepily for her robe, skipping her slippers as she maneuvered her way through the obstacle course of half-packed boxes to get to her front door.

"Who is it?" she muttered, coming eyeball to eyeball with her unknown visitor through the peephole.

A lumbering fellow stepped back from the door, a thick index finger tapping his breast pocket on which was written, Cavanough Movers. He mumbled the name as he pointed.

Angel put the chain on the door and opened it a crack. "What do you want?" she asked.

"You Angela Welles?" he grunted.

"Yes."

"Well, then this is the place. I've got a couple of cartons to deliver to a Miss Angela Welles, 397 Commonwealth Avenue, Boston, Mass."

"Give me a break," she said, glancing over her shoulder. "I'm already swimming in cartons. Where are they from?"

"Straight from sunny Miami, Florida, lady. I've

got four other drops today, so can we get this one started?"

Angel scowled. "Miami?"

The mover glanced at a pink sheet in his hand. "4211 Carlton St., Miami."

Angel's scowl deepened. That was Lou's address; the office and headquarters of the Chapman Detective Agency. Obviously, these cartons had to be part of Lou's estate. But what was confusing was why they were arriving at this time. Metcalf had made it clear that the will was going to be settled down in Miami after the funeral. This inheritance delivery was three days early.

"Okay if I bring them up?"

She nodded, closing the door for a moment to undo the chain. Then, belting her bathrobe more securely, she swung the door open wide.

"Can I see your delivery order?" she asked.

The big guy handed it over to her with a bit of a flourish. He might be feeling overworked, but it wasn't often he got to feast his eyes on a woman as beautiful as Angela Welles. He even managed a crooked smile. "Here, you read, I'll get to work." He turned and headed down the hall, opting for the stairs instead of the elevator.

Angel felt a gnawing sensation in the pit of her stomach as she read the pink sheet of paper. The cartons were from Lou all right. *Directly* from him. His signature was scrawled across the bottom line. Lou had lousy handwriting. It took her several seconds to make out the date beside the signature. It was exactly two days before he died. So, these items

29

weren't part of his estate after all. Lou had sent her this stuff himself. The question remained. Why?

"Good morning," a deep baritone greeted her.

Angel looked up to find Max approaching her from down the hall. "Oh . . . hi," she said distractedly.

"Not more bad news, I hope," he said, wiping his brow. He'd just finished a five-mile run and he needed a shower badly, so he kept a good six-foot distance from Angel.

If the smell of manly sweat bothered her, she didn't show it. She smoothed her tousled hair and smiled. "Well . . . in a way. As if I didn't have enough cartons to decorate this apartment, some more are on the way." She folded the pink sheet of paper as she spoke. "I . . . uh . . . forgot about the shipment. There were some things I had sent out with a moving company from Miami . . . and . . . they're just arriving now."

"Kind of slow moving, aren't they?" he quipped. Okay, so it wasn't the greatest joke, but he didn't get Angel to crack even a faint smile. His glance grew curious. "Are you okay?"

She smiled then, but it was as phony as a three-dollar bill. "I'm fine." She quickly glanced down the hall as the elevator doors slid open and the mover stepped out with two large cartons. Angel was worried that Lou's name might be on them and she was anxious for Max not to make note of that information. Her smile turned cool and she gave him a brief nod of dismissal. Max gave her a speculative look.

30

"How about some breakfast later?" he asked as he headed toward his door.

Angel's eyes were focused on the boxes. "I'm afraid I'm going to be tied up this morning. How about lunch instead?"

Max unlocked his door. "Okay. I'll stop over at twelve."

She nodded, relieved to see Max disappear into his apartment before the mover got to her door.

This whole business was growing more confusing and Angel wanted some time to sort it all out. Why had Lou arranged to have her get these boxes? He'd never said anything about them to her. He always did play things too close to his chest. Of course, he probably figured he'd still be around to let her know about them before they arrived. A cold chill ran down Angel's spine. Or had he figured just the opposite . . . that he might not be around. That would explain a few things, Angel realized. But it was still too early in the game to know for sure. It was too soon to know anything for sure. Then again, Angel didn't know how much time she had to sort it all out.

She would have liked to bounce some theories off of Max. He impressed her as streetwise, shrewd, and tough. But she was scared that if she took him into her confidence at this point he might bolt. Angel did not want that to happen. If there was going to be trouble down the line, Angel was smart enough to know she wouldn't be able to handle it on her own. And since Max was the only man she thought she might be able to trust in this situation, the only man she knew who could not in any way be involved with Lou Chapman's personal or professional life, he was the choice candidate. It didn't hurt that she knew he found her compellingly attractive. That she found him equally compelling, however, was a definite negative. Angel needed to keep her wits about her. And Max Gallagher's sensual appeal had a way of muddling her thoughts. That wasn't good. She knew it wasn't good. But she told herself she could handle it.

The mover dumped the boxes unceremoniously into the middle of her living room, got her signature verifying delivery, and left. Angel put up some water to boil for a cup of instant coffee, threw on a pair of jeans and a T-shirt while the water heated up, ran a brush through her hair and dashed back into the kitchen just as the kettle erupted into a low, mournful whine.

Setting her coffee mug on a pile of books that were still waiting to be sorted and placed on the nice built-in bookcases along one living-room wall, Angel attacked the first of Lou's cartons. She ended up using a kitchen knife to pierce the packing tape. Lou didn't have to worry about the boxes coming open in handling. He'd sealed them tighter than a drum. Then again, Angel thought, feeling a lump rise in her throat, poor Lou didn't have to worry about anything anymore. Another part of his inheritance. Now, she had his worries.

That wasn't fair, she told herself. No one was holding a gun to her head. She could turn her back on the situation. She could skip the funeral, have

Lou's cartons shipped back to his lawyer, Metcalf, with a brief but firm note informing him that she wanted no part of Lou Chapman's estate and she especially wanted no part in what she was fast becoming convinced was a very sticky situation.

Angel sighed, ripping open the first box. No harm in just seeing what it was Lou had sent her.

Inside the carton was a stack of manila files. Names were typed on each file. They started with Aarons and ended with Morton. Angel proceeded to open the other carton, not surprised to find the rest of the alphabet covered, or almost the rest. The last file bore the name, York. No Z's. Maybe if Lou had lived to practice a little longer he would have gotten a client named Zinger or Zucker. Zucker rhymed with sucker, Angel mused. That's what she was all right. A prize sucker. Lou knew she wouldn't turn her back on him. That hadn't changed either in three years. Something smelled fishy clear from the aquamarine waters off the Keys direct to Angela Welles's beautifully chiseled nose. Lou knew all about Angel's ability to pick up the scent of trouble. Angel couldn't help thinking he was banking on that talent of hers. That was Lou Chapman for you. Even from the grave, he couldn't let a case go. But what case? One that had gotten Lou down to Key West? Or another one that he was working on at the time? She had a whole alphabet of names to choose from . . . or almost a whole alphabet.

"Damn it, Lou," she muttered out loud. "I gave up playing Doctor Watson to your Sherlock Holmes when I gave up playing wife." She rubbed her nose and broke into a grin. "You are a bum, Lou Chapman. You knew I'd get hooked. Was that what that strange disturbing phone call of yours was really about?" Three weeks ago, out of the blue, Lou telephoned. She hadn't heard from him in over a year. She had no idea he knew she was packing up and leaving Miami. But Lou had so many connections in town, she should have realized she wouldn't get as far as the local supermarket without word getting back to him. Not that she was ducking out or anything. It didn't matter that Lou knew she was leaving. The truth was, it didn't matter to Angel whether he knew she was heading up north or he didn't know. It had been a long time since she'd shared her itinerary with her ex-husband.

Just as she started reflecting on that brief final phone call from Lou there was a knock on her door. She glanced down at her watch, only to remember she hadn't put it on.

"Who is it?"

"It's me. Max."

She didn't know what time it was, but she knew it couldn't be anywhere near noon yet.

He knocked again. Angel frowned. There was no time to reseal the boxes. She got to her feet and walked over to the door. "I'm kind of busy, Max."

"I have something for you. Open the door for a minute."

Angel hesitated. Then she opened the door a few inches.

Max was freshly shaven, his hair still damp from a shower. He smelled very good. So did the mug of freshly brewed coffee he was holding. Correction. Two mugs.

"I know you turned down breakfast, but I thought you might like some of my special blend of Mocha Java and French roast. You looked a bit overwrought before." He extended one hand, bringing his own mug to his lips with his other. "Tastes great."

Angel's lips compressed. "I already made myself some coffee."

Max was not to be dissuaded. "This is better." His eyes narrowed slightly. He shook his head slowly, his gaze on her violet eyes. "Devil or angel," he started to croon in a low, husky voice, "I can't make up my mind." A cunning smile curved his lips. "What do you say, Ms. Welles?" The question was tinged with seduction, but there was also a hint of anger there.

Angel felt some anger of her own. Or maybe it was simply a defense. She wasn't sure. All she knew was that she didn't like Max Gallagher's insinuating tone. Even if it was legitimate.

"Let's talk, Angel."

"Later, Max."

"It would be a shame to let this terrific coffee get cold. We better talk now."

Angel shrugged. "Okay, but just for a few minutes. I told you I was busy this morning."

He stepped inside and handed Angel a mug. She cupped it in her hands as he started down the hall. "I'll grant you, Ms. Welles, we're not exactly confidants as yet," he drawled as he ambled in the direction of the living room, "but considering the fact that I accepted your offer to hold your hand during a plane ride down to Miami and to continue holding it through the funeral of your ex-husband, I'd say that I at least deserve to be dealt a fair hand."

Angel followed close behind him. "I have no idea what you're talking about, Max." Her tone was arch. She caught hold of his sleeve. "Let's sit in the kitchen. It's the only room in the house that isn't cluttered with boxes. I'll even whip up some eggs to go with the coffee."

Max came to a stop. "I thought you were too busy for breakfast."

Their gaze held for a few tense moments. "Okay, spill it out, Max. What's eating you?"

"I want to know why you lied to me, Angel."

"Lied? About what?"

He gave her a long look. "About those newly delivered cartons, for starters."

Angel let go of Max's shirt sleeve and turned right into the sunny eat-in kitchen with its cheerful yellow, blue, and white flowered paper and bright yellow cabinets. The brightness didn't lift her mood. "How did you know about the cartons?"

"I saw the mover while I was getting my mail downstairs. He flashed that pink delivery sheet in my face and asked if you were a resident here. I guess that temporary label on your mailbox must have fallen off." Max didn't bother to take a seat at the kitchen table. He just leaned against the wall and took another swallow of coffee. "I'm great at speed reading. I caught the name . . . Chapman. I thought only doctors and teenage boys wrote that bad."

"Okay," she said, after gulping in a deep breath, "those boxes were part of Lou's estate. In a way I didn't lie, though. They are mine . . . now."

He gave her another of those long, wary looks. "Something tells me there's more here than meets the eye, Angel. You look nervous. Now that I think about it, you looked nervous yesterday, too."

"You're confusing nervousness with grief," she said defensively.

He moved closer to her. "But you told me yesterday you weren't exactly a grieving widow. Now that was one statement I did believe."

Angel glared at him. "How dare you? I am broken up about Lou's death. He meant a lot to me at one time. He still does mean something to me."

"I believe that, too," Max said, his tone a fraction more tender.

Angel clutched her hands together, but when she saw Max's gaze move to her meshed fingers, she dropped her hands to her side. "Why don't we just drop this whole thing?" she said wearily.

"Does that include our flight together to Miami?"

Angel stiffened a little, but she kept her composure. "Including the flight."

Max's eyes narrowed almost imperceptibly. He stood there silently watching her for several moments.

Angel could feel his gaze practically piercing her skin. This was a crazy idea, she told herself. What made her ever consider dragging a complete stranger into her private affairs? And yet in an even crazier way, Max Gallagher didn't seem like a stranger to her. There was a connection between them. She'd felt it from the start. So had he. Wasn't that why he hadn't simply turned and left as fast as his feet could carry him?

Max studied her face. The way the sunlight hit it, she was half in shadow. It gave her an air of mystery. As if she needed any outside assistance.

"Are you in trouble?"

Angel didn't answer Max's question. She looked up at him for a moment and then her gaze slid off his face.

He walked over to her, pulled out a chair and spun it around as he sat so he could lean his arms on the back of the chair as he confronted her. "Was Chapman in trouble then?"

Angel's violet eyes sparkled. "Lou was always in trouble. But he got paid for his trouble. He got paid quite substantially."

There might as well have been a hook stuck into him because he could feel Angel reeling in her line —with him as the catch. If he had any sense, Max would have let go of the bait, pronto. But instead, he went on. "You think there was some monkey business down on that fishing boat in the Keys, don't you?"

Angel smiled ruefully. "Lou's death was listed as an accident. Metcalf didn't elucidate the details." She hesitated. "But I intend to find out exactly what happened."

"Why?" Max's tone was sharp. He was angry,

but he wasn't sure of the reason. Maybe it was because he couldn't imagine any woman he'd ever known whose intentions would be so fierce if he were to kick the bucket mysteriously.

She made a quick, impatient gesture. "I told you. I still care about the guy."

"You still love him, you mean." Max's voice was tighter and angrier. He didn't bother to justify his feelings. He couldn't if he'd wanted to.

Suddenly Angel's cool, slender hand reached out and stroked his cheek. It was a decidedly more intimate gesture than that touch she'd initiated in the elevator two weeks ago. "I'm not still in love with Lou," she said in a soft, tender voice. She could feel her pulse racing in her head. She could feel the insistent beat clear down to her fingers.

Max stared into those blue-violet eyes, that beautiful mouth half open. Everything was working against his common sense. Himself most of all. "Angel . . ." Her name was a mere whisper of desire on his lips.

It was a toss-up as to who leaned forward first. For an instant, before their lips met somewhere in the middle, Max got a glimpse of her face unmasked. He could see fear there and pleading. And incredible, wrenching loveliness.

His open mouth moved on hers. He could feel her lips trembling. She lifted her arms and moved them around his neck. The back of the chair acted as a barrier. It was probably just as well. Things were already moving faster than a speeding bullet.

Angel closed her eyes tightly and lost herself to

the kiss. His tongue touched hers and she gave a low murmuring sigh, her fingers moving to his hair. Max knew how to turn a kiss into an artful erotic act. He was unhurried, deliberate, tantalizing. He ran his tongue slowly across her lips, her teeth, then slipped past to tease the tip of her tongue, then deeper still.

It was also a toss-up as to who pulled back first. Both of them were acutely aware of where a kiss like that could lead—if they let it . . . if they decided to be reckless. But the truth was, they were both scared. This attraction between them was so incredibly powerful. And they didn't know a thing about each other.

Angel got up from her seat. "You've kissed a lot of women." Her face was averted. "You're good. Very good." Her voice was breathless and her heart was still pounding against her chest.

"Do you always rate your men?" he asked cynically. Her remark had hurt. It was cool, dismissive. And Max was feeling very hot. Even if he had pulled back. "Tell me, how did Chapman rate? From the hints you dropped, he must have been a pretty experienced kisser himself. Was he good? Very good?"

Angel spun around. "You can be hard, Max Gallagher. Hard and cruel."

His eyes narrowed. "You're right."

Angel swallowed. "I think you better leave."

"You didn't answer my question."

Frustration overwhelmed her. "Dammit, what did you want me to say about what . . . just happened between us? That your kiss drove me wild, made me hear bells? That you're the best thing that ever happened to me? Did you want me to drag you off into my bedroom and throw myself at you? If you want to know the truth, your kiss scared the hell out of me. Because it did drive me crazy. Maybe there were even a few jingles. And the idea of dragging you into bed did cross my mind." She caught her breath. "And, yes, Lou was a pretty good kisser. But he didn't . . . put his heart and soul into it . . . like you do. He never made me feel that kissing me was, at the moment anyway, the most important thing in the world he had to do." On that last word she went storming out of the room.

Max sprang after her, catching hold of her arm and pulling her to a halt in the foyer.

Her eyes were a midnight blue now. "But you had to go and ruin it with your cutting wit," she muttered, feeling embarrassed and humiliated by her tirade. "Let go of me." She struggled in his grasp, but Max's grip merely tightened.

"How about giving me a second chance?" There was a tender, seductive smile on his lips. Angel knew he didn't expect an answer.

He traced a finger down her cheek. "Let's try for chimes this time." He pulled her into his arms, taking it slowly at first, lightly kissing her eyelids, the tip of her nose, her cheeks, the quirky corners of her lips. Angel felt as though she were floating in a pool of liquid sensuality. He molded her against him, against that strong, firm, virile body. Angel fitted perfectly.

When he captured her lips, she responded with an almost savage desire that stunned her.

Angel was wrong, Max thought. Although he had kissed a lot of women, kissing Angel was like nothing on earth. He hated to let her go.

When he did release her, Angel had to throw her hand out against the wall to keep her balance. This time there was no analysis, no comparisons. In fact neither of them said a word.

Max walked into the living room. Angel did not try to waylay him this time. He glanced at the newly arrived boxes.

"They're Lou's case files," Angel said in a low voice.

She walked over to the couch and sat down. "He sent them, or, that is, he arranged to have them sent." She paused. "It's not the first time. About a year ago Lou phoned me. I hadn't heard from him in ages. Occasionally he'd drop me a card from some port of call. He'd always write 'wish you were here.'" Angel shrugged. "It was a kind of joke. I told you we kept things amiable. But when Lou called me he seemed on edge. Oh, at first he ran the old routine by me. Told me how much he missed me, how often he thought about me. Did I want to get together for old times' sake? But when I didn't play my part, he dropped the game and came around to the real reason for his call. He asked me if I would mind holding on to some papers for him. It turned out his place had been ransacked the night before. Whatever the intruders were looking for, though, apparently they didn't find. I agreed to hold the papers for a while, but before we settled on the arrangement, Lou was adamant about my not breathing a word of it, not even the fact that we'd spoken on the phone, to anyone, but especially not to Rick Seidman."

"Who's Rick Seidman?" Max came and sat down beside her on the couch.

"Lou's competition. He ran another investigation agency in Miami. I was working for him at the time. He hired me right after I left Lou. Lou didn't mind. Rick wasn't in Lou's league, so he was no real threat. And I needed a job. While we were married, I used to run Lou's office. Mostly filing papers, answering the phone, making appointments, that sort of thing. But, every now and then, I'd do some legwork for Lou. I did the same for Rick." She smiled. "I was pretty good."

"What happened after the phone call?"

Angel scowled. "I got a parcel in the mail the next day, stuck it in my dresser drawer and then, two weeks later, Lou sent me a note with a Miami box number on it and asked me to send the parcel to that address. So I did."

"That was it?" Max looked puzzled when Angel nodded.

"I guess Lou decided since I'd agreed to temporarily look after that one parcel, he could count on me to do it again. Oh, he didn't send me stuff very often. Maybe three, four times at most. Always with a note telling me to keep the delivery to myself. On one occasion anyway, I understood why Lou was so anxious to keep the information from Rick. They were working on the same case that time. Only Lou's client was the wife and Rick was being paid by the husband." She gave Max a wry look. "Like I told you, Lou always went for the female clients. And Vera Hargrove was very female."

Max reached out and took her hand, making a sweeping gesture toward the boxes with his other hand. "You think this delivery is a similar deal? You think Lou wanted you to hold on to this stuff for safekeeping?"

Angel frowned. "I said that Lou sent me a few parcels before, but this . . . these boxes must contain *all* his files. Lou never said a word about it when I spoke to him."

Max cocked his head. "When was that?"

Angel was quiet for a moment. "Two days before I left Miami. It was another of those calls out of the blue." She hesitated. "Only this time he didn't ask me to hold anything for him. He did ask me why I was leaving town, why I'd quit my job with Seidman."

"Good questions," Max said.

Angel shrugged. "I needed a change. I wanted to get out of the South and I thought Boston would be a nice, civilized city," she replied. Then tears misted her eyes. For a moment Max wasn't sure why.

"Lou sounded . . . different on the phone. I don't know. He seemed lonely. When he started talking about missing me, I . . . I had the feeling he meant it." Her eyes lifted to Max's. "Crazy, isn't it? I mean . . . three years later and all."

Max shook his head slowly. "No, not crazy. I doubt any man could get you out of his mind for good."

Angel didn't really hear him. Her eyes closed. "He asked me if I would meet him for a drink. He named a spot that . . . that used to be our . . . special place. It was very romantic, soft lights, a piano bar playing mood music."

"Did you meet him?"

"No. I'd gone by that bar a few months back. It had changed." She paused. "So had I."

Tears fell down Angel's cheeks. "I told him just that. He seemed . . . hurt."

She stood up and walked aimlessly over to the window. "If I'd known that it would be my last chance to see him alive . . ." She didn't finish the sentence.

Her back was to Max. He saw her body shudder, but there was no sound of crying. He let her be. He sensed that that was the way she wanted it.

Finally she turned around. "Maybe," she said in a strangled voice, "if I'd met him that day—"

"Don't play that mind game," Max cut her off sharply. "You have no cause to blame yourself for anything that happened to Chapman. He got paid to look for trouble. Isn't that what you said? Well, I guess in the end he paid the price. Accident or not, Angel, he was a big boy. I'll bet he knew what he was doing." He stood up then and walked over to her. He rested his arms firmly on her shoulders.

45

"That's why you're so set on finding out what happened. You feel guilty. Well, you know what I think? I think you don't owe Lou Chapman a thing. But you do owe yourself a chance to start fresh." His eyes seared into hers. "Just as you planned to do when you packed up and left Miami. That was your goal, wasn't it?"

Angel didn't answer.

"Wasn't it?" he persisted.

Angel nodded faintly.

"Okay then," he said firmly. "What you need to do is send these boxes back to Chapman's lawyer and forget . . . the whole thing."

Angel's large blue-violet eyes looked up beseechingly at Max. "Does that mean you won't come down to Miami with me on Saturday?" The vibrato in her voice was especially thick.

Max met her gaze directly. "It means that I don't want either of us going down there." His hands moved up to her face. He brushed his lips lightly against hers. "What do you say, Angel? We both could use some starting over."

Angel smiled faintly. It was a nice thought. But she knew there'd be no starting over until she put a finish to old business.

CHAPTER THREE

Angel had spent half the afternoon sifting through Lou's files. There were thirty-four in all, most of them thinner than a ham sandwich, but there were a dozen that were filled to overflowing,—long, complicated cases that Lou had worked on for stretches of several months. Three of those thick files bore names that Angel was familiar with and she set those aside. None of the others rang a bell, which meant that all of those clients had to have signed on after she'd stopped playing wife and file clerk for Lou.

After a quick solitary dinner in the kitchen, Angel went back to the living room and was just starting to go through the first of the three files she'd set aside when there was a knock on the door.

She knew it was Max without asking. His knock was beginning to sound familiar. Still, she took a quick check through the peephole before opening the door.

"There's a good basketball game on TV," he said as he walked into her apartment.

"My TV set isn't working."

"You could come over to my apartment and watch."

"I'm not crazy about basketball."

He gave her a playful look of disappointment.

"Sorry." She grinned.

He walked into the living room. Apparently, watching the game wasn't all that urgent. He glanced over at the three files on the coffee table, the first of which lay open. There was a photo on top. Max walked over and lifted it up. He let out a long, low whistle. The woman in the photo was a cross between Marilyn Monroe and one of those high-priced call girls Max used to see around Vegas casinos in his younger, wilder days.

"Look familiar?"

Max's eyes shot up to Angel's face.

Angel laughed. "That wasn't a personal question. I thought you might have caught Janine Dion in a movie. She made a couple of those grade B college antic flicks."

"No. I don't go for those kinds of flicks." He grinned.

Angel picked up a typed sheet of paper from the top of Janine's file and scanned it. "Well . . . then maybe you caught her in one of her . . . earlier films. Seems Janine had a couple of lean years out in Hollywood and made a few movies that she wasn't terribly proud of."

She tapped the paper in her hand. "It's all here in black and white. This was Lou's system. He always started by asking his clients to describe their problem in two sentences or less. He didn't want to waste time pulling teeth. He wanted his clients to spit out their problem without beating around the bush."

"And what did Janine spit out?" Max asked, sitting down on the couch.

Angel sat down next to him. "So you are a curious guy, after all."

Max's eyes trailed her face. "You knew that already." His tone was teasing.

Angel felt a warm sensation spread through her body. She focused on the sheet of paper. "It says here that Janine won a film test after coming in first in the Miss Sun Sweet Orange beauty contest in Miami two years ago. Stardom didn't follow immediately. But, it seems that when it did, an old boyfriend of hers, Ross Allen, who happened to be her costar and producer/director of one of her earlier, more immodest movies, hit her for some dough in exchange for the film. She hired Lou to get the film back."

"Did he?"

Angel placed the file on her lap and thumbed through the sheets. "Looks that way."

Max opened the cover of the next file. Another eight-by-ten glossy of yet another beautiful blond bombshell with a sultry smile stared up at him.

Angel tilted her head. "Lou always was popular with fair-haired damsels in distress. That's Wendy Shaw. She's a nightclub singer. Not a bad voice. Although the men go to see her more than listen to her. She's the star attraction of Anton's, one of the classier nightclubs in Miami Beach. Beautiful, isn't she?"

Max looked over at Angel. "I never did go for blondes myself." He omitted mentioning to Angel that he'd been particularly turned off by blondes after six months of marriage to one of those luscious fair-haired creatures. Not that he didn't believe for one instant that he couldn't get in plenty of trouble with a dark-haired beauty like Angel. He was beginning to worry plenty about that. And seeing her avid interest in these files only added to his worry.

Angel noted the sullen expression on his face. "What's wrong?"

His dark blue eyes narrowed. "I'm wondering why you're going through these files. I thought we'd decided you were going to ship these cartons back to Chapman's lawyer and . . . forget the past." His look was stark. "You're still going down to Miami for the funeral, aren't you?"

"I never said I wasn't," she said, her tone defiant. "Look, Max, I think there's something here, maybe in these three cases. Remember I told you that Lou sent me papers on clients a few times. Well, they involved these three women. Janine Dion, Wendy Shaw, and Vera Hargrove. Wendy Shaw hired Lou when she was accused of the attempted murder of her paramour, a very wealthy hotel owner and a very married man by the name of Derek Bendix. He was also an up-and-coming candidate for the U.S. Senate. The night before he was shot while walking down a dark Miami street, he and Wendy had had a blowup in her dressing room at Anton's. According to several witnesses she even threatened to murder him. The incident made Miami headlines." Angel gave Max a teasing smile. "Never make idle threats."

"Or idle promises," Max said in a low voice.

Angel averted her gaze, and scanned another sheet in the Shaw file. "According to this, Derek's wife, Paula, claimed she knew about the affair and that the blowup with Wendy came about because Derek had agreed to end it. However, Lou tracked down a good friend of Paula's, a so-called leading citizen of the balmy city, who was not eager for the limelight, but who had also witnessed the fight at Anton's that night. He finally admitted to Lou that he'd told Paula about the incident the next day and his impression was that Paula had known nothing at all about her husband's . . . extra-curricular activities." As she spoke she continued rifling through the papers. Her eyes widened as she came across one particular sheet. "That's interesting."

"What?" Max asked reluctantly. Damn, but the woman was good at hooking her catch.

"Metcalf was Wendy Shaw's lawyer. He got her off . . . with Lou's help. Lou got Paula Bendix to finally confess the truth: that after her 'good friend' had told her about her husband's affair with Wendy, Paula went into a rage, got hold of a gun, and took a pot shot at her philandering spouse. Metcalf is the same man who's handling Lou's affairs. He wrote me the letter." She picked up the third file. "Now that I think about it, he was Vera Hargrove's attorney, too." A magazine clipping fell out of the file as Angel opened it. Max picked it up.

Vera Hargrove was pictured at a charity ball. She was as beautiful as the nightclub singer and the actress. But she was a definite class above. Tall, slender, sophisticated, glittering with diamonds. And red-headed. Max noted that Lou wasn't totally discriminatory.

"The man next to her in that clipping is her husband, Michael Hargrove," Angel said. "He was the president of Weston Electronics. But it was Vera who actually owned the company. The company was going downhill. So was the Hargrove marriage. Vera hired Lou because she thought her husband was embezzling company funds. Michael in turn hired Rick Seidman, my boss at the time, to prove it was Vera's handiwork. Rick's involvement was real hush-hush. Even I wasn't supposed to know about it for some reason. It was Lou who told me. It was also Lou who won. Rick wasn't too happy about it. Neither was Michael Hargrove. He was found guilty and is currently pressing out license plates while he does big time in a Florida slammer."

As Max studied the clipping, he could feel Angel's gaze resting on him. "You're staring," he said, without looking up.

Angel didn't turn away. A lesser woman, Max mused, would have blushed and cast her eyes down prettily. But when he looked over at Angel, she continued to gaze at him unabashedly.

"I imagine you're used to women staring at you,"

she said with a faint smile. "You're a striking-looking man, very strong profile. Very appealing."

He eyed her warily. "If this is your way of trying to seduce me into changing my mind about going to Miami with you, forget it." He gave the files a sweeping glance. "I don't want any part of this business, Angel. I just got a little carried away on impulse for a moment there and forgot my current aversion to trouble. Maybe in the old days, I would have gone along for the ride, even if I knew it was going to be bouncy. Maybe, especially if I knew. I was a fool in those days. I used to walk into the fire with my eyes open. But I finally accumulated enough singe marks to smarten up. I would have thought you'd be smarter, too."

"I am smart," Angel said angrily. "I'm smart enough to know that Lou didn't accidentally fall overboard and drown. I'm smart enough to know that he sent me his files for a reason. I'm smart enough to know that there's something here that might be just the clue I need. Look, Lou knew me well enough to know that I'd take a look at those papers he'd send me for safekeeping every so often. Maybe he was counting on the fact that I would remember the names on those papers and weed out these three files."

"Why all three? Certainly you don't think this tantalizing trio here all got together and pushed Lou overboard? Anyway, all three of those women owed him a debt of gratitude, not a final dip in the sea."

"Ah, but what about Ross Allen, Janine's black-mailer? Or Paula Bendix, who, thanks to Lou, spent six months in prison on attempted manslaughter? And last, but not least, there's Michael Hargrove."

"I thought he was tapping out license plates. How'd he get on that fishing boat?"

Angel made an impatient gesture. "He could have contracted the job out."

Max took the Hargrove file from Angel and set it on the table. Then he turned her to him. "Angel, listen to me, none of what you're thinking makes any sense. This is all old news. Even if any of these characters had an ax to grind, why wait all this time to grind it?" His grip tightened. "Will you forget this nonsense, dammit? People might not take too kindly to your snooping into their old affairs. Lou might have drowned accidentally, but you start poking that beautiful nose of yours into other people's business and you might run into another sort of . . . accident . . . altogether."

Angel's eyes darkened. "Talk about minding your own business—"

Max shook his head from side to side, a slow smile curving his lips. "You're right. I should be minding my own business. I stopped walking into the fire four years ago. I have a steady job nine months out of the year coaching football at a private school, date nice, uncomplicated ladies occasionally, pay my taxes like a good citizen, and keep as far from trouble as I can get. And yet, here I am, staring straight into the biggest blazing inferno I've seen in a month of Sundays, feeling hotter than hell . . . and the heat feels . . . so damn tempting."

"Max . . ." Angel turned her head just as his

54

lips descended. "Don't," she whispered as his mouth landed on her ear instead of her lips.

"Why not?" he murmured, his warm breath making her tremble. "You're hot too." His hands slid down her arm. "Don't deny it."

She pulled away, the warm flush in her cheeks ready proof of Max's observation. "I'm not denying it. But we're both worried about a different type of trouble. For me . . . it's letting myself get caught up in another . . . intimate relationship. I walked into the fire blindly once. And once was enough. Talk about burns, I collected more than my share. It wasn't all Lou's fault. I felt stifled. Lou was a possessive man. I guess I'm just too tough-minded, too independent. I like my freedom, Max. I don't want it tampered with."

"Then why did you come on to me?" he demanded harshly. "Why ask me to go down to Miami with you in the first place?"

Angel lowered her eyes. "I thought I might need some protection."

"You wanted a bodyguard." His voice was hard as steel.

Angel's expression was strained. She was scared. But she was also determined. If Lou's death wasn't an accident, she had to find out the truth. She owed him that. She'd loved him once. He was a good man. She couldn't let it go. There was no one else likely to take up the investigation if she didn't. "I . . . wanted . . . a partner. I thought I could trust you. I thought you were tough . . . but tender." She looked away as his eyes met hers. "It was a crazy notion to believe you'd help me. I don't know whatever made me think . . ."

He pulled her to him. "Thinking too much can get you in trouble."

In his arms, Angel felt a light-headed weakness. "So can not thinking at all," she managed to murmur before his lips descended, this time landing right on target.

He kissed her harder this time, moving his hands up under her shirt, the heat between them spreading like a fire already out of control.

Angel sighed audibly as the kiss ended. *Face it,* Max thought, as his eyes met Angel's. You might have worked for years to keep from getting burned again, but you never came up with the fiery likes of Angela Welles. He eased one arm across her waist and lowered her back onto the couch. He felt her stiffen.

"You're ready to face a horde of possible murderers and now you're frightened. You don't have to be afraid of me, Angel," he whispered, his hands sliding over the broad swell of her firm, high breasts.

Angel wanted to tell him that it wasn't him she was afraid of. It was her own intense feelings that terrified her. All Max had to do was touch her and she forgot all about not getting involved. She forgot all about those past regrets, the feeling of hurt, the sensation of being closed in. When Max's palms cupped her breasts, his mouth on hers, she even forgot for a few moments that she'd ever known a man by the name of Lou Chapman.

Max's hand found its way to the snap on Angel's

jeans, but as he undid it, his palm spreading over the satin smooth warmth of her stomach, Angel's hand pressed over his.

"No, Max." Her face was buried in his neck and her voice was muffled. But Max heard her.

He lifted his head and looked down at her.

"I'm not going to leave it alone, Max." She turned her face away. "I can't. Making love to me won't change that. It . . . won't change anything." She didn't really believe that last line for one moment. In fact, she was terrified that her whole world would change drastically if she let herself succumb to this burning desire that Max Gallagher ignited. But if he didn't buy her statement, he didn't argue it either. He eased himself off her and got up. Without another word, he started out of the living room.

"Max . . ."

"You're probably right, Angel. You may not be able to leave well enough alone, but I sure as hell can. See you around, Angel." He gave her a Humphrey Bogart grin and walked into the hall.

Angel followed him. "You're not as tough as I thought." Her voice was low, seductive, taunting.

Max glanced over his shoulder. "Oh? And why is that?"

"Because you're running scared, Gallagher."

He arched a brow, giving her a hooded gaze. "Maybe I got the wrong message in the clinches, Angel. I could have sworn I'd gotten a tidy brush-off."

She leaned against the wall. "That's not what I'm referring to."

His mouth curved in a slow smile. "You don't give up easy, do you, Angel?"

"Did you think I was the kind of woman that would?"

He laughed. "No. No, you definitely impress me as the determined type."

She walked over to him. "Maybe I am whistling Dixie about Lou's death. Maybe once I get down to Florida and . . . check on a few items . . . I'll be able to put my mind at rest. I might even decide to take a little cruise to the Bahamas afterward. People are always saying summer's not the time to go down to the islands. Actually, it's the best time. No tourists. You get to have the beaches all to yourself. You get a chance to unwind, take life a little slower, easier, get to know people in an . . . unhurried way." She smiled at him.

Max couldn't help but notice that it was a breathtaking smile. The only trouble was, it didn't reach up to her eyes. Angel's eyes still held that cool, determined glint. She spun a good tale, all right, but Max was pretty sure she had another scenario in mind. She wasn't going to stop digging until she found what she was looking for. Oh, she might go down to the Bahamas, but not for the reason she was giving him. That magazine photo he'd glanced at, of Vera and Michael Hargrove at that charity bash, had been snapped at the Crown Colony Club in Rum Cay in the Bahamas. There was also a small notation under the photo indicating that the Hargroves owned a villa close by the club.

Max stroked her cheek. "What about Key West,

Angel? I hear that's a nice spot to unwind this time of year, too. Maybe you want to go out on one of those deep-sea fishing boats, catch a few . . . sharks. But then, you were probably going to get around to mentioning Key West at some point."

Her breathtaking smile slipped away and she let out a ragged breath. "I don't know anyone else who can help me, Max. And the truth is . . . I'm scared to go it alone."

He leaned forward, brushing his lips to hers. "No dice, Angel. I never was the Boy Scout type." He held her gaze. "If you really want to unwind, get to know a person in an unhurried fashion, try Cape Cod. Now, that's a place to really take things nice and slow. I think I might just head on down there this weekend. If you change your mind about Miami and want to come along with me, that would be great." He paused, his gaze taking in her slow burn. "Truth is, I hate making the drive alone. Oh, and talk about things I hate, Angel, being used goes on top of my list." With that, he turned and walked out of the apartment, closing the door firmly behind him.

Angel watched the door shut, her eyes flickering with anger and guilt. She knew she'd laid it on thick. She couldn't have been more obvious if she'd flashed her message on a neon sign. Still, she'd expected him to bite. Even if it was true that she was using him, Angel knew that Max was well aware there was more to what was going on between them than that. She'd banked on his awareness to get his cooperation. But it hadn't worked.

Okay, she thought, *so you'll go it alone.* She'd had a few lessons in the game. Lou had showed her a couple of tricks. And Rick Seidman had shown her some more. Problem with Rick was he could never keep his lessons strictly on a professional line. That was one of the reasons she couldn't turn to Rick for help. He might get the wrong message. And as far as Rick was concerned, Angel did not want there to be the slightest chance he'd read it wrong.

She walked into the living room, sank down on the couch and closed her eyes. There was another reason she couldn't turn to Rick for help. She didn't trust him. Although she trusted him somewhat more than she trusted that lawyer, Metcalf, or, as Max had put it, the tantalizing trio—Wendy Shaw, Vera Hargrove, or Janine Dion, Lou Chapman's three gorgeous clients.

There were enough motives for Lou's murder floating around to sink a ship, never mind a lone man. Vera Hargrove's husband, Michael, certainly had to have it in for Lou. He was doing time, thanks to Lou's digging. That gave Hargrove motive—but unfortunately, not means. Michael wasn't too likely to have managed a weekend pass for a quick trip to the Keys.

Janine Dion's blackmailer, Ross, however, was not behind bars, and he couldn't have particularly loving feelings toward the guy who'd squashed a nifty little blackmailing scheme. Then there was Paula Bendix. She could have it in for Lou on two accounts. One, he'd nailed her for the attack on her husband, Derek. And two, by doing so, Lou had inadvertently cleared the way for Wendy Shaw to go waltzing off with Derek.

Those were just the obvious suspects. Angel bet that Lou had had brief romantic flings with one, two, or all of his three delectable clients. Maybe one of them had wanted a story-book ending, a happily-ever-after fairy tale. Only Lou Chapman hadn't been the type to believe in fairy tales. How did that saying go? Hell hath no fury like a woman scorned. Vera, Janine, Wendy . . . any of the trio might fit that adage.

None of those people would have won good-citizenship awards. And if Lou were around he would have been the first to tell her to play it close to her chest. As Lou used to say, Think the worst. Then you won't be disappointed.

A sad smile came to Angel's lips. She should have followed Lou's sage advice where Max Gallagher was concerned. Then she wouldn't be feeling so damn miserable. With Max she'd made the grievous error of believing the best. It was the chemistry between them that had blinded her to the truth. Max Gallagher, she decided, was a typical man. He wanted everything to come easy and then he wanted to walk away with the same ease.

Angel stood up with a resolute sigh. Tomorrow was a new day. That was one of her adages, not Lou's. She glanced back at the three files on the coffee table, then bent down and scooped them up. Just in case she couldn't fall off to sleep right away, she'd do some bedtime reading.

As it turned out, she was more tired than she

realized. She fell asleep halfway down page ten of Lou's notes on the Janine Dion case. The bedside lamp was still on and when Angel woke from a disturbing dream in which she and Max Gallagher were racing down a dark tunnel together, menacing footsteps behind them, she reached out to switch off the light. The strange thing was, those footsteps didn't recede even though the dream had. She flicked off the switch, bathing the room in darkness, as she listened, her body trembling, to the distinct sound of creaking floor boards in the living room next door. Had she gotten around to laying the large area rug, she might never have heard the intruder. She might never have heard anything ever again.

That thought made her tremble in earnest, but she cautiously lifted the covers and eased her legs over to the side of the bed. Fortunately, the previous tenant had left the wall to wall carpeting in the bedroom, cushioning Angel's bare footsteps as she crossed the room. Before she got to the bedroom door, she picked up the heaviest object she could find, a bronze figurine of a ballet dancer that her parents had given her when she was fourteen and had been the lead ballerina in her dance school recital of the Nutcracker.

Her palms were sweaty and she gripped the figurine tightly for fear that it would slip out of her fingers. She was terrified, but it never occurred to her to simply bolt her door and stay put. A sense of rage at the audacity of someone invading her privacy superseded her fear. She was determined to ignore her pounding pulse and the tight constriction in her chest. Despite the muggy heat, Angel was shivering. She had no real strategy other than to bash the intruder over the head and ask questions later. Better still, let the police ask questions. If only she'd gotten around to purchasing that second phone she'd been meaning to get for her bedroom, she could have dialed 911 and the police would be on their way. As it was, the only phone in the house happened to be in the living room.

Angel inched the bedroom door open. It made a slight squeak. Her hand froze on the knob. Had the intruder heard? The footsteps had stopped. Angel took a long, shuddering breath. Did that mean the intruder had gone? Or was he or she standing in the living room silently waiting for her to walk into the lair?

Angel had her answer the next moment. There was a rustle of papers falling followed by a low curse. The intruder was still there all right. And apparently busy at work. Angel hesitated for a moment and then slid past the narrow opening of the door. Hugging the wall she sneaked down the five feet of hallway that led to the arched entrance to the living room. Cautiously, she peeked around the corner.

There was a man, his back to her. He was large, dressed in a dark shirt and trousers. He was holding a flashlight and he was leaning over one of the cartons.

Angel held her breath and ducked her head back. The man was going through one of the boxes of files that Lou had sent her. Despite her fear, she congratulated herself on her intuition that those files were important. She thought of the three files she'd removed to her bedroom. Was one of those what the intruder was looking for?

Angel risked another quick look. He was still going through the files. Gripping the bronze figurine, Angel took a few cautious steps. The noise of the rustling of papers muffled the sound of her footsteps. Besides, the burglar seemed absorbed in his work.

Or at least that was the way it looked to Angel. She lifted her arm up, ready to strike, as she took a few longer strides. Then, just as she was in striking distance, the man whirled around, flashlight in hand. The light blinded her and she struck out wildly. Hard fingers gripped her wrist as her arm flung forward and the figurine went crashing against the wall. The next moment her arm was being wrenched behind her back. Angel let out a painful cry, lunging with her other hand. She made contact with her assailant's face and she heard his low, angry curse. She clawed him in earnest, but he shoved her off with ease. Angel felt herself fly backward. She crashed into a lamp table stacked with books that she hadn't yet gotten around to putting away. The ceramic-based lamp and all the books went crashing to the floor, the table and Angel following. But she kicked out as she fell, managing to catch her assailant directly in the groin. He let out a sharp cry as he bent over. Angel grabbed a heavy book and threw it at him. His hand rose to thwart the attack and the book smacked against the flashlight which spun, glittered, then fell to the floor, the glare going out instantly.

For a few brief moments, Angel had the advantage. Bathed in darkness, she knew her way around the disarray better than her assailant. She managed to make it to the living-room arch, her thoughts now only of escape. She'd lost her weapon and realized too late just how meager it was against a good two hundred pounds of male brawn.

Then two things happened almost simultaneously. Those hard male fingers reattached themselves to her, this time circling around her left ankle. At the same moment that she went toppling face first to the floor, there was a loud pounding at her door.

"Angel? Angel, are you all right?"

"Max!" she screamed out as she hit the ground. She tried for a second scream, but her assailant lunged forward, landing on top of her. The air shot from her lungs, a fierce stab of pain filling her body. She felt she would suffocate from the combination of the man's weight and the sweaty scent of his muscular body.

From down the hall there was a series of smacking, thudding noises, and then a shattering sound as the thick, wooden front door gave way.

A shaft of light streaked through the darkness. A hoarse, angry sound echoed close to her ear as the attacker's hot breath washed over the side of her face. Then the man pulled himself off her and got to his feet just as Max came racing toward him. The assailant lowered his head like a battering ram and charged, so that both men collided in a struggling heap.

Desperately, Angel scrambled to her feet. She lunged at the intruder who had his hard hands coiled around Max's throat. What she failed to notice was that Max's hard hand was about to ascend up into the bastard's jaw. She ducked to the side, but she wasn't quick enough. The next moment stars flashed in her eyes and then there was darkness again as the floor seemed to come up to meet her halfway.

Cold water, half of it landing down her face, the rest of it choking her throat, brought her around. Groggily, she opened her eyes and saw Max looking anxiously down at her.

"The burglar . . . ," she muttered as he helped her sit up.

"He got away."

"Are you all right?" she asked anxiously.

Max grinned. "I was just about to ask you the same thing. You've got a hard jaw."

"You've got a hard fist." Gingerly, she rubbed her jaw. It was sore, but otherwise in one piece. His tag had stunned her more than anything else. "He was after the files. Lou's files. I caught him going through them. I bet he was looking for the ones I'd brought into my bedroom. I told you they were—"

Max pulled Angel to him so abruptly, she let the rest of her sentence trail off. His hand moved with a caressing gesture against her cheek, then he tenderly brushed his fingertips against her jaw. He bent as if he were going to kiss her. He did, but first he mur-

66

mured, "I guess you do need some looking after, Angel."

She received his kiss greedily despite her sore jaw. Afterward she murmured, "I knew you had some Boy Scout in you, Gallagher. You have quite a number of sterling qualities, as a matter of fact."

He wasn't so sure Angel was right. Or maybe she was intentionally overlooking some of his more tarnished traits. Like the fact that he kept jumping from the frying pan into the fire. Like the fact that he had always been a sucker for a beautiful dame. And they didn't come more beautiful than Angel Welles.

CHAPTER FOUR

It was ten A.M. when the plane touched down in Miami. A heavy humidity hung in the air. Even the air conditioning in the vast terminal couldn't counteract it. The cloying heat coupled with the dim, dreary indoor lighting cast a damp pallor over all the travelers, half of whom lay slumped in those hard, unyielding plastic airport seats that stretched along the windowed walls. Already, the sun was glaring, its rays penetrating the tinted glass.

There was a steady drone of noise as people scurried to the baggage claim area, Max and Angel following along with the other passengers. They had packed light, each reclaiming their one mid-size canvas suitcase from the conveyor belt.

"A miracle." Angel grinned. "They managed not to lose either of our belongings."

Max managed a quick grimace. He'd been out of sorts since they'd left Boston. Angel knew he had any number of misgivings about taking this trip, but he'd made up his mind to grin and bear it. Well . . . to bear it anyway. He hadn't so much as cracked a smile yet.

He took the case from her hand. Angel had enough to manage with her large tote bag and a smaller overnight case that she'd kept with her during the flight. She had no intention of letting this case out of her sight. It contained the three files she'd been carefully guarding since the break-in at her apartment three nights ago.

As they headed past the swarming hordes of people still anxiously awaiting the arrival of their baggage, Angel heard her name being paged over the loudspeaker, asking her to come to the TWA information desk. She gave Max a puzzled look. His gaze was truculent.

"I thought no one knew exactly when you were arriving." His tone was harsh and wary.

"I thought so, too." Angel shot him a cool glance. She was beginning to have her own misgivings about having coerced Max into holding her hand through this ordeal. All she needed right now was yet another adversary. Then she shook her head almost imperceptibly. No, she decided resolutely, she hadn't really coerced Max into coming along. He had made the final decision. Not that she wasn't greatly relieved. Her encounter with that intruder who'd broken into her apartment convinced her she was going to need some help. She just wished Max would be more gracious about giving it.

"We better go see who's paging me," she said finally, glancing around to see where the information desk was located.

"It's over there." Max pointed off to the left.

Angel noticed that Max hung back a little as they

walked across the terminal. When they were within twenty feet of the desk, Angel came to an abrupt stop as a man rose from a plastic seat nearby and stepped into view.

Her stop was so sudden Max nearly collided into her. "What the hell . . . ?"

"It's Rick," she muttered, her eyes narrowing.

"The private eye you worked for?"

Angel nodded as Rick Seidman began walking toward them. Max studied him carefully. Seidman was of medium height with a trim, compact body. He wore a pair of chinos and a pale blue short-sleeved shirt. Both items were rumpled. His hair was dark and curly. He could use a haircut, but the unruly look seemed to go with the rest of him. Max guessed him to be in his late thirties.

Seidman's smile was assessing as he drew near. Angel knew that while Rick had given Max only the briefest of glances, he was the one Rick was evaluating.

Angel waited for Rick's approach, her head tilted, mouth set in a firm line.

"Hi, beautiful. Welcome home." Seidman's voice was smooth, cool, self-assured. There was a look of secret amusement on his face as his hazel eyes met Angel's.

Max didn't understand what that look meant. But he knew he didn't like it. Nor did he like the familiar way Rick bent down and placed a moist kiss on Angel's toffee lips. Come to think of it, he didn't much care for the way Angel received the kiss.

"This isn't home anymore, Rick. Remember?"

Angel said with a teasing smile after the kiss was over.

"Home is where your heart is, Angel." Rick's glance slid by Max again.

Angel quickly introduced the two men, exchanging names only. She didn't bother giving out any information on Max. She had a pretty good idea that Rick had already done his homework on her new friend. Although outwardly Angel maintained a playful manner with Rick, inwardly she was seething. The bastard had been keeping a check on her. She was sure of it. That's how he knew when she was arriving in town. That's why he didn't look at all surprised at seeing Max. A pressing question whirled in her mind. Had he also had one of his cronies break into her place to get a hold of Lou's files? She knew Rick well enough to know she was going to have to keep things light if she was to get any answers. With a man like Seidman, you got more with honey than you did with vinegar.

"I have my car out front." Rick hesitated. "Listen, I was sorry to hear about Lou, Angel. I know how much you cared for the guy. We had our differences, but I respected him. We went back a long way."

Angel nodded. At least Rick hadn't tried to lay it on thick. He'd said only enough to be polite. Then again, he'd have to know Angel would be able to see through any hearts-and-flowers speeches. Over the years she and Rick had worked together, he'd badmouthed Lou on any number of occasions. Rick never did handle competition well.

"How did you know I was coming in?" she asked.

Rick grinned. "You're the loyal type, Angel. I know you."

"You even knew just what flight I'd be taking." She eyed him narrowly.

Rick gave an idle shrug. "You know me, Angel," was all he said.

"You still have a couple of hours before the funeral," Rick went on after a couple of silent beats. "I've got my car outside. I'll take you over there now if you want to . . ."

Angel shook her head. "No. I think we'll go the hotel and get checked in." She shot Max a quick glance, but a shutter had come down over his blue eyes and she couldn't get a reading.

"Where are you staying?" Rick asked casually.

As if he didn't know, Angel thought. He'd tracked all her other moves. Surely he'd gotten word of where she'd booked her reservations. "The Sea Beach," she said lightly. "You know I always had a fondness for that spot."

"Well, you'll like it even better now. They've just finished refurbishing their nightclub. And they hired one of Miami's top singers."

They'd started walking, Rick on one side of Angel, Max on the other. She almost messed up the pace on hearing Rick's last remark. Her woman's intuition told her that the singer was none other than the entrancing Wendy Shaw. Her shoulder brushed against Max's and she gave him a sidelong glance. His lips compressed and Angel felt certain he'd made the same guess.

"Wendy Shaw," Rick affirmed her unspoken conclusion after a brief silence. "You've caught her act, haven't you, Angel? She used to be the feature attraction over at Anton's."

Angel kept an even pace. "No. I've heard of her, of course." Her hand gripped her overnight case tightly. "She's supposed to be very talented."

"Very." The smile on Rick's face smacked of a more intimate knowledge than Angel had guessed. She eyed him curiously.

"If she's a friend of yours," Angel said casually, "maybe you can get Max and me a ringside table. I have a feeling I'm going to need to unwind after . . . by tonight." Her voice lowered an octave.

Rick put his arm around Angel and pressed his lips against her hair. "You know I'd give you the world, babe. A ringside table is a snap."

Tension was fast building inside of Angel. Nothing had changed as far as Rick's attitude or approach was concerned. She was the challenge he couldn't conquer, the challenge he never seemed to weary of. Probably because there'd been a few weak moments a long time ago when she was feeling very vulnerable and very lonely and Rick had made it clear that he was very available. But Angel had come to her senses before things got too intense. She realized she would only have been compounding her problems to go from the arms of one private eye into the arms of another.

Besides the handicap of his profession, Rick wasn't her type. He was too slick, too confident. And too secretive. Even though she worked for him for three years, she knew that he secreted away certain files that he didn't want her to see. And there were a few cases that he never seemed to keep any record of at all. Or if he did, Angel never saw the files. The only way she knew about those cases was from spotting a name showing up on his appointment pad on several occasions. And a couple of times, she'd gotten word from Lou. That was how she'd learned about Rick working for Michael Hargrove. At the time, she didn't make much of the fact that she never did file any papers on that case. But now, that fact had a lot more impact on her thoughts.

However, it was difficult to give those thoughts her undivided attention with Rick's arm slung possessively around her shoulder and with Max staring straight ahead, his expression hard and surly. She brushed her hand against Max's, hoping the brief contact would convey her true feelings. Max merely stuck his hand in his pocket and stepped up his pace.

Angel found his rigidity grating. Couldn't he tell in the slightest when she was putting on an act? Could he really think she enjoyed playing up to Rick Seidman?

Of course, she concluded, with a sad little wrench, that was exactly what Max thought. And why not? After all, he knew nothing about her. He had no way of knowing that she found Rick's touch particularly offensive especially as she compared it to the delirious sensations Max's caresses evoked in her.

Rick led them to a sleek gray Mercedes coup. Angel's brow shot up. "New car, I see. Business must be good."

Rick's eyes trailed her face. "Not as good as it used to be when you were with me."

Angel let the remark slide by. But when she looked over at Max she noted that it hadn't slid by him. He shot her a fierce gaze.

Rick followed Angel's glance as he wiped a bead of sweat from his brow. It had to be near one hundred degrees in the shade. "Ever been to Miami before, Gallagher?"

"A few times," Max answered Rick succinctly, pulling his eyes away from Angel.

She pursed her lips. In the pizza parlor, he'd told her he hadn't been here before. She wondered why.

Rick opened the front passenger seat, ushering Angel in before she could make any maneuver to slide in back with Max. She had no alternative but to get in front. Rick closed the door firmly once she was settled into the plush charcoal velour bucket seat and skipped around to his side of the car, while Max got in back, slamming the door harder than necessary once he was inside.

The drive from the airport to the Sea Beach took twenty minutes. During the ride, Rick did most of the talking, chatting amiably with Angel about mutual friends and acquaintances. His tone was warm with a distinctly seductive tinge. Every now and then, his hand shot out to pat Angel's knee. These intimate gestures were too brief for Angel to actually protest. Besides, she didn't feel comfortable making an issue of it in front of Max, who sat stiffly and silently in the backseat. He looked as if he were doing a dress rehearsal for the upcoming funeral service. Angel thought glumly that he'd make a perfect pallbearer.

When Rick pulled up in front of the Sea Beach, a small, sophisticated hotel a mile down from the bustling hotel strip, Angel was eager to send him on his way. But Rick wasn't going to make it easy.

"I'll get your bag, Angel."

"That's okay, Rick. Max can manage." She glanced back at him. Max remained silent.

"No problem," Rick said. "I'll just make sure you get settled."

Angel compressed her lips, irritated that Max was being no help at all in ditching her ex-boss.

They entered the cool mauve-and-mint-toned lobby. No gold and gaudy glitter so typical of Miami. Everything about the Sea Beach was understated. The tile floor was shaded a soft gray-green reminiscent of the Florida sea. The furnishings were a tastefully elegant blend of antique tables and credenzas intermingled with plush, modern sofas upholstered in natural fibers. And there was not a single potted palm in sight, a point Angel rated highly.

While she and Rick headed for the registration desk, Max strolled over to a large poster resting on an easel near the entrance to the hotel's supper club. Wendy Shaw, pictured here full-length in a clinging sequined gown, microphone in hand, looked as strikingly alluring as in that photo in Lou's file. The sultry smile on her face as she gazed out from the poster made it clear she knew just how alluring she was.

Max pivoted around and looked over at Angel, who was signing the registration card. Had she known all along that Wendy Shaw was singing here now? Is that why she chose the Sea Beach? His expression darkened. He didn't much care for that possibility and he planned to tell her exactly that as soon as that octopus, Seidman, took a walk.

Angel motioned to Max to join them. He took his time.

"You have to sign for your room," she said when he approached.

Max took up the pen and scrawled his signature. Then he flicked a glance at Rick. "Worried that Angel and I might be sharing the same room, Seidman?"

Angel's expression was startled by Max's remark, especially after he'd been so glumly silent since Rick's appearance. But Rick didn't even flinch.

"No, Gallagher. I wasn't worried. I know Angel."

Max's grin was decidedly lascivious. "Is that so?"

That remark managed to get a slight reaction from Rick. Max noted with satisfaction the pulsating muscle in the private eye's jaw.

"Well," Max said laconically, "why don't we go upstairs and freshen up, Angel? It's been a long flight and neither of us got much sleep last night." He took hold of Angel's arm at the elbow, gripping it firmly. "Will we see you at the funeral, Seidman?"

Rick looked as if he were entering combat. "I'll pick you up." His gaze rested exclusively on Angel.

"That won't be necessary," Max said dismissively. "We've arranged for a car."

Angel nearly tripped as Max strode off with her in tow.

"You are the most puzzling man I've ever met, Gallagher," she said with exasperation once they were alone in the elevator and it started its ascent.

He gave her a brooding look. "Nothing puzzling about me, Angel."

He was still gripping her elbow. Angel wrenched it free as the doors slid open on four. They weren't sharing the same room, but they were both on the same floor. Angel stepped out ahead of him, but Max's fingers again took hold of her as she got to her door.

"You're across the hall," she said coolly.

"Open the door," he ordered. "We've got a few things to get straight."

When she made no move, Max wrenched the key from her hand and opened the door himself. He gave her a not-so-light shove inside and then followed.

"I don't appreciate being manhandled," she said tightly.

"And I don't appreciate being made to feel a bigger sucker than I already feel. Why didn't you tell me that you and Seidman were more than working mates? You were bedmates too, weren't you? Were the sheets still warm when you left town?"

Angel laughed. It was the wrong thing to do. She

78

misjudged Max's degree of fury. In one swift, powerful movement, he hoisted her up and literally tossed her onto the large, pristinely done up bed. Angel's eyes flickered with rage as she fell onto the mattress.

"Are you crazy?"

As she started to rise, Max was there to shove her back down. "I want the truth, Angel. All of it. As far as I can see, you didn't need me holding your hand down here. Seidman's hand is positively itching to hold you."

"Don't be a fool, Max."

His mouth was set in a tight line. "That hasn't been easy to avoid since I met you, Angel."

Angel's eyes widened. "I didn't know you were the jealous type." There was a touch of teasing in her tone, but Max was in no mood for banter.

"There are a lot of things about me you don't know," he snapped.

"Like that you've been to Miami a few times. Why didn't you tell me?"

"Whoa there, Angel. I'm asking the questions right now." His fingers dug into her shoulders as he pinned her down on the bed.

"If you let me at least sit up, I'll consider answering you," she said. "Or do you plan to beat the answers out of me?"

His smile was shadowed. "I'll consider that. It depends on whether I like the answers you give me. The first one is what's going on between you and Seidman?"

79

"Nothing," she said hotly. "But even if there were, I don't see that I owe you any explanations."

"That's where we disagree, Angel. I figure that since I'm along for the ride, I deserve to know exactly what route we're following. And exactly who's following along with us. Did you know Seidman was having you watched after you left Miami?"

Angel tilted her chin. "How did you know that?"

He laughed dryly. "I know the type. I also figured that was the only way he could have known when you'd be landing in Miami. Unless you wired him and forgot to mention it to me."

"I haven't had any contact of any kind with Rick since I left Miami."

Max loomed over her. "And what kind of contact did you have with him before you left?"

"Not the kind you're thinking."

"Now why don't I believe you, Angel?"

"It's the truth, Max." She hesitated. "Okay . . . a long time ago, we did get a little . . . chummy, but that didn't last long."

"But you still kept on working for him?"

Angel shrugged. Or she made the vain attempt anyway. Max still had her in a viselike grip which didn't give her much freedom of movement.

"Okay, let's leave that one for a moment. What about Wendy Shaw?"

"What about her?"

"Why didn't you tell me you'd picked the Sea Beach because she was singing here now?"

"I didn't tell you because I didn't know." Her eyes sparkled. "But it is convenient."

Max shook his head wearily, then released his hold on Angel and rolled onto his back beside her. "I knew this was going to be one of my bigger mistakes."

Angel turned onto her side, propping her head up with her hand. She stared at Max's profile, thoughts completely unrelated to the mystery of Lou Chapman's death swirling in her mind. This was the first time she'd found herself in bed . . . or at least on a bed . . . with Max. Since the break-in at her apartment three nights ago, Max had been notably standoffish. Just as he resigned himself to joining her on the trip to Miami, he seemed also to have decided to play a cool hand in the romance department. While Angel told herself it was for the best— after all she was as eager as Max not to get seriously involved in a relationship—she couldn't get those sensuous moments they'd shared out of her mind.

Angel touched his face, running her fingers over the faint rough stubble of beard along his jawline. She felt the muscle beneath his flesh tighten. He took hold of her hand, withdrew it, studied it for another instant, then sat up. Angel felt a dull ache as she watched him hesitate for another moment and then rise.

"We better take this slow, Angel. My mistakes have a way of compounding themselves. And I end up paying a heavy price. My last one cost me a lot of dough and my self-respect."

He turned around and faced her as she sat up on the bed. "My ex-wife's family lives in Miami. We were married down here." He shrugged. "I had high hopes back then. Lots of them. I thought I had the world in the palm of my hand."

"What happened?" Angel asked softly. "What went wrong?"

"Everything." His smile was bleak.

Angel felt a wrenching in her heart, half for Max, half because she could so readily identify with his feelings. "I've been there, too," she said in a low voice.

Max gave her a long look. "Maybe you have." There was such tenderness in his voice, such empathy that Angel felt a strange mixture of desire and fear well up in her. It had been a long time since she'd felt drawn to a man the way she did to Max Gallagher. Or maybe what really scared her was that she had never truly felt this overwhelmingly intense pull before. Not with Lou, not with any man. Max Gallagher could mean countless complications.

They were both silent, but the room almost crackled with electricity. Max looked into Angel's eyes, large, exquisite eyes of the deepest lapis lazuli gems. They were luminous with emotions. She was the loveliest, most captivating and unique woman he'd ever come upon. A siren. How easily she had lured him. How willingly he had come.

He wrenched his eyes from her and turned away. "Anyway, after Laura and I broke up and she walked off with most of what I had, I came to the conclusion that the dough didn't matter nearly so much as my self-respect. It took a long time building it back up. It withstood a lot of temptations."

Angel rose and walked slowly over to him. "Is that all I am, Max? Just a temptation?"

Max smiled ruefully. "Ah, Angel. You're more dangerous than a mere temptation." His glittering eyes raked her face, then he brought her fingers to his lips. "You could be the straw that breaks the camel's back."

Her hands reached up toward his face, but Max took hold of her wrists. His eyes narrowed speculatively. "I don't play for keeps anymore, Angel."

She flashed him one of those breathtaking smiles of hers. "Neither do I, Max."

He was still holding her wrists, still studying her reflectively. Once again her smile did not reach her eyes. Max shook his head. "I used to gamble, Angel. Not just money. I gambled on people, on myself, on excitement. Some folk say being a gambler is the same as being an alcoholic. One swig and you're on the road to ruin again." His eyes were hungry, but the wariness had returned full force. "And you, Angel . . . you're the finest sparkling champagne . . . a real vintage year. I'm scared, Angel. Scared that I could grow too damn accustomed to the taste. I think I better play it safe and stick to beer."

He walked over to the door. "I'm leaving Miami Monday morning as planned, Angel." He cast her a glance over his shoulder, a wry smile on his lips. "So either you resolve things by then . . . or you're on your own."

Angel bristled. "I've been on my own before," she retorted.

He was about to give a comeback, but clamped his mouth shut instead and walked out the door.

Angel paced up and down her hotel room. She knew only half of her anger had to do with Max's ultimatum. The rest had to do with her feeling rejected and hurt . . . even if what Max said made sense for her as well as for him. For three years she'd told herself that she liked being on her own. She even believed it . . . most of the time.

She came to a stop. Max talked a good line, but she wasn't sure he could stick to it. A devilish smile curved her lips. If she knew what was good for her, she'd give him the benefit of the doubt. Then again, if she knew what was good for her, would she be down here in Miami determined to find out what really happened on that fateful fishing trawler off the Florida Keys that resulted in her ex-husband's demise?

She glanced at her watch. She still had an hour before she had to dress for the funeral. She walked over to her overnight case and plucked out the three files, one of which she instinctively felt held a clue to the puzzle. Maybe if she found it, she might be able to convince Max to switch his Monday plane reservation. She tried to concentrate on the papers, but the pages of the files blurred as she began to wonder if she could convince Max Gallagher about anything else.

CHAPTER FIVE

Lou's funeral was held at a small chapel off Euclid Avenue in Miami Beach. It was two o'clock in the afternoon and the temperature had soared to a hundred and three in the shade. Max pulled the rented Ford Fairlane into a parking lot across from the church. He got out first, walked around and opened the car door for Angel, offering a hand which she took with a small smile. She was dressed in a simple gray linen dress, her thick black hair brushed off her face and pinned at the nape of her neck into a twisted coil. She wore no makeup but the candy-colored lipstick she always used. Max walked beside her as they crossed to the church. He thought she looked subdued and probably more beautiful than ever . . . if that was possible. He tugged on his tie, a heavy sweat working up under the collar of his white shirt. He carried the lightweight tan jacket of his suit over his shoulder. It was too hot to slip it on a minute before he had to.

Angel walked with a fluid grace. Max had been worried about her after he'd walked out of her hotel room a couple of hours ago. He felt like a heel giving her his masterful brush-off right before the ordeal of the funeral. She could have been reaching out for some comfort. And he'd turned his back on her, his only concern his own neck . . . or more accurately his own heart. He didn't want it broken. That shouldn't be a crime, but he spent two hours pacing his room feeling guilty as hell.

Now he saw that Angel was doing fine. When he knocked on her door ten minutes ago to say the car had been delivered, she gave him a warm smile. He asked her how she was doing and she clasped his hand in a strictly platonic squeeze. She was fine, just fine. He was the one who was sweating.

A diminutive middle-aged woman stood at the heavy wooden church door. She smiled with just the right touch of respectful sympathy as Max and Angel approached. She handed the two of them hymn books and went to open the door for them. Max had to help her. The door must have weighed three times what she did.

Once inside the chapel, Angel came to an abrupt stop at the head of the middle aisle as those already gathered turned to see who the new arrivals were. Angel had told Max that few people were likely to attend the service, but even she had thought there'd be more than the handful of mourners that had gathered here this afternoon. She felt sorry for Lou, but maybe his policy of distrust had led to this less than standing room only crowd.

Angel glanced at the people sitting in the three front pews. There were six in all. She recognized four of them. Rick Seidman was sitting next to the radiant blonde, Wendy Shaw, the chanteuse, looking delectably sexy as she flashed Rick a beguiling smile. Rick didn't pick it up. His eyes were on Angel and Max. One pew behind them and off to the far left was another fair-haired lass, Janine Dion. She was dressed rather inappropriately, Angel thought, in a flimsy Hawaiian print dress that left little about the actress's assets to the imagination. A young man with bottle-streaked blond hair, his neck draped in gold chains, his skin tanned to match his glitzy jewelry, sat beside her. Angel didn't recognize him, but she watched him whisper something to Janine after giving her and Max the once-over. Janine, however, seemed too preoccupied in her own private rapture of self-involvement to pay much attention to what he was saying.

The last of the tantalizing trio, as Max had so aptly named them, sat demurely in the third row of pews. Vera Hargrove, dressed in a simple navy sheath with shoe-polish-white peter pan collar, gave Angel and Max a mere flicker of acknowledgment before she turned to the man sitting to her right, the pair exchanging what Angel thought were cautionary looks. This gentleman was older and was by far the most distinguished-looking mourner of the gathered group. He wore a well-tailored navy suit with crisply laundered pale blue shirt and maroon and navy striped silk tie. His hair was graying nicely, not a strand out of place. Yet he habitually brushed a palm across the side of his head to smooth out imaginary untamed wisps.

Max placed his hand lightly against the base of

Angel's back. "Shall we find a seat?" He spoke in a muted voice.

Angel leaned closer. "You mean before the house is packed?"

She chose two seats down front. There was no coffin on view as Lou's will had requested cremation and a simple memorial service. A young, attractive minister stood at the podium. He was about to begin the service when two more people arrived. He might have begun anyway were it not for the commotion that ensued as the two men slipped into back aisle seats.

It began with a loud gasp. Angel and Max turned to see where the sound had come from. It wasn't difficult to ascertain. Vera Hargrove had risen to her feet, her face paler than her starched white collar as she stared wide-eyed at one of the two men seated in the back. Angel's eyes followed Vera's. Her own intake of breath was audible.

"It's Michael Hargrove," Angel whispered into Max's ear.

"I thought he was a prison entrepreneur."

"I thought so, too."

Vera Hargrove was still on her feet, but the man beside her was doing his best to get her to sit down again. She flung his hand off, her face going from pasty white to scarlet. Then suddenly she stormed up the aisle, stopping in front of her husband. Seething with rage, she struck him across the face, hissed, "Murderer," and fled from the church like she was on fire.

Angel's blue-violet eyes widened as she and Max

exchanged a stunned stare. Michael Hargrove didn't bat an eye. He stared straight ahead of him, gave a brief nod to the minister as if giving his permission for the proceedings to resume, then opened his prayer book. The man sitting beside him waited a moment, stood up and quietly slipped out of the chapel.

The service itself went ahead without any further hitch. The minister had a deep baritone voice and a nice lyrical style. He kept his words about Lou Chapman brief, but he spoke with a flare for the dramatic. Angel thought Lou would have been pleased. Max handed her a hanky as she rummaged through her purse for that packet of tissues she'd bought just for the occasion and now couldn't find. She shed a few tears for auld lang syne and noticed that Wendy Shaw and Janine Dion also shed some tears into tissues.

The service concluded, Max and Angel walked up the aisle. Max took her hand and Angel squeezed it, this time with more passion. He slipped his arm around her. They both noticed that Michael Hargrove's seat in the last row of pews was now empty. Neither of them was certain he'd actually stayed for the service itself. He might have come merely to stir up some excitement and then, the deed accomplished, made his exit.

Janine Dion and her friend came up behind Angel and Max. Angel glanced at the actress over her shoulder, but Janine hastily averted her gaze. Angel was surprised to see that Janine's eyes were quite red from crying and there was a look of pain and discomfort on her face. And something else. Fear. Janine gave the barest nod and then squeezed past them as she rushed to the door. Her boyfriend's face totally lacked pathos. He followed after Janine, but only after he'd given Angel a look that made it clear he wouldn't toss her out of his bed. The look also said he was sure she'd want to climb in. Some people had more self-confidence than was warranted.

Angel grinned as Janine's companion moved on. She saw that Max wasn't amused. She heard him mutter the word "creep" under his breath.

His anger passed as they stepped outside and Angel swayed slightly against him. The contrast of the glaring hot sun after the cool dimness of the chapel upset her equilibrium, but Max thought it was the aftereffects of the funeral service.

"Are you okay?" he asked.

"Better than Vera Hargrove," Angel said, squinting up at him as Max's arm tightened around her waist.

"I don't like that look in your eye, Angel."

"You heard what she called Michael Hargrove. Murderer."

Max sighed heavily. "She could have been referring to anything. He sure as hell murdered their marriage."

"You're reaching, Gallagher." Those blue-violet eyes of hers glittered as she gave him a shrewd glance. "And you know it."

"I only know one thing."

Max didn't get to tell her what it was, however. The dapper man with nary a hair out of place who'd lost his companion, Vera Hargrove, before the funeral service, called out Angel's name.

"Ms. Welles, I'm delighted to meet you. I'm John Metcalf. I wrote you." He ushered Angel off to the side of the chapel's path as he introduced himself. Max followed behind.

Angel shook his outstretched hand. He had a firm grip, but his skin was slightly clammy. Angel had the urge to wipe her palm off on her dress, but she fought it. Instead she introduced Max.

"Mr. Gallagher. A pleasure to meet you." Metcalf turned quickly back to Angel. "May I say how sorry I am about that incident back in the chapel. One never can be sure how a person will react at a time of grief."

"I didn't realize Vera Hargrove would take Lou's death so hard," Angel said, a touch of facetiousness in her voice.

"Oh, I'm not surprised in the least. Not considering the circumstances. And . . ." There was a pregnant pause before he concluded the sentence, "not considering their relationship."

Angel scowled. "Their relationship? You mean Lou and Vera were—"

"Involved," Metcalf broke in, then pursed his lips as Rick Seidman and Wendy Shaw approached.

Angel shot Max a baffled look, then quickly greeted Rick who gave her a condolence kiss that smacked of more than sympathy. Meanwhile, Wendy smiled glamorously at Max.

Max wondered if Metcalf felt left out. He had a

poker face so there was no way to tell what the suave attorney felt.

"I got you that ringside table for tonight," Rick said after introducing the singer around. "We'll see you then."

Wendy continued smiling at Max until Rick ushered her off. Angel threw Max a smile that beautifully and intentionally imitated Wendy's. Only Angel's had a hefty dose of mockery tossed in.

"If you aren't too drained, Ms. Welles," Metcalf interjected, "perhaps I could drive you down to my office and we can go over Mr. Chapman's will. I assume you're only planning a short stay in Miami and I imagine you would like to settle things quickly."

Angel's glance went back to Max. Then she nodded slowly. "Yes, let's take care of the matter now. Mr. Gallagher and I will follow you in our car, Mr. Metcalf."

Nothing changed on Metcalf's face, but Angel had the distinct impression that the lawyer would have preferred to lose Max. After hesitating for a fraction of a second, Metcalf nodded. "Very well."

Fifteen minutes later, Angel and Max were sitting in plush leather armchairs in the cool cream and aqua office of John Metcalf. The place was showy. It looked to Angel like Metcalf had used the same decorators who designed the sets for "Miami Vice." Angel thought John Metcalf should have gone the whole route and hired the show's clothing designers to give him the same contemporary look as his office, because he didn't go with his place. On the other hand, Angel observed, Max fit in perfectly. He had the right look, the right air of tough, sensual ruggedness and a relaxed, easy manner that seemed to make John Metcalf uncomfortable.

"Perhaps it would be better to conduct our business in private," Metcalf addressed Angel as he removed a manila envelope from the top drawer of his mahogany desk. "I'm sure you could use a drink, Mr. Gallagher. There's a very pleasant pub right across the street."

"Are you thirsty, Max?"

He gave her a wink. "I can hold out."

"He can hold out, Mr. Metcalf. Why don't you go ahead?"

Metcalf cleared his throat. "All right." He opened the envelope, his movements meticulous as he carefully removed a typed sheet of stationery. "Actually it's quite brief and to the point. You, Ms. Welles, are Mr. Chapman's sole beneficiary. There is a small life insurance policy amounting to five thousand dollars, a savings account on which I've withdrawn the balance of twenty-three hundred and thirty-six dollars for you." He removed a certified check from the same envelope and slid it across the table. "Beyond that, there is Mr. Chapman's office and home furnishings and his professional and personal papers. Perhaps you would want to ask Mr. Seidman to help you with the professional side, Ms. Welles. He did phone me the other day to offer any assistance."

"That won't be necessary," Angel said with a pleasant smile. "Max and I will manage quite nicely. I assume you have the key to Lou's place for me."

Metcalf nodded. "There is one thing, Ms. Welles." He paused. "As I was sure Mr. Chapman would want, I took the liberty of checking his home and office yesterday to make certain everything was in order for you."

"Was it?" Angel asked.

"I believe there might be . . . certain papers of Mr. Chapman's that are missing."

"Papers?" This time Max asked the question in a slow, lazy voice.

Metcalf bristled. He obviously did not think Max had any right to ask questions. "I think some of your ex-husband's business files might be missing, Ms. Welles. There was a filled file cabinet that I recalled seeing on other occasions when I'd visited Mr. Chapman's office. Yesterday, that cabinet was empty."

Angel stood up, gathering the check. "Don't worry about it, Mr. Metcalf. What interest would I have in Lou's business files anyway?" She leaned over to take the letter and envelope from Metcalf's desk. "I assume these are mine." She tucked them in her purse along with the check. "Oh . . . and the key, Mr. Metcalf."

"It's in the envelope," Metcalf said stiffly.

Angel smiled. "Well, I guess that concludes our business, Mr. Metcalf." She looked over at Max, who was easing himself slowly out of the leather armchair.

"Will Ms. Welles find Mr. Chapman's bank book in there also?" Max asked laconically.

That question jarred a few of Metcalf's composed features. His jaw tightened, his pale blue eyes blinked and his mouth twitched. "The bank book? I closed the account out, Mr. Gallagher." He looked at Angel. "I thought you might be leaving the city before the bank opened on Monday morning. I was merely . . ."

"You were merely being helpful," Max said, pulling himself up to his full height now, which was at least six inches above Metcalf's. "I'm sure Ms. Welles appreciates it, don't you, Angel?" He didn't wait for an answer. "But Ms. Welles has a real thing for order, Mr. Metcalf."

Angel thought about the chaos of her apartment back in Boston and had to hold back a laugh.

"She would like to file Mr. Chapman's bank book away under account closed," Max added.

"I don't really see the point . . ." Metcalf began.

"Call it a sentimental whim. You know women, Metcalf." He gave the lawyer a broad wink. "Some things they just like to hold on to for old times' sake."

Angel took Max's hand. "You understand me so well. I guess that's why I rely on you so." She smiled at Metcalf. "Max is right, Mr. Metcalf. I would like that bank book . . . just something to file away in my drawer of memories."

Metcalf's face was a little red under his Miami tan. He walked over to a fancy oak file cabinet and withdrew a folder. Inside was the bank book and several other papers. He withdrew only the bank book.

"Anything else that Ms. Welles might want to tuck into that memory drawer, Metcalf?"

The lawyer gave Max a searing glance. "The rest are my personal papers, Mr. Gallagher." He didn't hand over the bank book. He merely placed it on his desk.

Angel plucked it up and put it in her purse. "Thank you, Mr. Metcalf. It's been a pleasure." She paused. "Oh, there is one other thing, Mr. Metcalf. You mentioned before that Vera Hargrove and Lou were . . . involved. I assume you meant personally involved."

"It isn't my place to discuss the matter, Ms. Welles," Metcalf said officiously.

"You also mentioned that Mrs. Hargrove's outburst might have had something to do with the circumstances of Mr. Chapman's death," Max added in that same laconic tone he'd been using all along. "What did you mean by that?"

Metcalf clearly didn't like being the one on the witness stand, but he said crisply, "You'll no doubt find out, if you haven't already, that it was Mrs. Hargrove's yacht that Mr. Chapman was out on that day." He pressed his palms together and turned his back to them in dismissal.

Max guided Angel to the door. With his hand on the knob, he glanced over his shoulder at Metcalf's back. "I assume Mrs. Hargrove was with him at the time."

"I believe Mrs. Hargrove told the police she was

at her hairdresser's in Key West when Mr. Chapman was off . . . fishing." Metcalf turned to face them. "The Key West police are quite satisfied that there was no foul play in the death of Lou Chapman. His death by drowning was ruled an accident. A most unfortunate accident. The waters were rough that day and while I understood that Lou Chapman was a superior fisherman, he took reckless chances. He must have made a catch that was more than even he could handle and he was dragged overboard. There were several witnesses on the boat who confirmed what happened."

"Yeah"—Max nodded slowly—"it must have been some ornery fish that got him."

Angel bid Metcalf a brief good-bye. Max said nothing in parting. Neither did Metcalf.

In the car, Angel tossed her arms around Max. "You were terrific back there. And what ever made you think of asking Metcalf for the bank book?"

"I'm always a little leery of a guy that's too helpful. I started thinking that maybe Metcalf wasn't eager for you to see the way the entries ran."

Angel withdrew the bank book from her purse. She let out a low whistle as she opened it. Without saying a word, she passed it to Max.

He saw the notation that caused Angel's response. A withdrawal dated June twenty-third for thirty-four thousand dollars.

"He must have withdrawn the money just before he left for the Keys," Angel said. "I wonder why Metcalf didn't want us to know that. Not to mention why Lou took off for the Keys with all that cash."

"I wonder where it went." Max gave her back the book and pulled out of the parking place.

"Good question. You don't think Vera charged Lou for services rendered, do you?"

Max grinned, but as he turned the corner the grin faded. His eyes shifted to the rearview mirror several times. He hooked a left at the end of the street.

"Wrong direction. The hotel's back the other way," Angel said.

Max picked up some speed as he guided the car onto the causeway.

"Max, where are you going?"

"We're being followed, Angel."

She shifted in her seat and looked back. "It isn't a Mercedes."

"Maybe your friend Rick has more than one car."

"Slow down a little and let me try to get a look at his face."

It was the wrong move to make. For one thing, the face was totally unfamiliar to Angel. For another, it gave the driver of the navy new model Pontiac sedan a chance to pull forward. When Max slammed down on the gas pedal, it was too late. The heavy Pontiac peeled into the next lane and a shadowy figure in the backseat, who hadn't been visible before, stuck a glittering black revolver out the window.

Angel shouted a warning to Max who swerved wildly onto the shoulder of the road, shoving Angel down at the same instant. The bullet pinged into the metal of the rear bumper. Either the gunman was a poor shot or he merely wanted to let them know that they weren't welcome in Miami. Max was willing to bet on the latter since they were easy targets even for a novice. And neither Angel nor Max thought the hoods in that Pontiac were amateurs. Having delivered the message, the Pontiac peeled off down the road.

Angel and Max weren't going anywhere. The front end of their rented Ford had kissed the guard rail and smoke was pouring from the hood. The car rental people weren't going to be too happy. Max figured that if it hadn't been for the seatbelts he and Angel had been wearing they'd be in even worse shape than the car.

A patrol car pulled up less than two minutes later and Max gave the cop a description of the car that had sideswiped him. Angel sat quietly in her seat saying nothing. She was badly shaken, but she was trying to keep calm. Max saw through her efforts and asked the patrolman to run Angel down to the hospital to make sure she was all right, while he waited for the tow truck that the cop had called in for.

"I'm fine," Angel insisted as Max helped her out of the car.

"Just this once, Angel," Max said in low tones, "do what you're told."

Angel had the distinct feeling that Max was worried that the Pontiac might make a return trip and he wanted her safely out of target range.

She was just as worried about Max's safety, but

99

she could see by the stubborn set of his jaw that she wasn't going to get anywhere by trying to argue with him. Finally, she gave a reluctant nod and let the patrolman help her into his cruiser.

The tow truck came by ten minutes later. There was no further sign of the navy Pontiac. Max spent a half hour down at the rental office filling out accident forms and then made one more stop at a hunting and fishing supply store before heading back to the hotel.

While he found it somewhat disturbing to see how easy it was to walk in off the street and purchase a handgun, he had to admit he felt more secure packing some protection.

When he got back to the hotel, he stopped in his room and tucked the gun inside his suitcase. Then he walked across the hall to Angel's room. She opened the door on the first knock and practically fell against him. He could feel her trembling as he put his arm around her.

"Next time," he said softly, "check who's at the door before you open it." He cupped her chin. "Are you okay?" She nodded. Then tears spiked her eyes. He lowered his mouth to hers. She responded hungrily then pulled away abruptly.

"Oh, Max, I'm sorry. I should have never dragged you into this. I could have gotten us killed." She lifted her eyes up to his. They were stricken.

She was absolutely right, of course. But for some crazy reason, the danger faded in the background as Max felt Angel's warm, inviting body pressed against his. All he could think of at that moment was the softness of Angel's mouth, the way it had felt to kiss her, the sweet urgency of her tongue stroking his. She was so incredibly lovely. Her hair had fallen loose and Max gently pushed the wild strands from her face.

"What would I have done without you, Max? If I'd been driving . . ." She gave the faintest glimmer of a smile. "I'm a lousy driver." She pressed her cool, toffee lips to his cheek. Max could smell the scent of her hair as it brushed his face.

"I should let you get some rest," he murmured, but he couldn't let her go.

She shook her head slowly, her eyes on his. Her pulse hammered in her head. An aching need enveloped her.

"Angel, if you know what's good for you, you'll stop trying to play detective and we'll go back to Boston." He tried to sound firm. He tried even harder to quell the husky yearning in his voice. He failed on both counts.

"If either of us knew what was good for us," she murmured in that rich vibrato, "would we be here together, like this now?" She let her hands creep up his chest, across his shoulders, around his neck.

Max ran his palms down the sensual inner curve of her back and down along the firm roundness of her hips. "I keep trying to stay away from you, Angel." He placed sharp, nibbling kisses on her toffee lips. "But I can't."

She looked up at him, her big violet eyes measuring him. "We're heading for big trouble, Max. You know that."

He took in a slow breath. "Trouble seems to be my life story."

Her eyes continued to cruise slowly over his face. "We can't let . . . things . . . get too complicated." Her voice was deep and breathy. She closed her eyes. "This scares me more than the rest, you know."

Max felt an aching warmth suffuse him. "I know, Angel."

A pink flush highlighted her cheekbones, a stray tendril of midnight hair dropped over one eye. Max cupped her face. Her skin felt like flawless silk. Then he brushed away the wayward strand and she opened her eyes and tilted her head back. His mouth moved over hers for a kiss that was pure honey.

Angel took an unsteady breath as her hands moved to his jacket. He slipped out of it and let it drop to the floor. She moved her hands down the front of his shirt, opening the buttons. Then she loosened his tie and slipped it over his head. Her fingers opened and the tie joined the jacket on the floor. Max was already undoing the buckle of his belt.

A wild, reckless abandon shot throught them both, obliterating their fear and caution. After everything else they'd been through together, this seemed the only finale that made any sense. There were some things in life that seemed inevitable. This was one of them.

Max finished the job of removing his slacks and the rest of his things, while Angel stepped back and began undressing. She moved with a sinuous grace as erotic as any movie sex goddess in her finest performance. Only Angel wasn't performing. She discarded her clothes with a complete, tantalizing abandon. Underneath the dress was a lacy black bra and matching bikini. She was entrancing, incredibly desirable. Max had known many beautiful women, but Angel was flawless. And she was utterly without guile. Max had never felt the kind of craving he experienced with her. It almost drove him mad.

Angel's hands were trembling as she attempted to unhook her bra. Her eyes were ablaze with longing, but her pulse was pounding so loudly in her head she felt dizzy with desire.

"Let me do that." Max's voice was low and husky. He moved toward her. As her gaze took in his strong, fine body her lips parted sensuously. She'd never seen a more perfect-looking man. The truth was, though, other than Lou Chapman, she was far more inexperienced in situations such as this than anyone would have imagined. She suddenly felt overwhelmingly nervous. Her hands dropped to her sides as Max's fingers moved slowly over the lacy material covering her breasts and followed a trail around to the catch of her bra.

Angel's smile was innocently alluring as Max hesitated for a moment. He didn't say a word, but she knew he wanted to make sure she wanted this as

103

much as he did. And she did. She leaned slightly forward so he could unfasten her bra with ease. Angel wasn't about to turn down any offers of assistance from Max Gallagher.

CHAPTER SIX

Max held Angel in his arms and felt the trembling course through her muscles. His hands moved down her body in long, sinuous strokes. She arched against him, breathless, feeling his caresses as the onset of a summer storm, gentle yet intense, crescendoing, sweeping her along in its tumbling wake.

Max drank in her beauty like a desert wanderer who'd found his oasis. His lips trailed her high-cheekboned face, her long swan's neck, her sweet toffee lips.

"Angel," he whispered, her name on his lips the loveliest music to Angel's ears. Her heart sang as Max broke through the wall she'd so carefully erected around it. She stroked the back of his neck twining her fingers in his thick burnished blond hair. She felt him against her like the quake of the storm, felt a jolt of lightning quiver down her spine. His scent was tangy, intoxicating. As she slid her tongue downward, she licked the saltiness of his skin, reveling in the taste of him.

Max cupped her face and kissed her with such

fierce passion it took her breath away. Then his tongue glided down the lovely column of her neck, trailing a delicious line to her breasts. He circled them with his lips, then sought the tender, ripe nipples that burned for his touch. She arched into him, her sigh vibrating deep in her throat like a cat. Max lifted her buttocks as his mouth trailed downward along her silken skin, his tongue stroking, questing. He could feel Angel tremble beneath him, her breath coming in rapid pants.

"Oh, Max," she murmured as she drew her long, graceful legs around him, a throbbing sensation radiating throughout her entire body. His lovemaking was so passionate, so all-absorbing that Angel grew wild with a consuming hunger for him. She had never felt so sensually alive in her life. Her lips moved to Max's chest and she felt his heart hammering so hard she feared it would explode. She ran her fingers over his gleaming tanned muscles, letting her hands snake down between their bodies, feeling his hardening length. He felt like fire, his body shuddering as she stroked him. Her legs entwined around him now as she moved beneath him in slow, tantalizing motions. Max groaned deeply as he entered her. The movement of their passion intensified as the gathering storm engulfed them. Rain clouds burst inside of her as elation and ecstasy combined to fill the very core of her being. Max's low throaty groan was triumphant as he finally fell against her, his breath hot on her thick midnight hair.

For long moments they clung to each other, neither wanting to break the spell, neither wanting to face the irrevocable meaning of the act they had shared with such abandon. He held her close, his strong, knowing fingers languidly trailing her back. Finally she lifted her head and Max could see the confusion in her eyes.

Gently, he pressed her head to his chest. "Not now, Angel. Let's not talk about it now." He shut his eyes.

After a while, Angel could hear Max's breathing, slow and deep. Carefully, so as not to wake him, she disentangled herself from his embrace. She took hold of the sheet and began lifting it around him only to pause and let her gaze drift unabashedly down his strong, vital body. A film of dampness made his golden skin glisten.

Ever so lightly, Angel touched his lips. She felt a deep desire to feel those lips devouring hers again, but now with the need came a disturbing sense of panic. It was dangerous to run on impulse. It was dangerous to let her emotions take the lead. With Max, both impulse and feelings had utterly over-whelmed her and she felt the danger like a heavy cloud looming above her. She turned away.

After a quick shower, she threw on a pair of jeans and a jersey and quietly left the room. Max was still asleep. Five minutes later, she returned from the lobby where she'd gone to retrieve Lou's files from the hotel safe.

When Max awoke, Angel was sitting at the desk sifting through the papers. He watched her silently, a sharp frown creasing his brow. He cursed himself for even thinking for a moment that what they'd shared together might bring Angel to her senses. As he shed the covers they made a rustling sound and Angel turned.

She smiled at him, but there was more bravura there than warmth. Max's scowl deepened.

This was not the afterglow either of them might have expected. The tension between them obliterated any hope of sustained intimacy.

Without a word, Max dressed. Then he walked over to the desk and gave the files a sweeping glance. "I want you to turn these over to the police, Angel. The game is over."

The contempt in Max's tone stung her deeply. She wanted to ask him if what had just happened between them was also a game, but she was afraid to ask. She was afraid to hear the answer.

Angel shivered. "What are the Miami police going to do? Lou died off of Key West. His death is out of their jurisdiction. And as for that Pontiac that ran us off the road, we didn't even get a look at the license plate. Neither of us could give the police enough of a description to give them the slightest lead." Her hand reached up to Max's arm. "I think the thing to do is go down to Key West and talk with the police there. But first I want to find out what could be in these files that someone could kill for."

Max's eyes darkened ominously. With one sweeping gesture he flung off her hand and sent the files flying to the floor. "You're dynamite, Angel, but I don't want to be around for any more explosions."

"Suit yourself." Angel's voice was hoarse with hurt.

If her pain moved him, he didn't show it. He merely turned and walked out of the room. She clenched her eyes tightly closed, willing away the tears. *Temporary insanity,* she told herself vehemently. It was as good an excuse as she could come up with for the passionate abandon that she'd experienced in Max's arms.

"I hate you, Max Gallagher," she muttered fiercely. And that was as good a lie as she could muster under the circumstances.

Slowly she bent down and gathered up the files. She put them in order and for the next two hours read through them. All the while she tried to push the memory of Max away. But it was impossible, thoughts of what they'd experienced together sticking to the screen of her mind like glue. Still, she forced herself to focus on Lou's notes, the newspaper clippings, photos, and receipts that accompanied each file. The Janine Dion file seemed cut and dried. Lou had found out that Ross Allen, the man who was blackmailing Janine, had a few unsavory aliases. By the time Lou brought them all to light, Ross Allen was in more of a bargaining mood. One item in particular turned things around for Janine. Ross Allen, under the name Robert Ashe, was wanted for questioning in Atlanta, Georgia, concerning an armed robbery. In exchange for Lou not informing the police of Robert Ashe's current whereabouts, Ross Allen eagerly gave up those films. The last notation in Janine Dion's file was that she and Lou had celebrated the return of the film with one humdinger of a bonfire. Angel had a feeling that wasn't the end of the celebration.

As for Wendy Shaw's file, Lou's notes included certain current information that Angel found interesting. Wendy Shaw had become engaged to Derek Bendix while his wife was doing her six-month stint for attempted manslaughter. But three weeks after Paula Bendix was released from prison, Bendix broke off with Wendy and went back to his wife. Some men, Angel mused, were a lot more forgiving than others. She felt a stinging pain, thinking that Max Gallagher did not strike her as the forgiving type at all. If she continued to pursue this case against his clearly stated wishes, he was very likely to walk out of her life for good. That realization hurt a lot more than she cared to admit. However, Angel wasn't all that certain Max wouldn't walk out of her life one of these days, anyway. He'd made it perfectly clear that he didn't play for keeps.

Resolutely, she began reading through Vera Hargrove's file. She had a gut feeling that the key to the mystery lay here. After all, Vera and Lou were intimately involved. The two of them were down in Key West together. It was her yacht he was on. And most significantly, Michael Hargrove, the man Lou had sent up the river as it were, was now back in circulation. He certainly was a tailor-made suspect. He had motive and means. Lou Chapman had not only ruined his life, he'd walked off with his wife, Vera. Men had been known to commit murder for less.

There was a light knock on her door. Angel's heartbeat quickened, thinking it was Max returning to apologize for his flare-up. Before she opened the door, she tucked the file in her overnight case. No need to add fuel to Max's rage. Only it wasn't Max at her door.

"Hey, you're not dressed yet. Wendy goes on at ten. She's going to join us for a drink first."

Angel glanced down at her watch. It was almost a quarter after nine. She nodded slowly. "I guess I lost track of the time."

"Are you okay? You look a little down."

Angel managed a faint smile. "I'm fine. Just give me ten minutes. I'll dress and meet you down in the club." She waited for him to head off, but he continued to study her thoughtfully.

"I'm worried about you, Angel."

She arched a brow, but said nothing.

"I have friends down at the police station. I heard about that report you filed this afternoon." His features hardened. "Go home, Angel. It's too hot this time of year down south. You made a smart move leaving." He paused, his features softening slightly. "Even though it hurt like hell to see you go."

"Wendy Shaw seems to be soothing some of that hurt," she said with a wry smile.

Rick grinned. "She grabbed me on the rebound. Just like you did once upon a time. You know where those things usually end."

"You mean Derek Bendix?"

"He dumped her. Wendy hired me to find out why. I never did come up with much of a reason.

111

Love's a strange and mysterious emotion." Rick gave Angel a seductive smile. "Anyway, after a while Wendy stopped caring all that much."

"How come she hired you instead of Lou? He'd done a damn good job for her the first time around."

Rick's grin broadened. "I could be bought for less. Besides, we hit it off right from the start." The grin faded. "And Lou was . . . otherwise occupied at the time."

"With Vera Hargrove?"

Rick sighed. "Personally, I don't know what Lou saw in her. She's a real ice princess. But she seemed to make Lou dance to her tune right from the start. Even if it was the wrong tune."

Angel frowned. "What do you mean?"

Rick bent down and kissed her cheek. "No more time for idle chitchat, beautiful. Wendy gets sore when I keep her waiting. See you down at the club." He turned abruptly and walked off.

Talk about dancing to a woman's tune, Angel mused. Wendy Shaw seemed to have Rick doing the jig.

She started to close her door when Max opened his door across the hall.

For a moment they stared at each other in silence. Max's grim look could have sunk a ship. It certainly sank Angel's heart.

"I was just heading down to the club," he said. As he opened the door wider, she saw that he was dressed in his tan suit again. He looked rakishly handsome, but his voice was so cool and dispassionate that it made Angel shiver.

"Rick stopped by to say he and Wendy were waiting for us." Her own voice was hollow and raspy and she found it too painful to meet Max's obdurate gaze.

Max nodded.

"I . . . thought . . . you might have left town," she muttered.

His eyes narrowed. "No change in my plans, Angel. My plane leaves Monday morning. Meanwhile . . . I figured I might as well take in all the sun and fun Miami has to offer."

She felt his words like a slap across the face. Her own features hardened to ice. As far as she was concerned, the fun was over between her and Max. She turned without a word, stepped farther back into her hotel room, and slammed the door.

When she walked into the supper club twenty minutes later, all eyes turned. Angel's riveting beauty was almost blinding, especially in the racy little black evening dress she was wearing. The front of the dress formed a vee that slid down to her navel, the sarong-style skirt was long, lean, and clinging. She took the breath away of every man in that club. Some women could do that. Angel did it best.

She walked through the crowded supper club, oblivious to the hungry looks. Her eyes were cool jewels as she cast a quick glance at Max, who was already seated with Rick Seidman and Wendy Shaw at the best table in the house.

"Angel, you look like dynamite," Rick said with

a lusty smile. He stood and pulled out the remaining chair for her. Wendy Shaw gave Angel a disinterested glance. Her eyes were happier focusing on Max.

Angel slid gracefully into the seat, shooting Max another look. Earlier this evening, he'd likened her to dynamite, too. Only the meaning behind his words were worlds apart from the meaning she saw written all over Rick's face. Angel knew that Rick Seidman liked playing with dynamite. She also knew that he was slick enough never to get too close and let it blow up in his face. That wasn't true of Max. It was the very fact that he could get too close which made their liaison so dangerous and yet so compelling.

Their eyes met, but Max's pulled away. Angel watched them focus on Wendy Shaw.

"What would you like to drink, Angel?" Rick asked as a waiter approached.

Angel looked over at the glass in front of Wendy. "What are you drinking?" she asked.

Wendy shrugged. "Tonic water on ice. I never drink before I go on. Liquor affects my voice."

Rick laughed dryly. "That's not all it affects."

Wendy threw him a dirty look. Angel had the distinct impression that Rick and Wendy weren't exactly winning the prize for the most loving couple. But then, neither were she and Max.

"I'll have the same as Ms. Shaw," Angel told the waiter. "Only throw a little gin in mine," she added. Her eyes slid by Max's. "There are some benefits in not having to perform."

Wendy leaned forward and squeezed Max's hand. In her low-cut white-sequined gown, the gesture was clearly meant to tantalize. From the look Angel saw on Max's face, Wendy was successful. Angel could practically hear him panting.

"How about a dance before I go on?" Her cherry-red mouth puckered prettily at Max.

He shrugged. "I might step on your toes."

Wendy's brown eyes sparkled. "I might like it."

Angel felt a strong desire to pick up the drink the waiter was placing in front of her and toss it at the chanteuse, but she merely sat stiff as a statue, trying to ignore the solicitous way Max helped Wendy out of her seat and tucked his arm around her waist even before they got to the dance floor.

"You look jealous, Angel." Rick touched her cheek.

Angel edged from his reach, tilting her head. "You don't."

Rick laughed. "I don't always show my feelings, Angel."

"That's true," Angel said slowly, eyes narrowing.

For a while neither of them spoke. It was Angel who broke the silence. "Tell me something, Rick. Why do you think someone wanted to take pot shots at me this afternoon?"

Rick took a long swallow of what looked like double bourbon. Then he held the glass between his two palms and glanced over to the dance floor where Wendy and Max were doing an extra slow fox trot. "I don't know, Angel. Why don't you tell me?"

She took in a deep breath. Maybe she ought to

say something, draw him out a little. She didn't see Rick as a suspect. If he'd wanted Lou out of the way, he wouldn't have waited until now. But he might know more than he was letting on. She wouldn't put that past him.

"I don't think Lou's drowning was accidental. I think Lou was murdered. And I think there's someone out there who doesn't want me to stir up any muddy waters." She leaned closer to him, but there was nothing seductive in her gesture. "I want to know what you think, Rick."

He let his eyes roam over her for a few moments before he answered. "I think you're asking for serious trouble, Angel, if you insist on following your instincts."

Angel sipped her drink. When she set it down she said, "Vera Hargrove seems to agree with me."

"She's just hot under the collar because her husband won his appeal and was acquitted of all charges."

"When did all that happen?"

Rick finished off his drink. "A couple of months ago." He turned in his seat to face Angel. "Vera Hargrove hired Lou again . . . this time for protection as well as to see if he couldn't come up with anything new to lay on Michael and send him back to the slammer."

"I assume you mean she wanted protection from her husband." She paused. "It seems Lou was the one that needed protection," Angel said in a low voice. "Vera accused Michael of murder. She could

116

have been talking about Lou. What do you think, Rick?"

"Like I said, Angel. I think you ought to mind your own business."

"You also think that it wouldn't be very clever to bite the hand that feeds you." Angel's eyes narrowed. "I bet Michael Hargrove is real grateful to you, Rick, for his acquittal. You were helping out behind the scenes, weren't you?"

Rick shrugged, watching Max return alone to the table. "Why ask the questions, Angel, when you have all the answers?"

"Not all the answers, Rick," she said in a tight voice, just as Max walked over to the table. He was alone. Wendy had headed backstage to get ready for her act.

Rick stood up as Max slid into his seat. "Well, I'll leave you two to enjoy the show. I've got a business meeting." He placed a hand on Max's shoulder. "Look after her, Gallagher. Angel's a very special lady."

Max gave Rick a cool, sly look. "Now I thought you were angling for that job yourself."

Rick merely laughed. "I never stop angling. But Angel refuses to bite. She's stubborn. You know what I mean?"

Max looked over at Angel speculatively. Slowly he shook his head. With a faint glimmer of a smile, he muttered, "Yeah, I know just what you mean."

Angel dared a small smile as Rick walked off. She was afraid Max wouldn't smile back. Her fears were justified. He didn't.

Angel grew frustrated. "Damn it, Max, doesn't what happened before mean anything to you?"

He leaned forward ominously. "I'll tell you what means something to me. Getting shot at means something to me. Since I quit pro football I was a happy-go-lucky guy without a care in the world— until I met you. Since then, I've been in one precarious situation after another." He gave her a pointed look.

Angel eyed him narrowly. "No one twisted your arm, Gallagher." Her voice was as husky as the old blues number Wendy Shaw had begun warbling. Angel only heard the first few bars as she rose and strode out of the club.

Wendy's eyes brightened as she watched Angel leave. She gave Max a dazzling smile. He didn't notice. His eyes trailed Angel's departing figure. He took out a cigarette. He was trying to break the habit, but he was having about as much luck at it as he was having breaking the habit of Angel Welles. Someone should have put a sign on her back: Caution . . . this woman is definitely going to be dangerous for your health. But he hadn't needed a sign to tell him that.

He watched her until she disappeared, unable to tear his eyes away. When she was no longer in sight, visions of Angel lying naked beside him danced in his head. He could see the long, lovely line of her throat, her mouth forming his name. Her kiss had been fire to a fast-burning stick of dynamite, the final explosion more powerful than any he had ever experienced.

He told himself he shouldn't have let it go so far between them. But he knew that it would have happened sometime. He'd known it from the first moment he'd set eyes on her. Angel was like a potent drug . . . dangerous but intoxicating. And Max was addicted. He took a long drag of his cigarette and let the smoke out slowly. The only way to cure an addiction, he decided, was to go cold turkey. His eyes drifted to Wendy Shaw who was singing her heart out for him. Now *there* was a woman who had mastered the adage "out of sight, out of mind."

When Angel exited the supper club, she hesitated in the lobby, contemplating whether or not to retrieve those files she'd again tucked away in the hotel safe. Who was she trying to kid? There was no way she could concentrate on the tantalizing trio right now. Her mind refused to dwell on anything but the intoxicating but nonetheless infuriating Max Gallagher. She almost believed those moments of ecstasy they'd shared earlier had been nothing but a fantasy. A fantasy gone miserably awry.

It had been so perfect, so unbelievably right. So how could something so right go so wrong so quickly? Angel knew Max would blame it on her continued interest in the tantalizing trio and what she believed was their link to Lou's death. But Angel was beginning to think Max was using that as an excuse. It wasn't her obsession with Lou's murder that Max was worried about. She believed that Max was afraid he was falling in love with her. Now that was a fear she could very much relate to.

She went upstairs to her room. As she unlocked

the door, opened it, and reached for the light switch, a drawling voice in the dark said, "Don't bother with the light, Angel."

She stiffened. The voice was unfamiliar and although the light from the corridor filtered into the room, the man stood in shadow off to the side.

"Close the door, Angel."

She hesitated.

"I have a gun. It would be a pity to have to waste such a beautiful woman."

Angel closed the door and stumbled forward into the room. "What . . . do you want?"

"You have some papers that belong to me."

"What . . . papers?"

The man laughed. The next moment a flash of light blinded her. The flashlight traveled provocatively from her face down to her feet and slowly back up again. "You sure are one beautiful angel, Angel."

"I might throw you a compliment about your appearance too . . . if I could see you," she said with a false bravado she hoped wasn't transparent.

The man laughed. "Cute, Angel. Real cute."

"I don't know what papers you're talking about," she said.

"Your ex-husband had them delivered to you. I just want a couple of items. You can keep the rest."

"You're the one who broke into my apartment in Boston," she accused.

"Sorry. I've never been to Boston." There was a long pause. "So, I'm not the only one who wants . . ." He let the sentence fade. "I don't like that. I don't like that one little bit."

Angel noticed that the man's drawl had vanished. At first she'd thought he was a real southerner. Now she saw that it was merely an affectation. She'd have to remember that when she reported this break-in to the police. A cold chill shot through her. If she lived long enough to report it.

The flashlight wavered a little and Angel could see that the intruder had been here awhile ransacking her room. "Look," she said, "you've scoured the place already. You know I don't have any of Lou's papers here. If you tell me what it is you want exactly, I'll send them to you when I get back to Boston."

Her suggestion made the intruder laugh heartily.

"I mean it." Her voice cracked. She cleared her throat. "What would I want with them, anyway?"

He stopped laughing abruptly. "Blackmail, Angel."

"Blackmail?"

His footsteps drew near. Terror paralyzed her, as all bravado vanished. She stepped back until she pressed herself against the door. The man was tall. And there was something oddly familiar about his cologne. She'd gotten a whiff of that scent quite recently. Before she had time to contemplate where, she felt the barrel of a gun pressed against her temple. "I really don't want to hurt you, Angel. But I've worked too long and too hard to let some broad screw up my life. Even a broad as beautiful as you."

"Everything Lou sent me is back in Boston." Her voice was trembling.

"Then you better call a friend back home and see to it that the package is delivered express mail. And you and I will wait right here . . . all night long . . . until it comes. Actually, that doesn't sound like the worst idea I've ever heard."

A knock on her door made Angel leap forward in shock. She fell against the man, which made it supremely easy for him to snake a thick, powerful arm around her waist and position the gun's barrel into her back. His breath was hot against her ear as he warned her to be silent.

The knocks got stronger, more insistent. Angel shut her eyes, praying it was Max, praying he would once again play her knight in shining armor.

"Ross. Open up. I know you're in there. It's me Janine."

Angel's brow creased in confusion. Janine? Ross? Not Ross Allen, the man who'd tried to blackmail Janine Dion. And then Angel remembered those papers in Lou's file on Janine, linking Ross to that alias, Robert Ashe, a man wanted for questioning on an armed robbery charge in another state. So those were the papers he wanted. He was scared that she might decide to play his own game and blackmail him. What was still thick as mud was where Janine fit in. Then Angel remembered where she'd gotten a whiff of Ross's cologne before. It was at the funeral. He was the man who'd been Janine's escort.

"Damn it, Janine," Ross hissed through the door. "I told you to wait in the car."

Her knock was loud enough to wake the dead. With a muttered curse, he hiked Angel up, lifted her away from the door and opened it.

When Janine saw Angel, she gasped. "Oh, God, Ross. What are you doing with her? Have you gone and completely lost your mind?" She hurried into the room, flicked on the light and slammed the door.

Max didn't make it past Wendy Shaw's second number. He was too tense and Wendy's love songs were only making him feel worse. He decided to call it a night. What he didn't know was that the night had just begun.

When he stepped out of the elevator on the fourth floor, Max spotted Janine Dion pounding in earnest on Angel's door. He shot over to the nearest doorway just as Angel's door opened. When he heard Janine's high-pitched exclamation, a cold chill ran down Max's spine.

What the hell kind of trouble had Angel gone and gotten herself into now?

CHAPTER SEVEN

Before Max went to Angel's rescue he decided that this time he had better be prepared. He hurried to his room, opened his suitcase and removed the small pistol he'd bought earlier that day.

He could hear Janine ranting inside Angel's room as he knocked on the door. His sharp rap brought an abrupt silence. He flattened himself against the wall.

It was Janine who opened the door a crack. She peered out, but Max was hidden from her sight. She opened the door a little more, this time taking a small step out. Max sprang on her, catching her by surprise. She stumbled in shock, finding herself a second later in Max's powerful clutches. He shoved her into the room, sticking behind her like glue.

If she weren't so terrified, Angel might have burst out laughing. It looked like the showdown at the OK Corral, each man pointing his weapon, each armed with a woman for a shield.

"Looks like a stalemate," Max said with a wry smile.

Ross glowered.

Janine took up where she'd left off. "Put that damn gun down, Ross, before somebody gets hurt. You told me you were just going to break in, get the papers, and scram."

"She walked in on me." Ross's voice was slightly embarrassed.

"And I don't have the papers here," Angel said indignantly.

"What papers?" It was Max's turn.

Angel sighed. "Ross thinks I'm going to blackmail him with some information Lou dug up on him."

Tears came to Janine's big blue eyes. "We're trying so hard to make a go of it. Ross had nothing to do with that armed robbery in Atlanta." She stared at Ross. "I told you all along the only answer is for you to turn yourself in to the Georgia authorities. If Lou found out about that Ashe alias, so can others. You can't spend the rest of your life running, Ross."

"Wait a second. Backtrack a little," Angel said. "You and Ross are . . ."

"Involved?" Max finished the question for her. He looked as surprised as Angel.

Janine smiled coyly. "I know. I know. He was a louse once upon a time."

Angel would have vociferously argued Janine's use of the past tense, but the gun Ross was still digging into her back kept her from voicing her opinion.

"You always fall for guys who've blackmailed you?" Max asked mockingly.

Janine gave an impatient pout. "Anyone can

125

make one mistake," she retorted indignantly. "I, for one, believe in forgiveness. Look, can't you fellows put your guns away so we can talk this thing over like . . . adults?"

Max eyed Ross. "What do you say, pal?"

Ross looked at Janine, then shrugged. "Okay, but no funny stuff."

"Who's in the mood for clowning?" Max said ruefully.

Both men, practically in unison, tucked their guns in their pockets and released the women. Angel let out a relieved breath. Janine flew to her boyfriend's side.

"If only Lou were still alive," Janine said, "everything would be all right now."

Angel, still shaken from the ordeal, sank into a chair. "Lou?"

"Ross and I saw him a few days before . . . he left for Key West," Janine explained. "He knew that Ross and I had gotten together. He was pretty surprised, too." She laughed softly. "We certainly didn't plan it. It was really an accident. My movie career was back on a downswing when I bumped into Ross in Hollywood at a bar on Sunset about four months ago. He'd had it with the film business, too. Anyway"—she smiled at Ross—"we got to talking, found out we had a lot in common. Ross felt real rotten about that dumb blackmail scheme. He was broke and he thought since I'd made a couple of big pictures, I could spare the cash. The crazy thing was, I probably would have given him some cash if he'd asked real nice instead of threatening me with that old film. It wasn't even smutty. Just bad. I was scared if any producers saw it they'd start having second thoughts about my talent." She shrugged. "They started having them anyway. So, Ross and I decided to quit the scene, come back to Miami, and go into business together."

"What kind of business?" Max asked.

Janine smiled seductively. "Why . . . body building. For men and women. We've only been at it for two months and already we have quite a large clientele."

Max gave Janine's shapely form a trailing glance. "I'm not surprised."

Angel shot Max a dirty look, then turned her attention to Janine. "Where did Lou fit in?" she asked.

"We asked Lou to help clear Ross of the armed robbery charge in Atlanta." Janine put her arm around her boyfriend. Since he'd put the gun away and released Angel, Ross Allen seemed to have lost his tough-guy stance. He even managed a warm smile for Janine.

Angel eyed the loving twosome speculatively. "Did Lou agree to take the case?" she asked.

"He not only took the case," Janine replied, "he told us not to worry about a thing. Lou was going to head out to Atlanta as soon as he came back from Key West."

"How long did he plan to be in Key West?" Max asked.

"Two-three days at the most," Ross said. "He told me to sit tight in Miami and he'd go to Atlanta.

He said he'd send for me when he'd dug up enough evidence to prove I wasn't involved in the robbery. I agreed to turn myself in then, although we were all hoping Lou would get the police to forget all about the alias Robert Ashe."

"Lou would have straightened things out. That man was the best," Janine said passionately, demurely brushing away an errant tear. "He believed Ross was innocent. He felt we deserved a fresh start." She took a deep breath, fighting back an onrush of tears. "If only Lou hadn't died."

Max leaned back against the door. "Chapman can't be the only talented private eye around. Why not find someone else to have a go at the case?"

"We were planning to do that," Janine said. "But then Ross went into a panic when he found out you had my file," she explained, turning to Angel.

"What made you think I had it?" Angel asked Ross.

"There was a crumpled piece of carbon from the bill of lading that must have missed Chapman's wastepaper basket. I found it behind the desk." He grinned, looking real proud of himself.

"What did you do with the carbon?" Angel asked.

Ross shrugged. "I crumpled it back up and tossed it into the wastepaper basket. I didn't think anyone else would have any interest in it."

Angel and Max shared a look that said different. If Ross was telling the truth about not having broken into her apartment in Boston and if Rick Seidman hadn't been behind it, that carbon sitting in

Lou's wastepaper basket meant anyone else who was browsing around Lou's office could have found it and realized she had the files. Which meant anyone could have been the intruder who'd paid her a late-night visit a few days ago. The field was wide open.

Janine walked over to Angel. "I know Ross was wrong to break in here like he did. But he was desperate."

"For his sake, your sake, and especially mine," Angel said ruefully, "your boyfriend had better learn some less criminal ways of dealing with his desperation. Otherwise that fresh start the two of you are looking for is going to turn rotten mighty fast."

Ross scowled, but he looked uncomfortable. Angel hoped some of her message had hit home.

Janine grabbed Angel's hand. "Ross will turn himself in. I promise. Just give us time to get a private eye. We were thinking about Rick Seidman."

Angel compressed her lips. There was a long silence. She looked over at Max, then said finally, "Why not try someone from Atlanta? You might be better off."

Janine turned back to Ross. He nodded slowly. She smiled at Angel. "Agreed." She paused, gingerly extending her hand toward Angel. "So . . . uh . . . no hard feelings?"

Angel arched a brow. "Let's not push it." But then she took Janine's hand and offered a small smile. "Good luck." To herself, she added, *You're going to need it.*

Max moved away from the door to let Ross and Janine leave. Angel thought he was going to follow them out. She was glad that he didn't.

"I guess I owe you . . . again." She gave him a weak smile.

Max didn't answer. Instead he fixed her with those dark blue eyes of his and leaned against the door.

Angel remained in the chair, crossing one long, glorious leg over the other. She tilted her head and looked across at him defiantly.

"Okay," she said, exasperated, "go on and say it . . . again. Give me the speech about how I'm going to get myself in serious trouble if I keep this up. Tell me I should go home and forget this whole thing. Tell me that one of these days I'm going to get myself in a jam and you won't be around to play Sir Galahad." She took a gulp of air. "Well, what are you waiting for?"

"There doesn't seem to be anything left for me to say," he said dryly. "You've got the speech down pat." He pushed himself off the wall. "And you aren't going to listen to your own playback any more than you are to mine."

Angel nodded her head slowly in agreement, even though Max didn't need a response. He already knew the answer as well as she did. With a faint, final smile he turned and walked out of the room.

Angel sat, arms folded across her chest, for a good ten minutes. Her head felt like a tape recorder that someone kept switching intermittently from fast forward to reverse and back to fast forward again. She tried to sort out the facts from her feelings, but Max Gallagher seemed to keep her feelings in constant motion. She raged silently against him for deserting her just when she needed him most. It didn't matter that she knew he was behaving with a lot more common sense than she possessed.

After a few more minutes, she decided to take a nice, long bubble bath and soothe her body even if her mind seemed beyond consoling.

She turned on the water, then opened up the complimentary plastic vial of bath gel and poured it in, watching the thick, green flowery scented liquid form iridescent bubbles. She slipped off her clothes and sank into the tub. She couldn't have been there more than a minute when she heard a sharp rap on her door. Her first reaction was irritation, but as she stepped out of the bubbly water and wrapped a bath towel around her wet body, a flash of panic swept through her. She walked cautiously into the bedroom, leaving a damp trail as she went.

The knock was loud, insistent.

She looked around the hotel room for some kind of makeshift weapon. She finally settled on one of her spiked heels, clutching the sole of the shoe as she edged toward the door.

"Angel . . . open the door."

It was Max. She let out a sigh of sheer relief and dropped the shoe to the carpet. "What do you want?"

"Open the door."

She opened it a crack. "I'm taking a bath."

He pushed his way in. Angel drew back her

131

shoulders, grasping the towel tightly at her chest. Max's eyes drifted reflexively down her body.

Angel's eyes registered haughty anger at his roving glance, but inside she seemed to melt like an ice cube touching a flame. What was happening to her? She couldn't understand this fierce arousal that would not relinquish its hold on her no matter how many lectures she gave herself about not getting too attached to the freewheeling Max Gallagher. Afraid of having him see her real feelings, she pivoted around and strode back toward the bathroom.

"I don't think we have anything more to say to each other, Max." Her voice was too breathy. She silently cursed herself. "And the water is getting cold." She took another step. Max was right behind her. His hand touched her bare shoulder. Just that brief contact was enough to transmit a hot liquid thrill to her body.

"Angel . . . we've got to sort this thing out."

"There's nothing to sort out, Max."

He refused to relinquish his grip. "This turns you on, doesn't it?"

For a moment Angel thought he was talking about his touch. Her face reddened. Max spun her around.

"The danger . . . the excitement . . . you think it's all one big thrill. I think you've been waiting around for a long time for something like this." His eyes fell across her bare shoulders. "You spent all those years playing girl Friday first to Chapman, then to Seidman, and now you've finally got your chance to play private eye." He lifted his gaze to her face before it drifted too low and he forgot his train of thought. "Only thing is . . . you haven't the foggiest idea of what you're doing. You have no plan. You just walk blindly into one catastrophe after another."

Angel glanced at him coolly. It took all her effort to remain calm as his fingers were burning reminders into her skin of past touches. "Not that it's any of your business," she said archly, "but I do have a plan." The towel was beginning to slip. She caught Max's eyes falling to her breasts. She wrenched herself free and grabbed the towel more tightly. "I thought you wanted out. Well, that's fine with me. So why don't you just leave?"

She stormed into the bathroom and slammed the door. Leaning against it to steady her breath, she pressed the brass button lock on the doorknob. After a few moments, she let the towel fall to the blue tile floor and she stepped back into the tub. The water was still warm, but the bubbles were skimpy at best. She turned on the hot water tap and some more bubbles burgeoned.

Angel couldn't hear the sound of the bathroom door opening over the roar of the bath running. It was the sudden cool draft across the back of her neck and shoulders that made her turn finally. She gasped in shocked surprise as she saw Max standing inside the bathroom.

"How did you . . . ?"

"See what I mean? You're careless, Angel. And you don't know the first thing about looking after yourself." He held up a Swiss army knife. "A five-

133

year-old could have undone that lock, for chris-sakes."

Angel sank deeper into the scanty bubbles. The water was still running. To reach for the tap meant exposing even more of herself. She let the tap go, feeling exposed enough already.

Max was the one to turn it off. Then he knelt by the tub. "Okay, let's hear this plan of yours."

Angel, who'd been busy gathering as many bub-bles as she could against her body, stopped and gave him a wary look. Was that a note of warmth she detected in his voice? Forgetting for the moment her extremely vulnerable position, she asked cautiously, "Why?"

Drops of water glistened on Angel's throat. The bubbles in the tub were popping fast. Max smiled. He had, although he hated to admit it even now, been bitten bad.

"Why?" he echoed, his voice sounding raw and strange to his own ears. "I'll tell you why. Because I care what happens to you, dammit. That's why. I don't even pretend to understand what's going on between us, Angel. I thought I had everything fig-ured out for myself. Then you come along and I can't think straight. Suddenly I'm taking chances again. Big chances." His voice had become a low croon. "Maybe taking chances is in my blood." He took a long deep breath, his eyes soaking in her exquisite naked body beneath the water. "Maybe you're in my blood, Angel."

"Oh, Max," she whispered. Her voice quivered. She felt light-headed, a little dizzy.

134

He touched a hand to her cheek. She turned her head and pressed his palm to her lips. His other hand moved against her hair.

"I guess," she said softly, "we're both taking big chances."

He lifted her out of the water.

"I'm going to get you soaked," she murmured as he pulled her into his arms. But Max didn't seem to even notice.

Her hands moved to his shirt. She undid the buttons with trembling fingers, then tugged the shirt off his shoulders.

Max leaned her up against the cool wall. Her body burned despite the coolness as his mouth cruised down her throat to her breasts, leaving a ribbon of fever along her damp skin. She could feel herself dissolving as his hard body pressed against her. They both felt the urgency like a fast-ticking bomb. She heard him fumble with his trousers. A moment later she felt them slide down his legs. One of her legs twined around him as he pinned her to the wall.

"Angel," he said in a strangled voice just before his lips found hers. Angel gave a low murmuring cry as his insistent tongue slipped silkily into her mouth. A wild, crazy hunger swept through them. Their kiss deepened, Angel clinging to him now, a throbbing coursing through her body.

He whispered her name again against her ear, his breath ragged and labored. Her arms flung around his neck. He lifted her, her back still pressed against the slippery tiles. Both legs twined around him now.

The contrast of coolness and heat sent delicious little thrills up her spine. His strong hands cupped her buttocks. She could feel him hard against her, lifting her a little more as he sought and found entrance. Angel arched into him, clutching him fiercely as he took her with mounting urgency. She wanted this feeling of oneness to go on forever as her whole body pulsated, low earthy sounds scraped from her throat as they shared in the sensation of fulfillment together.

She would certainly have sunk to the tiled floor if Max had let go of her afterward. But he had no intention of releasing her. He scooped her up in his arms. "Shall we try for a more conventional approach this time?" His smile was intoxicatingly sexy. Everything about Max reflected sheer sensuality and fire. Angel could not remember ever feeling more deliriously happy.

"You're insatiable," she murmured as she pressed her head to his shoulder.

He carried her out of the bathroom. "It's one of my finer qualities."

Angel laughed softly as they fell together onto the bed. "You're right," she said, his caresses stirring up rainbows just as she knew they would.

It was near dawn. Max had ordered up a bottle of champagne and a couple of turkey club sandwiches from room service. Angel was stretched out on the bed, her head propped up on a pile of pillows as she drank her champagne. Max sat cross-legged beside her, devouring his sandwich and finishing off his fourth glass of bubbly.

Angel watched him, a soft smile on her lips. "I've been thinking about something."

"Mmm?" He took another large bite of the turkey sandwich.

"About what happened before." She paused. "You do know what it means, don't you?"

He stopped chewing, his eyes narrowing. Then he swallowed quickly, too quickly. He sputtered and broke into a choking cough. Angel handed him her champagne. He swallowed half of it down before the paroxysms settled down. He wiped his mouth with the back of his hand and set the drink and the rest of his sandwich aside. His expression was very serious, very earnest.

"Look, Angel, I don't think we ought to make too much out of this. I mean . . . if I do think about it too hard . . . I might run like hell." Their eyes held. A hint of a smile tugged at Angel's mouth.

"Don't panic, Max. I wasn't about to propose."

His neck reddened. He smiled self-consciously and looked around at nothing in particular.

"I wasn't talking about us," she went on in a slow, teasing fashion.

Max gave her a quizzical look. "Oh?"

"I meant what happened before you walked into the middle of my bath and burst all my bubbles." Her blue-violet eyes sparkled as her gaze drifted down his naked body. Sated as she was, she felt a sharp twinge of arousal. So, she could see, did Max.

137

She could also tell that he wasn't exactly pleased with that fact. He twisted around, trying to be nonchalant as he pulled up the sheet around his hips.

Angel's smile broadened. "Where was I?" She gave his face a lingering look. "Oh, yes, Janine and Ross. Quite a pair, those two. Far be it from me to ever argue that love isn't blind."

Max did not miss the wry note in her voice.

"Anyway," Angel went on, "as far as Lou is concerned, I can't see any motive at all for either Janine or Ross . . . doing him in. If anything, they had everything to gain by Lou staying alive."

Max nodded slowly. "I guess that's true."

Her eyes shone. "So, that means we can chuck them from our list of suspects."

"We?"

She tilted her head, giving him a saucy look. "Don't you want to hear my plan?"

He shook his head. "From here on out, I'll do the planning."

"Oh, no, you won't," she said in a low, challenging voice.

He fixed her with a look that was almost menacing. "If I'm going to keep on sticking my neck out, Angel, we'll play it my way. Is that clear?"

Angel started to argue, but then she decided against it. At least she had Max willing to buy back into the case. "Okay," she said, albeit a touch syrupy, "what's your plan?"

Max grinned. He was well aware how hard it was for Angel to give an inch. "My immediate plan is to get some sleep. You better get some shut-eye, too, Angel." He leaned over and switched off the lamp, but the room still glowed with dawn's early light. Angel turned on her side to face Max. His eyes were closed.

"What if I had proposed to you, Max?" she asked in a low, tantalizing voice.

He took his time answering. "I thought you liked being single."

Instead of confirming his statement, she asked, "Don't you ever get lonely?"

"No," he lied.

"Have there been a lot of women . . ." She let the sentence trail off, feeling suddenly awkward.

Max's palm moved slowly up the curve of her hip. "I didn't take a vow of celibacy after my divorce, Angel, just a vow of detachment." He felt her stiffen and opened his eyes. He studied Angel carefully. "Up until now, I haven't had any trouble keeping that vow."

A faint smile curved her lips. Her hand moved to his chest. Max always did seem to come through. "I made the same vow when Lou and I split up."

He raised up on one elbow and watched her fingers sketching the lines of his shoulders and chest. He felt a shiver of delight at her tantalizing caress, his desire growing instantly. "How are you doing with your vow?"

She grinned slowly. "You mean now?"

He nodded.

"Lousy," she confessed, her hand drifting lower down his body.

"You're not following the plan, Angel," he said in a husky voice. "We're supposed to get some sleep."

Angel's eyes shimmered with tantalizing sensuality. "What if I come up with a better plan?"

"Trying to take over already, are you?"

She smiled alluringly. "Any objections?"

"I never did plan too well after a half bottle of champagne. Remind me to stay sober . . . after tonight."

He leaned down to capture her lips, but she blocked him by pressing her palms against his chest. "Did you mean it about never getting lonely?"

He took hold of her hands and brought them up high over her head. He pinned them there. Then his lips curved into a rueful smile. "I don't lie any better than I plan when I've had too much champagne."

She looked up into his eyes, the playfulness gone. "I've had my lonely times too, Max."

He felt a fierce rush of tenderness as he took her in his arms and kissed her. It was a good thing he didn't think too clearly when he was under the influence, or the disturbing thought might have come to him that he was falling helplessly, hopelessly in love with an angel.

CHAPTER EIGHT

The surf broke along the shore in long, smooth swells as Angel walked barefoot in the sand. It was seven thirty in the morning and the beach was deserted. Or so Angel thought.

She turned, pulling her short terry cover-up around her bikini-clad body, as she heard her name called out. Rick Seidman, looking out of place in crumpled khaki slacks and an out-of-style Madras plaid jacket, strolled toward her.

"The sand is going to take the shine off your shoes, Rick," Angel said facetiously as she glanced down at Rick's scuffed loafers that he wore without socks.

He grinned and stepped out of them. Angel had started walking again and he picked up the loafers, hurrying to catch up with her.

"You're up bright and early," Rick said casually.

Angel cast him a sidelong glance. "So are you."

Rick shrugged. "Truth is, I haven't been to bed yet. I wanted to talk with you, Angel." He cleared his throat lightly and looked out at the crystal-clear

141

ocean. "I've been hanging around waiting. I didn't want to interrupt anything . . ."

Angel felt her cheeks reddening, but she gave Rick a sharp look. "What did you want to talk about?"

"Who is this Gallagher?"

"Don't tell me you're slipping, Rick. I was sure you knew all there was to know about him."

"All except what he's after."

"Well, why don't you ask him the questions?"

Rick caught hold of her arm, forcing her to a halt. "I'm asking you, because I happen to care about you. I don't want to see you getting hurt. This pal of yours has had his share of trouble. And his share of wives."

"One wife doesn't make him a bluebeard, Rick. One ex-wife," she corrected.

"And one messy divorce. Not to mention a few scrapes with the law. When he was a football player he was known for his hot temper and his risky moves. And since he's been off the team, he's made it a habit of never sticking to one dame too long."

Angel laughed. "And I accused you of slipping. Tell me, Rick, what does the man eat for breakfast?"

Rick's brows shot up. "I figured you already knew that."

Angel glowered. "This conversation is a waste of a beautiful day." She shrugged off her terry robe. "I'm going for a swim."

She tried to dismiss the feel of Rick's roving eyes on her skimpily clad body as she raced toward the water and dove in. The chilly ocean did nothing to cool her off. She swam in long, easy strides, cutting across the waves. She hoped he'd get the message that their conversation was over, but Rick didn't wander off. He remained where she'd left him. He watched every stroke she took. Finally, exhausted, she headed back to shore.

Rick had the terry cover-up waiting for her. She tried to grab it from him but he was bent on helping her on with it.

"Angel, you're barking up the wrong tree." His tone was casual, but his expression was anything but.

She felt his arms move around her along with the robe. "So are you, Rick," she said acidly, wrenching herself free. She whirled around to face him. "I have a strong feeling, Rick, that there's a lot more you could tell me. And I'm not talking about Max Gallagher. I'm talking about Lou. About why he went down to Key West with a pocketful of cash. About what his relationship with Vera Hargrove was all about." Her eyes narrowed. "About what your relationship with Vera's husband, Michael, is all about." There was a pregnant pause. "About who killed Lou. And who wants me to stop snooping around."

Rick's face stiffened. "Whatever I do know, Angel, is strictly confidential. You know that. You know the rules of the game." His smile was a little too paternal. His hands moved up to cup her face. "Or maybe you don't, Angel. Maybe that's why you're behaving so foolishly."

Angel looked at him evenly. "You're a first-class heel, Rick."

"Angel."

"Or maybe you're worse than that," she said threateningly. "Is that why you're so eager to get rid of me? Are you scared, Rick?"

Rick laughed softly, his fingers moving down to her shoulders. The grip was firm. Angel knew she wasn't going to get free of him until he decided to release her. "I'm just your everyday gumshoe trying to make a buck, Angel. Just doing my job. As for Lou, all I can say is, he was probably just doing his job, too."

Angel's gaze was shrewd. "Are you telling me his trip to Key West was more than a pleasure cruise?"

Rick's laugh was stronger. "You're a clever woman, Angel. Just be careful that you don't get too clever for your own good."

His hands still gripped her.

"In this business," she said blithely, "it always pays to be careful. Lou taught me that."

Rick shrugged. "Too bad he didn't follow his own advice." He let her go. "Or maybe he died trying."

Angel swallowed. Rick started to walk away. She ran up to him, grabbing hold of his arm now. "I'm going to get to the bottom of this, Rick. If you ever do want to have a serious talk, I'll be happy to listen."

Rick smiled at Angel and then glanced back toward the hotel, thirty yards up from the beach. "Hey, your boyfriend's awake. Does he always look so sour in the morning?"

Angel's eyes followed Rick's. She saw Max sitting at a large picture window in the dining room. Sour was an understatement. His expression was tight-lipped and grim as their eyes met. Angel had the feeling he'd been watching her and Rick for a while. And misreading what he saw. She dropped her hand from Rick's arm, feeling Max's eyes measuring her.

Rick laughed. To make matters intentionally worse, he leaned over and gave Angel a fleeting kiss before he walked off.

Angel had to change out of her wet bathing suit before she could walk into the dining room. She hurried, concerned that Max would duck out before she could explain what had really transpired between her and Rick. Not that she was certain Max would believe her, even if he did stick around and wait to hear the story.

He was still there when she entered the dining room ten minutes later. Only he was no longer alone. Wendy Shaw had joined him at the table. It looked to Angel as if she'd joined him at the hip.

Angel hesitated at the entrance as she watched Max put a cigarette between his lips and light it. Wendy's hand snaked out and took the cigarette from his mouth. She placed it between her own ruby-red lips and smiled. Max took out a second cigarette for himself.

Angel arrived at the table amid intertwining smoke rings. Max looked up and gave her a cool smile. Wendy's smile was even cooler.

Angel slid blithely into a seat and lifted Max's menu from his place setting. "What's good?"

145

No one answered.

Angel looked up and directed her gaze to Wendy Shaw. "I ran into Rick on the beach. Did you two have a fight?"

Wendy seemed thrown by the remark, but she didn't answer.

"I think he's worried about you, Wendy. I think he believes you haven't really gotten over Derek Bendix. It was a raw deal, his dumping you for his wife after she'd actually gone and shot him. I bet that made you see red."

Wendy Shaw was certainly seeing red right now. She snubbed out her cigarette and rose abruptly from the table. "I don't know what Lou told you . . . but I never threatened Derek when he went back to Paula. It was good riddance as far as I was concerned. The man was becoming downright paranoid, thinking I'd pull the same stunt as his wife and have him gunned down for leaving me. And then he goes and hires Lou to protect him. Why Lou ever took the case is beyond me."

Angel stared at Wendy thoughtfully and then she gave Max a quick look. His expression gave nothing away.

Wendy's ruby lips formed a pout. "Lou knew me better than that." The pout gave way to a seductive smile as the chanteuse looked across at Max before giving Angel one final lingering gaze. "Lou knew me much better than that," she finished huskily. Then she turned with a graceful pirouette and slinked off.

Angel's eyes sparkled as she watched Wendy walk

away. She smiled brightly but when she turned back to Max the smile died off her face.

"You have the wrong idea about Rick and me," Angel said in a low voice. "You've been wrong about us from the start."

Max blew a thread of smoke and watched with narrowed eyes as it moved in Angel's direction.

"Cigarettes are bad for your health. Don't you read the Surgeon General's warnings?"

"That's one of my weak points. I tend to disregard the warning signs at first." He took another long drag of his cigarette. "It takes me a while." Max leaned closer toward Angel. "Sometimes a brick has to fall on my head."

"I was trying to get some information from Rick."

"And what was he trying to get?" Max shook his head. "Never mind. I may not be a detective, but I think I have enough clues to figure that answer out myself."

"Whatever he may want," she said softly, "he's not going to get."

"Don't underestimate Seidman, Angel." He blew some more smoke in her face, this time more slowly. "Come to think of it, don't underestimate me. I don't like women who bounce from my bed into another man's arms . . . even if all she's after is . . . information. Maybe I don't like the way you work, Angel. And I definitely don't like the fact that you're planning all the moves again."

Angel felt a cold fury attack her. "First of all, it was my bed, not yours. Second of all, I wasn't bouncing into Rick's arms. Nor was our conversation part of any plan. He followed me out on the beach." She glared at him. "And third of all, I don't like your insinuations, Max. I thought you knew me better than that." She stood up, miming Wendy Shaw's pout. "I thought you knew me much better than that." She got the singer's inflection down perfectly. But before she turned to walk away, her expression revealed the hurt she was really feeling.

Max found Angel out in the lobby. She was sitting in a pale blue and salmon striped moire silk armchair reading a note. When Max got closer he saw that the note was written on fine cream-colored stationery. There was a faint scent of roses wafting up from the sheet.

Angel didn't look up right away. When she did, her eyes locked with Max's. Neither of them said anything. He eased his long, muscular frame into a matching armchair next to her. Her eyes flicked involuntarily over his body. His clothing fell away in her mind and she could picture him naked with perfect recall. When she met his gaze again she saw the wry twist to his lips. She looked away.

"You know what this means, don't you?" He eyed her with a faint smile.

Angel's expression was bemused, but there was a flicker of apprehension there as well. She knew he was talking about their fight, but she changed the subject. "That Wendy Shaw might have had a motive for killing Lou?"

Max stretched his hand out. His fingers were cool and tender along her cheek. He ignored her and

kept talking. "It means that I'm the jealous type."
His lips drifted to her bare shoulder. She could feel
her nipples harden beneath the thin cotton of her
sundress.

"Max . . ."

"About what happened last night, Angel . . ."
He guided her face toward him. "It was the best.
You're the best."

"Damn it, Max. You've got me on a roller-coaster
ride. Why do you have to be so infuriatingly charming, so . . ."

"Irresistible?" He was laughing at her, but Angel
couldn't dredge up any anger. He was irresistible.

"This ride we're on is fraught with every possible
danger. You know that, Max." She regarded him
balefully. "Things are moving too fast. What do we
really know about each other?"

"We know that we think remarkably alike, Angel.
We both know what it's like to have loved and lost.
We both have hot tempers . . . and hot passions."
His hand stroked her shoulder. Although it might
have looked like an innocently idle gesture to other
people strolling across the lobby, it was turning Angel's insides to liquid fire. "And," he whispered, his
breath warm against her cheek, "neither of us likes
to operate under any restrictions or any conditions.
That's the only way either of us can play it, Angel."

The problem was, Angel had moved beyond that
point. Somewhere along the line, she had started to
realize, like it or not, that she was playing a different
game than Max. She was playing for keeps. And she
couldn't have picked a more unwilling partner for

the game than Max Gallagher. She told herself the only solution was to quit playing altogether. She wasn't at all confident she could follow her own good advice, but there was too much at stake not to give it her best try.

She manufactured a cool, confident look as she met Max's gaze. "I think we ought to read over Wendy Shaw's file again, see if Lou made any notes about taking on Derek Bendix as a client. If what Wendy told us is true and he hired Lou for protection against Wendy, he must really have been worried that she might go after him for leaving her. I don't think Wendy's the type to soil her own hands. I bet she'd hire some thug to do the dirty work for her. Which would make Bendix even more worried. Any face in the crowd could be the hit man. Maybe Wendy first had the thug take on Lou so he wouldn't be able to interfere with her revenge plan." Angel knew she was talking too fast. She wasn't even sure if she was making any sense. Her eyes skidded off Max's face. He looked none too pleased by the detour in the conversation she'd so obviously taken. She looked down at the piece of classy stationery in her lap. She'd almost forgotten all about it.

She handed it to Max. "This was left for me at the desk. The desk clerk just handed it to me."

He made no effort to take it. His eyes never left her face. They were dark and angry. "I can't figure you out, Angel. Every time I think I've got a clue you throw me a curve. I'm talking about you and me and you're talking about Wendy Shaw and the case." His tone was harsh and angry.

"You were the one who told me not to read too much into what was happening between us, Max. I'm just following your advice."

"I don't think that's what you're doing."

Angel arched a brow.

"I think I've got you scared, Angel." She started to protest, but Max cut her off. "Just like you have me scared. Okay," he said, studying her solemnly, "let's stick to business for now. We don't really want to scare each other off altogether." He lifted the creamy, scented note from Angel's hands.

A slow smile curved his lips. "The plot thickens," he said wryly after reading the formal invitation requesting Angel to be Vera Hargrove's guest for a week at her tropical villa on Rum Cay in the Bahamas. He glanced over at Angel. "Vera must have been pretty sure you'd accept the invitation. She didn't even bother with an RSVP."

Angel took the note back and studied it for a moment. Keeping her eyes cast down, she asked, "Ever been to the Bahamas?"

He laughed softly. "Never have. But I hear it's nice and quiet there this time of year. Not too many tourists. Maybe we'll have a chance to unwind a little." His last remark held a teasing note.

Angel gave him a rueful smile. "I wouldn't bet on it."

"Ah, but I'm still a gambler at heart, Angel."

His hand found its way to her shoulder again, but Angel hastened to disentangle herself. "I think I'll buy a few things for the trip." She stood up. "And

I'll make plane reservations. Can you be ready by this afternoon?"

Max rose. "I could use a few things myself. Why don't I go along with you?"

Angel's eyes narrowed. "I don't need a watchdog, Max."

"Now there, Angel, we strongly disagree. Every time I turn my back, you get yourself into trouble."

Angel was beginning to get the feeling that she was going to be in serious trouble no matter which way she turned.

"What do you think?" Max was holding up a sizzling red-hot orange print shirt in front of his chest as the salesman in the men's shop smiled encouragingly.

Angel grimaced. "The Florida sun is warping your sense of style." She walked over to a counter and lifted a soft beige cotton jersey. "This is more like it." She held it up for Max's inspection.

He quirked his dark brows. "A little drab, don't you think?"

Angel shrugged. "It depends on who's wearing it."

Max grinned. He walked over to her, pretending to give the shirt a closer examination. "Or who's taking it off?" Amusement glittered in his eyes.

Damn the man. Why did he insist on making trouble?

She set the shirt down. "Maybe it is too drab," she said coolly. She glanced down at her watch, then lifted two parcels from the counter. She'd

152

picked up some more sun tan lotion, a couple of T-shirts and one more sundress that was dressy enough to wear to any formal dinners in Rum Cay. There was one more stop she wanted to make before she returned to the hotel to pack and this one had nothing to do with shopping. She had a feeling Max would try to talk her out of it, so she decided, rather than have an argument, the easiest thing would be to ditch Max and make the stop on her own.

Meanwhile Max decided to buy the beige jersey. While he was fishing for a credit card in his wallet, Angel said, "I should pick up one more bathing suit. There was a little boutique down the street. I'll run over and find something and meet you back at the hotel in about an hour."

"We have to be out at the airport by four," Max reminded her.

"I won't have that much to pack. I have plenty of time," she said as she headed for the door.

Max eyed her curiously as she darted out. He tucked the credit card back in his wallet. "I think the wife's right," he said briskly to the salesman. "The shirt is too drab."

As Max made a beeline for the door, the man shouted out, "What about the Hawaiian print you were looking at? The wife couldn't say that one is too drab."

Max gave a dismissive wave as he exited. He spotted Angel hurrying down the street. He jogged after her.

"Never did see a woman so eager to buy a swimsuit. Slow down. You have plenty of time. You only have to throw a few things in a suitcase."

Angel shot Max an irritated glance. "Where's the shirt?"

"I changed my mind."

She came to an abrupt halt. "Look, Max, I don't need a round-the-clock shadow." She held up her hand. "Save the speech about my getting into trouble. How much trouble can a woman get into buying a bikini?"

Max wrinkled his brow in mock thoughtfulness. "Well, now . . . it doesn't seem like much could happen. But I was wondering how much trouble a woman could get into paying a visit to the Fontaine Hotel. That is the spread that Derek Bendix owns, isn't it?" He skimmed her arm and took hold of her hand.

Angel snatched it away indignantly. "Who said anything about paying Derek Bendix a visit?"

"I know how your mind works. You're taking charge again, Angel. I really don't know what I'm going to do about you. I thought we agreed that I'd do the planning from now on."

Angel frowned. "Well, doesn't it make sense to have a talk with him?"

"Why sneak around behind my back?"

"I didn't want to hurt your ego. You might have felt bad about not having thought to pay him a call yourself."

Max gave her an assessing look. "I might have . . . if I hadn't called him from the hotel before we left on this shopping excursion. He agreed to meet

154

with me for a little chat." He bent down and kissed the tip of her nose. "You were up in your room powdering your nose while I was making the appointment."

Angel's look was a mixture of surprise and indignation. "When were you going to mention it to me?"

"I figured you'd be so busy shopping, I'd just amble over and have a chat with him on my own."

"Oh, you did, did you?"

"See"—he grinned—"I told you we are a lot alike. We both had the same idea."

"Not so long ago, Gallagher, you weren't any too sure you wanted any part of this business. Then you tell me you'll make all the plans. And now you're pushing me out of the picture altogether."

"I'm not pushing you out of the picture, Angel." His grin broadened. "I couldn't manage that even if I wanted to."

Angel looked into those mesmerizing blue eyes. There was a devil lurking there. A devil she couldn't resist.

She tilted her head at a jaunty angle. "What time is our meeting with Derek Bendix?"

The Fontaine Hotel was a first-class Florida holiday spot, the kind rich, elderly widows vacationed at during the cold northern winters. During the summer months, however, you could stay at the posh hotel at off-season rates. Even at that, they were pretty stiff, but the July clientele reflected the difference in price. Lots of tour groups, families recuperating from a weekend in Disney World, conventioners. The place was hopping.

Max led Angel around a central atrium overflowing with flowering plants and tiny waterfalls amid the greenery. The air was smothered with the scent of tropical blossoms. To the left of the atrium was the lavish clover-shaped outdoor pool area where men in brightly printed Bermuda shorts and matching jackets trimmed in terry sat playing pinochle around umbrella-shaded outdoor tables. Other tables were occupied by wives in equally bright sundresses, busily playing mah-jongg or simply gossiping, while they sipped tall, pastel drinks garnished with paper umbrellas. What looked like whole campfuls of children filled all four clovers of the swimming pool. Everyone seemed to be having a grand time.

Derek Bendix's private office was to the right of the atrium. The PRIVATE was written across the door in bold black lettering. Max knocked.

The door sprang open immediately. "You're ten minutes late, Mr. Gallagher. My husband's schedule is very hectic. He will only be able to spare you five more minutes." Paula Bendix stared at him coolly. The gaze was even cooler when her eyes met Angel's. Paula Bendix was a severe-looking woman. She was tall and thin, but she lacked anything in the way of style or glamour. In fact, she seemed to go out of her way to look plain.

"We apologize, Mrs. Bendix," Angel said pleasantly. "We won't keep your husband long."

"You're Lou Chapman's ex-wife."

Angel nodded. "How did you know?"

"Derek told me you might come to see him as well." She absently tucked a loose tendril of hair back into her sleek, coiled knot. It was the only loose strand in an otherwise perfect coif. "Just why do you want to talk with my husband?" The question held a demanding note.

Angel was debating her answer when she heard a sharp voice coming from inside the room. "Don't keep my guests waiting, Paula."

Paula hesitated then opened the door marked PRIVATE all the way. She stepped aside and let them in.

Derek Bendix's private office was all an office in a swank hotel ought to be. One large wall of glass overlooked the gleaming Atlantic. The other three walls were paneled in very expensive burlwood. The floor was covered in glistening white imported tile over which was an extraordinarily lush Persian carpet in the palest tints of mauve, mint, and ivory. The furniture was old as in fine antiques. Angel thought Derek Bendix had better taste in decoration than in wives.

The once Senate hopeful moved in a graceful sweep across the room. He shook Max's hand heartily and when he took hers, he was slightly less zealous and slightly more seductive as his other hand briefly joined in the shake. Angel could imagine him taking over a Congressional meeting with ease. And she had no doubt he'd have an even easier time taking over at Senate supper parties. He had the looks of a politician, along the Kennedy lines. He was tall,

157

athletic-looking without being overly muscular, with a thick crop of fading auburn hair that fell in attractively haphazard waves.

Lou's files indicated that Derek Bendix was in his early fifties. He looked younger than that. He looked much younger than his wife. And yet Paula Bendix was only forty-two according to Lou's notes. Maybe, Angel mused, those six months of prison life had aged her. Then she found herself wondering if it had also made her bitter. Bitter enough to take some revenge of her own on the man who'd been responsible for sending her up the river?

Angel scowled. She already had more than enough suspects to cope with. And so far, she couldn't even prove any crime had been committed. She glanced up at Max. He moved his gaze away from Paula Bendix and smiled down at Angel. She had the feeling his thoughts were running in the same direction as hers. Sometimes it was very comforting to know their minds ran along the same track.

Sometimes it was anything but.

CHAPTER NINE

"Can I offer you some coffee? Tea? Perhaps a drink?" Derek Bendix asked.

"No thanks," Angel said. Max concurred.

Angel saw Derek shoot a quick glance at his wife. He was diplomatic enough not to overtly show his irritation at her presence, but he couldn't quite squash the momentary flash of annoyance as his eyes swung away from her. Paula, however, showed positively no sign of anything other than that cool, severe, and quiet rage.

She was also the one to launch the discussion. "What is it you want to talk with Derek about?"

They were all still standing, like guests at a cocktail party. Only there were no cocktails and no party. Derek had his hands clasped in front of him. He unclasped them and moved over to his wife's side. As he put his arm lightly around her shoulder he motioned to a pair of Queen Anne chairs across from him. "Please forgive my wife's manners. She's been overwrought. I'm afraid your visit brings up some painful memories for her. Please. Sit down." He looked at his wife.

Angel was surprised to note the tender look he gave her. She reminded herself that Bendix had a politician's way about him. But, for some reason, she had the feeling the look wasn't artificial.

Derek guided Paula to a delicately designed Louis XIV loveseat done in a heather-shaded damask. He held her hand as he sat beside her. "I don't believe in keeping anything from my wife." He cleared his throat, a line of red rising up from his neck. There had been a time he wouldn't have been able to make that statement and have there be any truth to it. Then again, Angel couldn't be sure there was any truth to it now. It was just another of her gut feelings.

She and Max sat down in the Queen Anne chairs. Angel smoothed her cool blue sundress over her knees. "I certainly don't want to cause you any pain, Mrs. Bendix. Obviously, you and your husband have been through a great deal." She paused. She could feel Max's eyes on her. She knew he wouldn't be any too pleased at her taking charge of the conversation. That, however, wasn't likely to stop her. "I've gone through a . . . painful experience myself . . . recently. It was a terrible shock to learn of Lou's death." This time the pause was longer. "It was even more shocking to learn that it might not have been . . . an accident."

Angel heard Paula Bendix take in a sharp breath. Derek Bendix took the news with a bemused frown. "You mean . . . murder?"

She liked that about Bendix. He called a spade a spade. "Yes."

"You're not really all that surprised, are you, Bendix?" This was Max's first comment. It was a doozy. Derek Bendix's face turned red. Red with rage. "What the hell is that supposed to mean?"

Angel narrowed her eyes. She wanted an answer, too.

Surprisingly, it was Paula Bendix who appeared the least distressed. "You're right, Mr. Gallagher." Paula seemed relieved to get the cards on the table. "My husband and I have discussed that possibility. Lou Chapman was in a very risky kind of business. Although I've no doubt his clients . . . and personal friends"—she cast Angel a weak smile—"were fond of him, he made a lot of enemies."

"Sometimes," Angel said in that rich vibrato of hers, "a friend one day could be an enemy the next."

"Or vice versa, Ms. Welles." Paula leaned slightly toward her husband. "I know what the two of you are thinking. That Lou Chapman was responsible for my spending six months in prison." Paula Bendix's lips quivered slightly. "Six horrible months." She shut her eyes for a moment. When she opened them again, she looked surprisingly less severe. Angel thought she looked almost beautiful. So, apparently, did her husband, who gave her a loving smile and touched her cheek.

"We are trying very hard to put the past—" Derek began, but Paula pressed his hand.

"No, darling. I want to have my say. I know I was against this meeting, but I see now that it's pointless to run from what people are bound to be thinking." Paula Bendix met Angel's gaze evenly. "I did hate Lou Chapman once upon a time. Maybe I even hated him enough to kill him." A wisp of hair fell from her knot, and she ignored it. "But if it weren't for Lou, Derek and I wouldn't be together now." Tears welled up in her eyes. "Lou came to visit me in prison. You might say he served as a mirror to my soul. I did take that shot at my husband. I timed it just after the argument Wendy Shaw had with Derek, so that . . . so that the police would believe she was guilty." She gripped Derek's hand. "I never intended to seriously harm . . ." She couldn't go on for a moment. No one in the room rushed her. "I was out of my mind with jealousy. I loved Derek so terribly much. I couldn't bear to lose him."

Angel felt a lump in her throat. She gave Max a surreptitious glance. There was a tender look of compassion on his face. Angel felt a poorly timed surge of arousal. Max Gallagher had a way of doing that to her. She tried to focus her attention solely on Paula and Derek Bendix.

"Lou came to see both of us . . . often," Derek said. "He was some detective. He even managed to piece together the fact that Paula and I . . . well, that we loved each other. My wife and I have made our mistakes, but we've paid for them. Paid heavily. Lou Chapman helped us to see the light."

"You hired Lou yourself a few months ago," Max said.

Derek's eyes shot up. "How did you know?"

Max shrugged. "Good training, I guess."

Angel stifled a laugh.

"Yes, I did hire Lou," Derek admitted.

"Because of threats to your life made by Wendy Shaw." Max spoke slowly.

Derek laughed dryly. "Threats to my career is more to the point. Although Wendy certainly knew that my aspirations for political office were a very vital factor in my life." He cast his eyes on Paula. "Not the most vital factor, however."

Paula smiled. Her face really did turn pretty when she smiled. "Derek is planning to run for U.S. Senator again next year. We think the public will be able to accept what I did as an act of love and they'll see how strong our marriage is now. Wendy Shaw was very upset when Derek decided that he wanted to give our marriage another chance."

"That woman is nothing but a little gold-digger. Oh, she threatened to have me killed. She'd done the same thing last time I tried to break up with her. But she wasn't interested in seeing me dead. All she wanted was cold, hard cash. I wrote some . . . rather intimate letters to Wendy." He looked sorely uncomfortable. "A long time ago. Wendy threatened to turn them over to one of those scandal sheets as soon as I announced I was running. Plus she hired her own detective to keep an eye on me." He leveled his gaze at Angel. "I believe you worked for Rick Seidman."

"That was a long time ago," Angel said in a low voice.

"Well, Seidman watched my every move for about two months. I guess Wendy was hoping to get some more current blackmail fodder. She couldn't believe I'd actually gone back to Paula."

"Wendy was certain there was another woman in the picture," Paula said. "She assumed Derek and I were together only because he wanted to run for office and thought it best to present a united front. Meanwhile, she was convinced, he was . . . fooling around on the sly."

"I told her I was in love with Paula," Derek broke in. "A few long evenings talking with Lou Chapman made me see that more clearly. But Wendy tuned out everything I tried to explain to her."

Max smiled. "Wendy must be deaf as well as dumb. It's obvious to any fool that you and your wife . . . have something very special."

Paula Bendix actually blushed. Angel felt another flash of arousal. How wonderful it would be to have something very special between her and Max. She sensed that they did have it, but because it lacked a sense of permanence, it wasn't as special as what Paula and her husband shared.

"Do you think Wendy Shaw could have killed Lou?" Angel asked Derek, distressed by the sudden breathiness in her voice. She kept her gaze averted from Max, but seeing the two lovebirds hand in hand on the sofa only served to remind her of what she was beginning to want so desperately for her and Max.

"If Lou had died a month earlier and you had asked me that question, I might have said yes," Derek said. "Wendy wanted a lot of money in exchange for those letters. The ante kept going up when Seidman came up batting zero on my extracurricular activities. Lou stood in the way of her collecting. And I think she might have considered hiring someone to get him out of the way." He paused for a moment. "Someone like Rick Seidman, maybe. She sure was playing up to Seidman for something. Wendy always had an ulterior motive. With me, it was money. With Seidman . . . possibly it was for services he might be willing to render."

Angel compressed her lips. She didn't like Rick Seidman. And she'd stopped working for him because he played by his own rules far too often. And Angel didn't like those rules one bit. But murder . . .

"However," Derek broke into her thoughts, "Lou died after things were settled between Wendy and me."

"Settled?" Max queried.

"Using Lou as the arbiter, Wendy and I negotiated a settlement." He glanced at his wife. "Paula wanted it that way, even though Lou felt confident he could get the letters . . . by other means." He shook his head wearily. "We all have to pay for our mistakes. So I paid Wendy for mine. It wasn't as much as she wanted. But she was satisfied. Especially as Lou held it over her that if she got too greedy he might have her brought up on charges of threatening my life, since we had witnesses." He took his wife's hand. "Of course, we wouldn't have allowed that in truth. It would have been too . . . déjà vu, if you know what I mean."

Angel and Max both knew what he meant.

Derek stood up. "Paula was right. I do have a busy schedule. Summers are hectic at the hotel because of all the conventions." He looked at Angel evenly. "I don't blame you for looking into this business, Ms. Welles. As my wife said, we had already discussed the possibility that Lou was murdered. We were both worried that suspicion would fall on Paula. Especially as she and I were visiting friends in Key West the same weekend Lou was down there." Derek shrugged. "I am trying very hard to keep my record unsmudged, Ms. Welles. But I suppose you'll find out if you continue to pursue your investigation that Paula and I even got together with Lou for drinks the first night he was in town. Please understand that we do not want to be in any way involved in this, if at all possible. Bad publicity at this time . . ."

Max rose slowly. "On the other hand, Bendix, you and your wife owe Chapman. Angel and I aren't interested in dragging you or Mrs. Bendix into the spotlight. We just want to find out the truth. What did Lou talk about that night you got together for drinks down in Key West?"

Angel noticed that Paula's severe look had returned full force. "We talked about the weather and baseball. Nothing else," Paula said, resurrecting her icy tone.

Derek Bendix smiled faintly. "Paula was bored. She's not much of a baseball fan."

Max met Derek's gaze. "I suppose Chapman mentioned he was staying over at the Hargrove villa."

"I suppose he did. Yes, he mentioned that he was Vera Hargrove's guest."

"Did you know he was also her lover?"

Derek frowned at Max, giving Angel a quick glance. "Don't you think that's a rather indelicate question?"

Max shrugged. "I think murder's rather indelicate, too."

Max was smiling.

"You're pretty proud of yourself, aren't you?" Angel was smiling, too.

The cab pulled out of the circular drive of the Fontaine Hotel.

"You were pretty good yourself in there," Max said with a wink.

"We're getting to be quite a team."

Max gave her a sidelong glance. "Not bad for beginners."

"We'll get better with practice."

Max's smile broadening. "I'm counting on it."

Angel turned to him, her expression sober. "What happens after that?"

The four o'clock flight from Miami landed Angel and Max in Bimini at five P.M. Rum Cay was a small dot of an island just north of Bimini. Vera Hargrove had noted in her invitation that her private launch would be at the Bimini Harbor the following morning at nine to transport Angel across.

The people of Bimini refer to their island paradise as a magical isle. It was a place where you could forget all your depressing yesterdays, wile away your todays in tropical splendor and weave fanciful dreams about all the glorious possibilities for tomorrow. It was also, Max mused, a perfect spot for romance. And Angel Welles was the perfect woman for this perfect spot overlooking a perfect multihued sea.

Angel, however, was not in the mood for romance. Or, more accurately, she was too much in the mood. She'd been giving herself some more of her sound advice all the way down to the Bahamas. Seeing the Bendixes earlier, engulfed in the kind of loving relationship that had not only weathered a lot of storms but seemed more seaworthy than ever, left Angel feeling that she didn't want to settle for less. She wanted a man who she could go through hurricanes, tornadoes, and old age with. She wanted that man to be Max Gallagher. Max, however, wanted a no-strings affair. Angel had a depressing feeling that they were both going to lose out on what they wanted.

"You're awfully quiet," Max said gently. "Disappointed that we shot down two suspects with one stone?"

Angel smiled wistfully. "No, of course not. It's to our advantage to narrow down the field. Our field being the Hargroves."

Max nodded. "You thinking about that flare-up of Vera's at Lou's funeral?"

She wasn't, but she said, "Yes."

He set his case down and turned Angel to him. "Look, we've got about sixteen hours before we arrive at Vera's place. What do you say we take the night off? Get a classy room somewhere, have a romantic dinner, go dancing under the stars, take a late-night swim." His hands moved across her shoulders. "Let's just be two people getting to know each other better. Two ordinary people off for a brief holiday. What do you say?"

"I say two rooms," she snapped irritably.

Max frowned. "What's got into you, Angel? Your mood swings are leaving me spinning."

Angel turned. "Let's just check in somewhere." There was a poster advertising the Buccaneer Creek Hotel on one of the terminal walls. She nodded in the direction of the advertisement. "How about there?"

She started walking, leaving her suitcase for Max to manage along with his own. Her overnight case with the files on the tantalizing trio was back in Miami locked in the hotel vault. Angel decided it would be too risky to bring them to the Hargrove villa. Besides, she'd read through them a half-dozen times already and could find nothing that would offer any helpful clues. She concluded that whoever had broken into her Boston apartment must have thought there was something in those files that hadn't actually found their way there. Or else Angel was overlooking something.

She, as much as Max, wanted a night off, but Angel had no intention of spending it in the arms of her no-strings-attached partner in crime. She tried to convince herself it was for the best. Even if she was letting some fantasies creep in about a romantic lifelong relationship with Max, the odds of it ever working out were slim. Not only was Max averse to restrictions, constraints, responsibilities; she hadn't done so well in those departments either. No, she told herself firmly as she climbed into a beat-up old cab outside the airport, better to get herself back on an even keel. She was determined to see to it that Max didn't get the opportunity to rock the boat too much.

Max had other ideas. When they got to the hotel he left Angel to pay the cab and he strode into the lobby ahead of her.

He was already signing in when she arrived. He pocketed the key.

"Where's the key to my room?" she said archly.

"In my pocket."

"You did get us two rooms?"

"I got a suite. Same thing." He gripped her elbow and led her toward the elevator.

"Wait a second," Angel balked. "They're not the same thing. I want my own room." Her voice had raised an octave and a young couple already standing at the elevator turned to gape.

"See, you're attracting attention. Now calm down. It was all they had available. Turns out this is the most popular hotel on the island. They're nearly full up."

"We'll see about that." She tried to wrench herself free, but Max's grip tightened.

"I don't appreciate not being believed, Angel."

"I don't appreciate your thinking that I'm a pushover." She blushed. Why shouldn't he think it? She'd let him push her into bed on more than one occasion. She'd even done some tugging of her own. But that was because she'd been mesmerized by his irresistible charm, hypnotized by his seductive allure. She hadn't been able to think straight. She hadn't known what the cost would be. What was it Derek Bendix had said? We all pay the price for our mistakes. Angel felt she was already paying for the mistake of falling in love with Max. And her assets for paying were fast dwindling.

The elevator doors slid open. "Come on, Angel. The suite has two bedrooms. You can have all the privacy you want."

Instead of sounding irritated by her sudden virtuousness, his tone was quite tender. Angel admitted that his mood swings had her spinning, too.

The suite Max had gotten for them turned out to have only one bedroom, but the adjoining sitting room had a day bed in it. Angel didn't leave Max a choice. She walked directly into the bedroom and slammed the door.

Max didn't try to open it. He merely leaned on the other side. "Do you mind telling me what you're so all-fired angry about? A couple of hours ago we were talking about being a team."

There was a long silence.

"Oh, I get it," Max said finally. "You're worried

171

that I might take the partnership too seriously. You want to make sure I get the message that . . . you're not that kind of girl." There was a touch of cruelty in his tone. "Well, don't worry, Angel. I wasn't thinking of proposing. I don't want to be tied to a ball and chain any more than you do. I have no plans to ever get hitched again."

There was still absolute silence on the other side.

"Okay, so I got a little jealous back in Miami," he said hesitantly. "But the truth is, that isn't really my nature. It was just . . . well, we had spent that very night together." He listened. "Angel, do you hear me? We're both free agents. Nothing's stopping either one of us from being with anyone we want. I'm not like Lou, Angel. I'm not the possessive type. Fact is, I hate that type as much as you do. My ex-wife was that way. Every time I went on the road with the team she imagined I was fooling around."

Max heard footsteps and leaned away from the door. Angel opened it slowly. "Were you?"

"Was I what?"

"Fooling around?"

Max gave Angel a long, lingering look. "I was tempted a few times. But I didn't act on my temptation. I guess I was pretty cocky back in those days. I was a big man, a football star. I was going right to the top. After hours, there were always women just itching to get to know me better. Not just me. All the football players. We were celebrities." His mouth curved in a teasing grin. "Of course, some of us were better-looking celebrities than others. Except when I was in the hospital nursing injuries, I was pretty easy on the eyes."

"Modesty certainly isn't one of your virtues." Angel's expression was sullen.

"What is it, Angel? What's bugging you?"

"Nothing."

"Nothing?"

"It's getting more risky, that's all." She looked away.

Max guided her face back to him. "If something's important, isn't it worth taking some risks?"

That question could be read in a lot of different ways. Angel knew how she wanted to read it. She was tempted to tell Max that what was happening between them was important, desperately important. Terrified as she was, she was willing to take the risk of trying to make it last. But Max had told her that he didn't want to look too deeply into their relationship or he just might run. Angel knew she couldn't push it. That was one risk she didn't want to take.

But she couldn't completely drop it either. "Do you ever think about the future, Max?"

"What do you mean?"

Angel walked back into the bedroom, over by a large window that looked out onto the glistening sea. Max followed her.

"Do you make plans, think about what you want your life to be, say ten years from now? What do you want from life?" She kept her eyes focused on the view.

Max's hand drifted up to Angel's hair, his fingers

173

gently threading through the strands. He studied her in profile, thinking again how utterly exquisite she was. His thoughts quickly moved to how much he wanted her. And then to how risky that could be. Was he willing to take those risks?

She turned to meet his gaze. Her blue-violet eyes searched his face. He felt as though she could glimpse into his soul. He wasn't even sure he could accept the intensity of his feelings, much less give Angel a glimmer of how mesmerized he was by her. A sense of panic struck Max. This obsession he was feeling for Angel was far too dangerous. If he wasn't careful, he just might lose that self-respect he'd worked so hard to rebuild. In a voice that was far cooler than he felt, he said, "I never did go for making long-range plans. I prefer to let the future take care of itself. It makes it more unexpected, surprising."

"And you like the unexpected?"

Max found himself smiling. "Up to a point."

"We've certainly had our share of the unexpected." Her blue-violet eyes sparkled.

"We're certain to have some more."

Angel bit lightly on her bottom lip and tilted her head up a little. "Not if we've very cautious."

His glance was deceptively innocent. "But we aren't very cautious, you and I."

"No . . . no, we aren't."

Max leaned toward her ever so slightly. "So I guess that means there are bound to be more surprises." His lips met hers. The kiss was warm and tender.

Angel's eyes widened. "Was that one of the surprises?"

Max shook his head slowly, that demon look sparking his eyes. Angel's heart quickened. She felt a sharp twist of desire.

Max pulled her into his arms. She clung to him, locked against him as if by a magnetic force. His fingers were cool and firm against her bare back as he drew down the zipper of her sundress. Passion soared. The warm, tropical air shimmered in its dusky glow. With trembling hands, Angel traced the contours of his face. Then her hands slid inside his shirt and rippled over his broad shoulders.

A bittersweet agony of longing rolled through Max. He kissed her again, gliding his tongue over the sensual curve of her lips. His hands trailed down her spine. He moved her away only long enough to let her sundress slide to the carpet. Then she was hard against him again, his kisses falling in a warm, random shower upon her face.

The longing grew within Angel like a painful and yet glorious tension as she arched instinctively against Max, feeling his hammering need just as she felt her own hungry desire. He was so strong, so powerful, so confident.

She pressed her cheek against his shoulder. His caresses were wonderful, the anticipation of fulfillment enthralling. But, in truth, neither Angel or Max would have called what was happening between them surprising.

CHAPTER TEN

"No, Max." Angel tugged away from him.

Max stared at her, incredulous. "No, Max?"

She bent down and grabbed up her sundress. "I know you find it hard to believe, Mr. Gallagher, but as irresistible as you are, I do have some sense of self-preservation." She was clutching the dress to her bare breasts, aware that her chest was still heaving with breathless desire, aware that her lips were swollen from Max's passionate kisses—aware that her attempt to fend off Max Gallagher's ardent lovemaking was the most difficult thing she'd ever tackled in her life.

"Self-preservation?" Max's tone was dry, but there was a hint of amusement there. He was far from accepting Angel's sudden protestations.

"Stop echoing me, Max. I don't want to make love with you. Is that so hard to comprehend?"

Max's dark eyes squinted in mild puzzlement. "I don't—comprehend—you, in the least bit, Angel."

"No, I don't suppose you do." She left off admitting that she didn't understand herself very well these days either. "Would you please leave so that I can get dressed?"

Max laughed. "I see. I'm allowed to remove your clothes, but not help you back on with them."

Angel held the dress against her more tightly. "You're not likely to be much of a help in that regard."

"You're right there, Angel. I much prefer seeing you—unclothed. You're incredibly beautiful. I've never set eyes on a more perfect body."

"Coming from a man of your experience, I take that as quite a compliment."

Max cocked his head. "I never said I was that experienced."

"You didn't have to. Rick did a bit of checking on you. He spared me the details, but he gave me a clear enough overview."

"And my past exploits disturb you?"

"No," she protested too quickly. "Not at all."

"Then why don't you want to make love, Angel? What's all this about self-preservation?"

"I . . . I just don't want things to get too serious, that's all. I do find you . . . very attractive, Max. But I . . . don't want to get hung up on you." She averted her gaze, not wanting Max to see that what she didn't want to happen had already occurred.

She needn't have worried. Max was focused on her words, not the hidden meaning behind them. "I forgot. You're the lady that doesn't play for keeps. Of course, it would be foolish to let yourself get too

177

involved. It makes the end so messy." His tone was cool and tinged with bitterness.

Angel's eyes shot back to him. "You don't play for keeps either, Max. I thought we both saw eye to eye on that."

Max didn't answer. The silence between them stretched. Angel was still clutching her dress against her naked body, feeling more ludicrous and more exposed by the minute. As for Max, his expression was unreadable. Angel found it infuriating not to have a clue to his feelings, but at the moment she envied him the ability to be so inscrutable. She felt that she was wearing her own feelings on her sleeve. Or on her naked arm, in this instance.

When he did finally speak his words were an abrupt command. "Get dressed."

"I will as soon as you leave the room," she answered tersely.

"And if I don't leave, are you going to stand around like this all evening?" He eyed her with a sardonic smile.

Angel's jaw twisted with fury. This was fast becoming an insane match of wills. "I did not invite you in here," she announced archly.

Max ignored her, pulling out a pack of cigarettes from his shirt pocket. He tapped one out and lit it. "Don't you feel just a little foolish, Angel? After all, I already know every inch of your body. A very exquisite body . . . but, then, I've already told you that."

Angel surreptitiously glanced at the bathroom door. Getting to it meant crossing the room, which in turn meant passing Max. Would he make some attempt to stop her? Angel knew that if he so much as touched her, her fragile resistance would shatter. She hated herself for feeling so incredibly vulnerable, but she could do nothing to dispel her desire. This battle over getting dressed was a ridiculous device for keeping her mind off the real issues between them.

"I thought we could go out for a nice, romantic dinner, but if you aren't going to get dressed," he drawled, a thread of smoke drifting out from his lips, "I may as well call up for room service. That's really not a bad idea. I like eating in bed with you." He walked over to the night table and picked up the receiver of the phone.

"Why are you playing this game, Max?" Angel's eyes locked with his. She could hear the buzz of the phone.

Slowly, Max hung the receiver back in the cradle. He scanned her for a long moment, up and down, then snubbed his cigarette in the ashtray beside the phone and walked toward her.

"I've got a crush on you, Angel. You are the most fascinating, irrepressible woman I've ever met. And certainly the most beautiful." He heaved a deep sigh. "I knew you were trouble right from the start." He stood very close to her, close enough for her to feel his hot breath against her cheek, but he made no attempt to touch her.

"I thought you were used to trouble," was all Angel could manage, in a small voice at that.

Max's mouth quirked in a twisted smile. "I'm

179

also painfully familiar with where it always lands me." A sudden shield came down over his face. He stepped away. "Okay, Angel. You win. I'll be downstairs in the bar if you . . . need me."

Max was nursing his third bourbon straight up when Angel walked into the hotel bar. He swiveled in his stool and watched her move gracefully through the crowded lounge toward him. His weren't the only eyes on her. Every man in the room was feasting on the sight of Angel Welles, all of them, Max felt certain, undressing her with their eyes. He told himself he ought to feel victorious for being the only one who'd had the opportunity to actually do it for real, but right now he simply wanted to punch out every pair of male eyes in the bar. And he'd told Angel he wasn't the possessive type.

She passed by him as she swung her lithe body up on the next stool. Max was sharply aware of the muted scent of her tangy perfume. She hadn't put the blue sundress back on. Instead she was wearing a slim black cotton knit tank dress with a very low scooped neckline and a provocatively leggy slit.

Angel gave him a sunny smile.

Max downed the third bourbon and nodded toward the bartender for another.

"What about that dinner you promised me?" Angel asked him.

Max leaned closer to her, almost losing his balance. He had to grip the edge of the bar so as not to slide off his stool. "See," he muttered, "it almost happened again."

"What almost happened?" She eyed him with amusement, at the same time being sharply aware of how incredibly sexy he looked, his blond hair rakishly mussed, enhancing a face that was magnificently handsome and heart-poundingly alluring.

"I almost landed flat on my ass again," he replied, giving her a thorough scrutiny from slightly glazed eyes. Then he muttered something under his breath that Angel couldn't quite make out. When the bartender brought over a refill, he grabbed it eagerly. "That's what happens when I'm dumb enough to get hooked on a woman." He downed a good third of the bourbon in one long gulp.

Angel pried the glass out of his hands. "Come on. I better get some food into you before you do land on your ass."

He shook his head, reaching for the glass. Angel was still holding on to it.

"Are we going to play more games, Max?" she asked soberly as he struggled for the drink.

He grinned. It was crooked. "Okay. Okay." He let go of the glass, letting his hand drift instead over hers. "No games."

His hand moved seductively up her bare arm. Angel began to wonder if he was as sloshed as he seemed.

"Let's go dancing, Angel."

"If you intend to lead, you better eat first, or I'm afraid I'll be dragging you across the dance floor."

181

He gave her a raking glance. "I always lead, Angel. The question is, will you follow?"

"Come on, Max." His hand had crept up to her neck, his fingers lightly caressing her. His touch flickered through her like a lick of fire.

"I am crazy about you, Angel."

She smiled tremulously. "I'm crazy about you, too, Max."

He shook his head a little as if he were trying to clear it. "You are?"

Her blue-violet eyes shone. "Um-hmm."

His expression turned wary. His hand moved away from her. "You're just nervous I'll walk out."

"I don't want you to walk out, Max," she told him honestly.

He pointed an accusing finger at her. "See. I knew it. This is all part of your con to keep me interested in the hunt."

Angel scowled. "Let's get something to eat, Max."

She stood up, but Max didn't budge. "Are you really crazy about me, Angel?"

She was aware that half the people in the bar had heard Max's ardent question as clearly as she had.

"Max . . . let's get out of here."

He broke into a slow smile, his eyes burning into her. "I think you really are crazy about me."

A middle-aged man sitting on the stool to Max's right poked him in the shoulder. "Of course she's crazy about you," he announced, giving Max an inebriated smile. Then he slapped him solidly on the back. "Happy hunting, buddy. Only wish I could switch places with you."

Max swiveled round abruptly in his seat and grabbed the startled drunk by the collar. "Watch your mouth, pal," he warned in a low, menacing voice.

"What did I say?" the drunken man whined. "I didn't say nothing."

Max tightened his grip. "Well, watch your thoughts."

"Max, stop it," Angel pleaded in a low voice as the bartender came hurrying over to restore peace.

With the same swiftness as it took hold of Max, the fury left. He released his grip so suddenly that the man slid off his stool and landed with a heavy thud on the floor.

Max stood up and blithely glanced down at him. "Like I said, you go looking for trouble and you land flat on your ass every time." He teetered slightly as he swung an arm around Angel and led her out of the bar. Actually, she was doing more of the leading, but Max was too out of it to notice, much less to balk.

Angel managed to maneuver him out to the dining terrace of the hotel. She hoped that the fresh sea air and some nonliquid nourishment would bring Max around. She was right. After a thick, steaming bowl of conch chowder followed by hot, spicy crab fritters, Max's head began to clear. It also began to throb, a condition that wasn't much helped by the goombay music being beaten out on maracas, drums, and guitars by an exuberant group of musicians decked out in colorful calypso garb.

"Couldn't you have found someplace quieter?" He pressed his hands against his temples.

Angel grinned. "I thought you wanted to go dancing."

"I had something a little less high-spirited in mind."

"There's a supper club on the roof terrace of the hotel. We could try that."

Max's brow furrowed. "Does it spin?"

She laughed. "Maybe we better have some coffee first."

Angel and Max were finishing their coffee when the calypso band ended a rousing number and then thankfully started its break. Max heaved a sigh of relief. Then he gave Angel a sheepish smile. "I did a pretty good job of making a fool of myself before, didn't I?"

"Don't go modest on me now, Max. You did a great job."

They both laughed.

"I haven't finished off that many bourbons in one sitting in a lot of years." He reached across the table and took hold of Angel's hand. "I used to drink like that to fight off the demons."

"What do you mean?" Angel asked softly.

He drew her hand to his lips and lightly nibbled her fingertips. Angel shivered at the tender seduction.

"I made a lot of lousy choices back in the old days. I guess it came from growing up in a crummy neighborhood in Detroit and dreaming too many big dreams. I was reckless. And stupid. I was determined to get what I wanted, to hell with how I got it. And to hell with the consequences. When things blew up in my face I blamed the explosion on the demons inside of me, always egging me on, clouding my vision. They made me greedy. They made me believe I was entitled to have it all . . . the football career, the beautiful wife, a ton of money. And then they snatched it out from under me. My football career ended, the wife sued for divorce claiming mental cruelty, and I lost every last cent to my name."

"For a few months after that, I tried to drown those demons in alcohol. I was angry, bitter. I felt I'd been handed a bum deal. And then one day it came to me that there were no demons. There was just me. I was the one screwing up my life. I made all the wrong choices. I was the one who blew it. No one but Max Gallagher. So I told myself I would chalk up those dumb, reckless years to experience and I'd make some changes. No more greedy dreams, no more big-shot plans. I decided to clean up my act."

A wry smile curved his lips. "I have managed, for the past four years, to live an uncomplicated, uncluttered life and, miraculously, I've also managed to stay out of trouble."

Angel gave him a saucy smile. "It sounds awfully dull."

"It's had its few high points. It hasn't all been dull."

"None of those high points lasted very long, though."

Max met her gaze evenly. "That's the way I wanted it."

"And now?"

He didn't answer right away. When he did speak his voice was very husky. "I'm not so sure I want it to end, Angel." He looked at her with eyes that revealed sharply etched desire and a clear hint of vulnerability. It was a double-whammy combination.

"You aren't still a little tight?" Angel asked warily.

"I've had soberer moments."

She tilted her chin. "Are you going to have regrets in the morning?"

His eyes flashed. "That depends on whether I wake up in your bed or mine."

Angel looked at him with arched brows. "We haven't gotten to the dancing yet, Max." She hesitated. "Anyway, since neither of us is in all that much of a rush to see this end, why don't we take it a little slower?"

"A little slower?"

"You're echoing me again, Max."

He grinned. "Okay. Let's go dancing."

It was a little before eleven P.M. when they stepped out on the hotel's rooftop terraced supper club. The stars were out and there was no goombay music up here to jar the nerves. A tuxedoed trio was playing soft, soothing mood music while a handful of couples danced on a small parqueted square of flooring. Tables spaced far enough apart to afford intimacy and privacy were strategically placed around the dance floor and along the railing of the terrace. Far below, a midnight-blue surf lapped rhythmically onto cooling tropical sands. Evening-gowned waitresses moved about discreetly among the couples taking drink orders, their steps guided by a shimmering moon and candlelight. It was as romantic a spot as they had on the magical isle.

A pretty blonde was leading Max and Angel to a table, but before she got them there, Max swept Angel into his arms and whirled her onto the dance floor. Angel laughed softly as he guided her into a tricky little two-step routine that would have done Fred Astaire proud. Then, with a flourish, he spun her away from him, then twirled her back into his arms.

"You take my breath away," she said, having to cling to him to follow his fancy maneuvers. "And I accused you of still being tight!"

He pulled her very close so that her long legs pressed into his. "I am still tight," he whispered hotly into her ear. "No inhibitions." He twirled her again, then caught her up, moving both arms around her waist. "There's no telling what I might do next, Angel. That's fair warning."

Before she could say anything, he dipped her low to the ground, holding her there. "You follow wonderfully." He grinned. "For a change."

"Let me up, Max."

"I won't let you land on your pretty behind, Angel." He swept her upright. "This time we're both

187

going to try to keep our feet on the ground." He twirled her in his arms as the dreamy music wafted around them. Then abruptly he came to a halt, looked down into her starlit eyes and cupped her face in his hands.

"Max, we're supposed—"

She didn't get to finish the sentence. Max cut it off with a soft, tender kiss that fast threatened to become torrid. Angel might have let it happen if the music hadn't ended and she hadn't felt dozens of eyes on them. As she gently but firmly pushed Max away, she was especially drawn to one particular pair of eyes studying her from a table that was very close to the dance floor.

The man smiled faintly as their eyes met. Angel narrowed her gaze. The lighting was very dim, but the face seemed familiar.

It came to her as Max whirled her around for a second dance. "Do you see who's here?" she whispered against his ear. "Michael Hargrove. Now what do you suppose he's doing in the Bahamas?"

Max nuzzled his face into her delicately scented silken hair. "I thought we were taking the night off."

"Why don't we go over and say hello?" Angel said, paying no attention. "He's alone. And he keeps looking over at us."

Max merely pulled her tighter. She stumbled over his toes as he tried another fancy step. "You're losing the rhythm, Angel."

"I'm losing patience, Max. Come on. He looks

like a man who wants to get something off his chest. We might learn something."

Max released her reluctantly. "I already am learning something. You've got a one-track mind, Angel. And it isn't the track I'm on."

She teased his lips with a light kiss. "You can handle a detour."

Angel was already heading in the direction of Michael Hargrove when Max mumbled, "That's what you think."

Michael Hargrove stood up and pulled out the chair next to him. Angel slid gracefully into it. Max was left to fend for himself. He had to walk around to several tables before he came back with an extra chair.

When he sat down beside Angel, she was busy giving Michael Hargrove an assessing study. Hargrove looked a little pale and strained even against the soft, forgiving candlelight. He toyed absently with a damp cocktail napkin that was weighted down by an untouched drink.

A striking-looking brunette glided over with an order pad. Michael Hargrove gave the waitress a quick glance. "Can I get something for you to drink?" Hargrove asked, directing his question solely at Angel.

Max thought he'd make himself known. "I'll have a bourbon, straight up."

Angel's eyes narrowed on him. Max got the message.

He gave the waitress a put-upon smile. "On second thought, make that a ginger ale. On ice. Easy on the ice." Michael Hargrove was giving him a distracted look. Max grinned. "I hate to bruise the soda."

Hargrove blinked several times in a row. The strain was getting worse. Except for the eye fluttering and the tension rippling all the muscles of his face, Angel considered Hargrove an attractive man. She hadn't really had the chance to study him at the funeral. Now she saw that he was much thinner than he appeared to be in that magazine clipping from Lou's file. No doubt the prison fare hadn't been up to par with his culinary tastes. He had a square-cut, smooth face, neatly trimmed brown hair, and very intense eyes, the color of which was hard to guess in the dim light. He was wearing a well-cut dinner jacket, only it looked as if it had been cut to his pre-prison frame.

Hargrove leaned closer to Angel. He might not have touched the drink in front of him, but Angel could smell alcohol on his breath. He didn't seem drunk in any way, though Angel could see his hands trembling.

"Someone is following me." His words were muffled, his gaze stark. He gripped Angel's hand. "I need help. I don't know who else to turn to."

"What kind of help?" Angel asked cautiously.

"Someone tried to run me off the road this afternoon."

"Join the club," Max said wryly. "Did he take a pot shot at you as well?"

Hargrove looked puzzled. "No. What do you mean, join the club?"

Max had finally gotten Hargrove's full attention. "Never mind. Why would someone want to run you off the road?"

Michael Hargrove scowled. "She tried to set me up once and failed. And now she's trying to do it again. Only, this time I won't let her. I'm not taking the rap for Chapman's death. I didn't kill him. If anyone wanted him out of the picture, it was Vera."

Angel stared into Hargrove's face. "I thought Vera and Lou were—"

Hargrove cut her off. "She's a witch. An evil witch. Lou Chapman finally started smartening up. He was beginning to get the real picture of what she was up to. He kept up the pretense, but he was playing her along. Only he underestimated my sweet, insidious wife. She realized that he was on to her game." Hargrove stopped talking abruptly when the waitress returned with one ginger ale, very little ice. He ran his hands up and down his untouched drink as he waited for her to leave before continuing.

"I've been keeping my eye on her. I figured that was my safest bet. If I knew her every step, I'd be okay. Only it made her very nervous. She's scared. So now she wants me out of the way." Hargrove's eyes flicked wide open. "Another . . . accident."

"Are you saying that Vera is responsible for . . ."

Angel didn't have to finish the sentence. Hargrove finished it for her. "She killed him. And I have proof."

"What kind of proof?" Max broke in.

Michael Hargrove shook his head. "Not here. We better not talk here. It's dangerous. She's got someone following me now. I have to be very careful." He glanced furtively around the terrace. "Listen, I've rented a cottage on the outskirts of the island." He scribbled directions on Max's napkin. "I'll leave first. I know Bimini like the back of my hand. If someone follows my car, I'll be able to lose them. Give me around forty-five minutes, then ride out to my place. I have some things to show you that will prove very interesting."

He went to stand up, but hesitated. "Please be careful. Vera is a woman who will stop at nothing to get what she wants. I managed to outsmart her once. She thought she had me for embezzlement, but I finally came up with proof that exonerated me. The only pity is, I couldn't prove she was the one who set me up." His eyes darkened. "But now, I can prove she murdered Lou Chapman." He gave a short, dry laugh. "So, I guess that makes things more than even."

He stood then and turned to go.

"Just one question," Max stopped him. "Why us? If you have some kind of evidence, why not go straight to the police?"

Hargrove scowled. "It isn't exactly concrete evidence. It will take a smart detective to fit together some of the missing links."

Max shot Angel a glance. "Who says we're detectives?"

Hargrove shrugged. "You aren't sightseers." He focused his gaze on Angel. "I know you want to see the person who murdered your ex-husband brought to justice, Ms. Welles. I believe in justice, too," he said enigmatically.

"What about Rick Seidman? Why not hire him?" Angel asked. "He's the one who helped clear you of the embezzlement charges, isn't he?"

Hargrove compressed his lips. "Yes. Yes, he did help me. But to be perfectly honest, that help he gave me cost me a fortune. I can't afford Seidman and let's face it, the man doesn't work for the joy of it." He glanced over his shoulder. "I have to go. You will come?"

He didn't wait for an answer. Angel watched him rush off, then turned to Max with a wry smile. "I guess he thinks I come cheap."

Max grinned as he stroked Angel's cheek with the back of his hand. "Then the man's a fool. You are priceless, Angel."

CHAPTER ELEVEN

The Buccaneer Creek Hotel clerk was very accommodating. All Angel had to do was flash the middle-aged plump man a come-hither smile and he went off to his cubicle of an office and got on the phone to arrange for an unorthodox late-night car rental. Then all Max had to do was slip the guy fifty bucks so that his memory would fail him should anyone ask if Mr. Gallagher or Ms. Welles had left the hotel to go for a midnight drive.

"Why did you do that?" Angel asked as Max took her elbow and led her through the lobby.

"I'm not taking any chances. If vivacious Vera is having old Mike followed, that means she could have someone trailing us as well."

Angel's brow furrowed. "So how do we get out of the hotel without being seen?"

Max slid a muscled arm around her shoulder. "A piece of cake, sweetheart," he mumbled through clenched teeth.

Angel threw him a desultory look. "Max, this isn't some Bogart movie. Do you have a plan?"

"Do I have a plan?"

"Stop with the echo, Max. I'm serious." She hesitated. "Hargrove got me a little spooked. If Vera is trying to have him killed . . ."

Max shed the teasing grin, his expression all at once deadly serious. "Do you want to call the whole thing off, Angel?"

She didn't answer.

"We could go to the local police, tell them what Hargrove told us . . ." Max began.

"Then what? Hargrove said the proof he had isn't substantial. Anyway, I have a feeling, if the police showed up at Hargrove's place, old Mike would make like he never even heard of us. The man is terrified, Max. And he's not likely to believe the police are going to be able to do anything about his problem. To be honest, I don't blame him." She smiled balefully. "No, we've got to go out there and see what he has to show us."

Now it was Max's turn to be silent.

"Do you want out, Max?" she asked softly.

He drew her closer. "What do you think?"

She smiled. It was a most tantalizing smile that covered her whole face. Those lapis lazuli eyes positively shimmered. Max felt a very untimely rush of hot desire. He had never known another woman who could arouse him to distraction with a mere curve of the lips. Angel had a smile like no other he had ever seen. But then Angel Welles was unlike any woman he had ever known.

"We better go upstairs and change," he said abruptly, clearing his mind of lust-filled thoughts. "I'll call down to the desk and have the bellboy drive the rental car down the road and pull it into a driveway of one of the cottages and then bring the keys up here. We'll go downstairs, dressed like we're going to take a midnight swim."

"Then what?"

"We'll try to find a dark spot of beach and make a run to the car."

"That's your plan? We make a run for it?"

"You've got a better one, Angelface?"

She scowled, then broke out into a faint smile. "Okay. Sounds as good as any."

Max grinned. "I knew we could see eye to eye."

Ten minutes later, Angel and Max were padding through the hotel lobby in their thongs. The effect that the alcohol had had on Max had worn off. Angel was wearing a flowered beach dress over her bikini. Her jeans, T-shirt, and sneakers were hidden in the middle of her rolled-up beach towel. Max was wearing a terry beach robe over his bathing trunks; his traveling clothes were secured inside his beach towel as well.

They weren't the only ones out on the Buccaneer's private beach, but the stretch of sand was large enough to give the dozen or so couples out for midnight swims plenty of privacy.

"What do you think?" Angel asked as they walked along the shoreline to a deserted spot.

"Hard to tell if anyone is following us. We better take a dip, just in case."

It was the last thing Angel felt like doing, but she agreed with Max that they couldn't afford to take any chances. She set her towel down and kicked off her thongs. As she started to lift the beach dress off, Max was there to help.

His hands skimmed her body as he removed the dress, then his eyes trailed down the skimpy black bikini. His approving look sent shivers up Angel's spine that radiated to every limb. "This is business, Max." Her voice was husky.

Max took off his robe. Angel's eyes involuntarily swept his tanned, tautly strong and perfectly proportioned form. Her lips parted slightly.

"There's a couple down the beach skinny dipping." His hand reached round to the tie of her bikini top. "When in the Bahamas . . ."

Angel ducked away. "Max, be serious. We can't fool around now." Her voice was even huskier. She needed to cool off. Bolting, she raced into the darkness of the sea.

Her breath caught as she plunged into the water. It caught again as Max, who'd reached her with a few powerful breast strokes, swept her into his arms and kissed her wet lips.

"Max . . . no," she protested as he lifted her high enough for his mouth to center around a bikini clad nipple. His warm breath and the sensuous movement of his lips made the nipple harden instantly.

"Max . . . yes," he murmured insistently, his teeth catching the top of the bra. With a quick tug, the bra slipped down over her glistening wet breasts.

"This is crazy," she gasped. "We'll be seen."

"Only in shadow." He captured a nipple, his mouth irresistibly persuasive. Then he drew her against him, his mouth seeking her lips. He kissed her lightly. "We do want to be convincingly innocent."

Angel threw back her head in a delightful peal of laughter. "Innocent?"

"You're echoing me, Angel." He kissed her again, harder, deeper.

A sigh of pleasure escaped her. But she refused to let herself get completely out of control. Wriggling from his arms, she swam in strong, graceful strokes toward the shore.

Max swam for a couple more minutes, just to cool down. Then he joined her on the sand.

"That was some plan you worked up," Angel bantered.

Max grinned, but his eyes were darkly serious as he scanned the beach. "What do you think? Did it work?"

Angel tilted her head. "It worked almost too well." A smile touched her lips. "We do have to watch ourselves, Max. We seem to both have a tendency to get carried away even in the midst of danger."

"They say that danger heightens sexual arousal."

Angel did her best to pat herself dry without unfolding the towel completely to reveal the change of clothes. "Who says that?"

Max still had one eye on the beach. The other was on Angel's delicious body. "Sigmund Freud, I think." He gave a brief laugh. "Or maybe it was James Bond."

"Whoever said it," Angel mused, "I do think

there's something to it." She gave Max an assessing glance. "Does that mean when the danger is over, we're likely to . . . cool down?"

Max focused his attention fully on Angel, amusement flashing in his eyes. "I find it hard to believe the danger will ever be over for us. I predict a future fraught with untold perils, Angel." Despite the glint of amusement, Max's voice had taken on a very serious note. "The question is, will we survive them?"

It was another one of those questions that Angel could interpret in several different ways, none of which was particularly comforting to contemplate.

"Shouldn't we get going?" she asked. "It will take us at least ten, fifteen minutes to get to Hargrove's cottage. And we're already late getting started."

"I'm sure Hargrove will wait for us." He stood up and took hold of Angel's hand, drawing her up beside him. "But you're right. This seems as good a time as any. I still can't be sure whether or not we're being watched." He motioned with an almost imperceptible nod of his head toward a darkened beach cabana about fifty yards away. "We'll stroll in that direction. Keep the pace easy. It's nice and dark there. Once we reach it we'll duck around back, change quickly and make for the road. The car's parked close by."

Angel nodded, but her throat had gone dry and a wave of fear mingled with the rush of adrenaline that shot through her.

It wasn't easy keeping a leisurely pace. Angel kept imagining dark shadows creeping up behind her, but she knew better than to turn her head and check it out. Max's strong arm around her waist gave her comfort, however, and she found herself musing for the hundredth time how glad she was that she had him to depend on. The way things were developing between them, she was beginning to believe she'd be able to depend on him for a long time to come. What surprised her was that the notion was extremely appealing. And frightening at the same time.

They changed hurriedly behind the wood and straw cabana, listening all the while for the sound of approaching steps. But this stretch of beach was relievedly silent.

Max took Angel's hand and risked a brief, passionate kiss before they set off. Their car, a nondescript blue Ford Escort, was parked in the driveway of a darkened beach bungalow. They scrambled in quickly, Max behind the driver's seat. He released the emergency brake and let the car roll backward until they hit the street. Angel scanned the road.

"Looks good," she said, tossing her wet bathing suit and beach dress onto the backseat and vigorously towel-drying her black locks.

Max started the engine up and headed down the thankfully desolate street. Angel reached over and gave his wet hair a brisk rubdown with the towel. "I guess we were overly cautious for nothing," she said, admiring the tousled look of Max's hair. "You are an incredibly good-looking man, Mr. Gallagher."

He shot her a sidelong glance. "Sorry we didn't fool around more in the ocean?"

Angel laughed softly. "We're not out of the woods yet. Someone may be lurking around Hargrove's place. And you know what they say about sex before battle. It drains you of the combative edge."

"Who says that?"

"It was either Napoleon or Muhammad Ali."

Max grinned. "I have my own theory," he teased as one of his hands left the steering wheel to circle the top of Angel's jean-clad thigh.

"This isn't the time for theorizing," she said. There was a little catch in her throat. She fumbled with the napkin on which Michael Hargrove had drawn directions to his cottage. "Turn left when you get to Dolphin Street. According to these scribblings we stay on Dolphin until we pass the Emerald Beach Hotel."

Max picked up a little speed once he turned onto Dolphin, seeing that there wasn't another car in sight. "What do you think Hargrove meant about Lou being onto Vera Hargrove's game?"

A puzzled frown formed on Angel's face. "I wonder if it has something to do with her company, Weston Electronics. Somebody was playing with the books there. If it wasn't Michael, maybe he's right. Maybe Vera set him up and was smart enough, even when he won his appeal, to make sure the finger couldn't be pointed at her. Come to think of it, there were several notes in Lou's file on the Hargrove case having to do with the possibility that some of the money coming through Weston Electronics was syndicate funds which were being laundered. And it was clear from some other notes of Lou's that he was looking for some evidence that would firmly link Michael Hargrove to the mob, but he couldn't come up with anything concrete." She turned fully in her seat toward Max. "Maybe Lou didn't give up the search even after Michael Hargrove was convicted and sent to prison. What if he kept on looking and finally found something? Only what he found didn't link old Mike to the syndicate. It linked his last client, Vera Hargrove."

"Why would Lou bother to track down that kind of info after Michael went up the river?"

"You'd have had to know Lou to understand. To him a case wasn't over until he was satisfied he'd done the best job he could. And that meant never leaving any loose ends. He was a man with an uncompromisingly curious mind. And he followed his own strict code. One thing I can say about Lou. He was always true to his code."

Max felt a sharp pang of jealousy. "Too bad he wasn't always true to you." It was a crummy remark and Angel didn't deserve it. He felt like a heel, but a jealous heel nonetheless. There'd been a tender tone in her voice when she was talking about Lou, a tone he wanted reserved strictly for him. Man, he was really in a bad way if he was actually feeling jealous of a dead guy. "I'm sorry, Angel. That was an uncalled-for remark."

She studied him for a moment. "You're right. But a true one, anyway."

"The man was a bastard for hurting you. And a fool not to be satisfied with the very best."

There was a faraway look in Angel's eyes. "The man was a man, like many others."

Max looked across at her. "A pretty strong generalization. I didn't cheat on my wife."

A rueful smile formed on Angel's lips. "You just didn't act on your fantasies. Maybe if you'd stayed married longer, you might have."

"Is that why you're so down on marriage?"

"I'm down on giving some man the right to make demands on me. Any demands. The fact that Lou cheated on me was only part of it. He had all these expectations. And I was supposed to live up to them. Somewhere along the line I lost sight of who I really was. That's when I knew I had to get out, before I was swallowed up completely."

"How did Lou react when you told him you wanted out?"

"He didn't believe me at first. I'll admit I wasn't initially all that convincing. I was in love with him. And he knew it. What he didn't know was that my feelings weren't strong enough to keep us glued together."

"Are you still in love with him, Angel?"

She didn't answer right away. "I still love him. But I'm not still in love with him."

"Is there a difference?" There was a bite to Max's tone. He didn't think there was one.

"A big difference," she said tenderly, her eyes resting on his grim profile. "I love Lou. But I happen to be in love with you, Max."

A high-current voltage seemed to suffuse the inside of the car.

"You missed the turnoff, Max. We just passed the Emerald Beach Hotel."

He pulled the car over to the side of the road. Angel was expecting him to throw the gear shift into reverse and back up, but instead he came to a complete stop. His hands stayed on the steering wheel, his eyes stayed straight ahead on the empty road.

"I did make a lousy husband, Angel. And you're right. Somewhere down the line, if Laura hadn't gotten that divorce when she did, I would have strayed."

"Too many temptations?"

Max shook his head. "Too little love. The difference between your marriage and mine, Angel, is that there was never any real love between me and Laura. Oh, there was passion. For a while, anyway. But we never communicated. We were little more than cardboard images to each other. I was the hotshot football star. She was the blond bombshell that any guy on the team would have given his right arm to have. We made a great-looking picture, but that's all it was. There was nothing beneath the surface."

He gave Angel a fleeting glance, then continued staring straight ahead of him. "It's different with you and me."

"It is?" She asked the question in a very nervous voice.

He squinted into the darkness. "I'm in love with you, Angel. I think it's the real thing."

"And that scares you." Her voice was even more

breathless than usual. Her heart was skipping a few beats.

"It doesn't scare you?"

"It absolutely terrifies me."

Max's mouth curved into a slow grin, then he threw the car into reverse. "Let's get this visit to Hargrove over with, so we can go back to the hotel and still each other's fears."

Five minutes later, they were both feeling a little light-headed when Max turned the car onto a dark, dirt path whose only marker was an off-kilter gray mailbox labeled Oxman. According to Michael Hargrove's hastily drawn map there was only one other cottage past the one belonging to Oxman. That was where Hargrove would be holing up waiting for their arrival.

Angel checked her watch against the glow of the dashboard. It was nearly twelve thirty. They were about a half hour late, but they saw a light on in the far cottage and a small dark sports car pulled up in the drive beside it.

The cottage, like Hargrove himself, had seen better days. It was really little more than a bungalow, the kind a native laborer might aspire to, but definitely not the sort of place a man like Hargrove, who used to play host at a lofty seaside villa on Rum Cay, would have ever been caught dead in . . . in the good old days.

As Angel scanned the one-story shack with its noticeably askew front porch, she said, "I guess Rick Seidman really did take old Mike to the cleaners if this is all he can afford these days."

"Well, it is off the beaten path," Max observed, pulling the Ford up behind what his headbeams now could identify as a racing green Triumph. "He still has pretty nice wheels."

"Are we sure they're his?"

Max gave Angel a shrewed glance. "That's one of the things I love about you, Angel Face. You've got good instincts."

Angel grinned. "You ought to trust them more, Gallagher."

He winked. "Stay put while I see if there's any registration or some other form of identity in the car."

"Isn't it a little late for that? Whoever that car belongs to will have heard us pull up."

Max reached around his seat and grabbed for his towel. He unrolled it to reveal the small gun that he never let get too far from reach.

Angel gripped his hand. "Do you know how to use that thing?" She shut her eyes. "Oh, God, what am I asking? You don't really think you're going to need a gun, do you?"

"Just to make a point, if one needs making." He gently disengaged his hand from Angel's grasp and pocketed the gun. "Believe me, I hope as much as you do that I have no call to use it." He hesitated, his eyes darkening. "But I can and will . . . if it comes to that."

"Max."

He drew her into his arms. His caress was strong and soothing. At least momentarily.

"Be careful, Max," she whispered.

"Get behind the wheel, Angel. If things don't look kosher, we'll make a quick exit."

She nodded solemnly, all light-headedness vanishing.

Max moved stealthily over to the Triumph. Angel saw a brief light go on as he opened the glove compartment. A few moments later, he was waving her to come out of the car.

Angel breathed a sigh of relief although she wondered why the house seemed so still. Hargrove had been so antsy back at the supper club, she would have expected him to come racing out the front door of the bungalow once he was sure it was them.

Hargrove not only didn't come racing out to greet them, he didn't answer Max's knock on the door. Max knocked again. He glanced down at Angel. "Maybe he fell asleep." A brief smile touched his face, but it didn't ease the tension.

Angel's hand moved to the doorknob. Max slipped the gun out of his pocket and nodded. She felt blood drum through her head and she had to fight off a sudden wave of dizziness as she turned the knob.

The door gave way with a creak. Max grabbed her harshly and pulled her away from the opening.

"Get back to the car and wait for me." He hissed the order into her ear.

Angel shook her head. "I'm staying with you."

Max scowled, but knew he stood little chance of getting Angel to cooperate. "Okay, but stay behind me. And run like hell for the car if there are any surprises."

The sound of Max cocking the gun sent a cold shiver up Angel's spine. She found herself clutching the back of his shirt. Max glanced over his shoulder. "You okay?" he whispered.

A quick, tense smile played across her face. It didn't reassure Max, but he smiled back. His smile didn't reassure Angel, but she let go of his shirt.

Max swung the door open a little wider and cautiously peered inside. The house was as silent as a tomb. And as disorderly as if an earthquake had struck smack dab in the center of it. Since no earthquake had hit Bimini that Max knew of, that left two possibilities. Either Michael Hargrove was one hell of a slovenly housekeeper or there'd been one hell of a brawl here. He pushed the door further until it opened fully and flattened against the wall. If anyone was hiding behind it he or she would have had to be thinner than a pancake.

"Wait here," Max ordered.

His words fell on deaf ears. Angel was right behind him when he walked inside. She let out a long, low breath as she took in the overturned furniture, the broken mirror, the lit lamp hanging precariously on its side on a small desk in which every drawer had been pulled out, its contents scattered over the floor like confetti that someone had forgotten to shred.

One wall of the studio bungalow made up the kitchen. It, too, had been gone over with a fine-tooth comb, the shelves swept bare of the meager assortment of canned goods and even the few stale items in the refrigerator ransacked and left to marauding insects on the mottled gray Formica counter.

Angel was closest to the bathroom door. She heard a rustling noise and froze, stark eyes darting to Max. He motioned for her to remain where she was. As if she could have moved if he'd wanted her to. She felt rooted to the spot.

Max moved with amazingly little sound to the bathroom door. His hand gripping the gun was steady enough, his face a fierce study in concentration. Once he was at the door, he waited there for a few moments, motionless. A soft thud could be heard behind the door.

Max turned the knob very slowly and inched the door open a crack into the darkness. The light from the main room fanned into the bathroom in a tight arc. There was no sound now. Max stepped off to the side. Then with the tip of his shoe he pushed the door open a little more.

Suddenly something darted out from the darkness of the bathroom. Max leaped back. Angel screamed. Then with mutual sighs they saw that the shadowy figure was merely a cat, a mottled alley cat who seemed supremely irritated by the intrusion.

"Max, look." Angel pointed to a trail of bloody red paw prints left by the streaking cat.

Max was busy eyeing the open bathroom door, making sure nothing larger came darting out of the darkness. He pulled his eyes away to see what Angel was pointing at.

His expression was puzzled. "The cat doesn't seem hurt," he observed as he shifted his gaze to

209

watch the creature leap nimbly up to the kitchen counter and blithely begin nibbling some cat food from an open tin.

Their eyes both turned back to the dark bathroom, their thoughts following the exact same disturbing line.

Angel made a vague sound in her throat as Max's hand reached the light switch along the bathroom wall and flicked it on. Her hand went up to her mouth in horror as she stared in revulsion at the small pool of blood on the gray linoleum floor in front of the shower.

Max stepped into the tight, airless room. The medicine chest had been torn from the wall and landed in the sink. The mirror must have cracked on the porcelain basin and there were shards of glass all over the floor. The shower curtain, a putrid green plastic affair, was drawn closed. Max wasn't all that eager to open it. He had a pretty good idea what he was going to find there. Or more to the point, who.

He glanced back at Angel. She was standing in the doorway. She looked frail and vulnerable, but she was holding her own.

Max met her frightened gaze. "Go outside, Angel."

She bit down on her lower lip, shaking her head.

"Angel."

"Go on, dammit. Open the curtain. The suspense is killing me." She made an effort to give the remark a wry twist, but her deep vibrato voice came off scared and very shaky.

Max still had the gun cocked, but he doubted anyone would be darting out of the shower. He pulled back the curtain.

He was right on one account. No one came leaping out.

But he was wrong, too. No one was slumped there dead, either. The shower was empty.

Angel stared, open-mouthed. She was more than a little relieved not to come face to face with a murdered Michael Hargrove, but she was also puzzled.

She gave Max a rueful smile. "Okay, Gallagher. You're the one with the plan. Now what?"

CHAPTER TWELVE

The Bimini police inspector was a large man with dark brown hair, all of his features on the heavy side. Angel guessed him to be in his mid-fifties. He walked at a slow, leisurely pace across the room, his thick lidded eyes cast down at his small note pad. He was surprisingly light-footed considering his enormous girth.

As he read over the information Angel and Max had given him, the inspector toyed absently with the frayed collar of his short-sleeved white shirt. A bead of sweat ran down his neck. He swiped at it randomly, but it kept running. It was a hot night, stifling in the tiny bungalow.

The inspector did not look happy as he reviewed his notes. Evidence of mayhem in the bungalow without a conveniently located victim seemed to particularly irk the policeman. Not that Angel blamed him. It did make his job more difficult. However, her sympathies lay far more with poor Michael Hargrove. Though she tried to avoid thinking the worst, her guess was that he'd been attacked and very likely murdered here in his bungalow and then dragged off somewhere so that his body would not be discovered. However confident he'd been back at the supper club, Hargrove had apparently been unable to ditch the man who was following him after all.

"You say that you met Mr. Hargrove at the bar of the Buccaneer Creek Hotel and he invited the two of you back here for drinks?" The question was asked politely, but there was an edge of irritation in the inspector's voice.

"Actually," Angel interjected, "it was the rooftop supper club of the hotel."

The inspector looked up wearily and gave her a raking glance. This was coupled by an abrupt halt in his leisurely stroll across the room, a stroll that frequently required him to skirt the toppled furniture, the general debris and his assistant, a lean, wiry young man with shiny black hair, who was crawling about the floor apparently checking for clues and leaving a trail of ash from a cigarette which seemed to be affixed permanently to the left-hand corner of his mouth.

"The question on my mind, Ms. Welles, is why Mr. Hargrove would ask you here," he made a sweeping gesture with his hand, "for drinks when you were already at a bar? Why not simply have your drinks there?"

Angel shot Max a surreptitious glance. They had decided, after calling the police, that they would say as little as possible about Hargrove's real reason for asking them to the bungalow. For one thing, the police inspector was unlikely to be able to do very

213

much with the information Hargrove had related to them, the details of which were vague at best. And they had no proof that there was any foundation at all to Hargrove's accusations against his wife. Angel and Max had checked the bungalow thoroughly before the police arrived for those interesting items Hargrove had mentioned having at the supper club. Not surprisingly, those items had disappeared along with Hargrove.

The other reason Max and Angel decided to play things close to the chest was that they didn't want to risk being detained by the police and even possibly being suspected of wrongdoing.

"To be honest," Max said airily, "Mr. Hargrove only invited Ms. Welles back here. I don't think drinks were all he had in mind. I appeared on the scene a few minutes after he'd made the invitation." He gave Angel a rueful glance and then smiled shrewdly at the inspector. "I wasn't about to bid my date good night and let her go off on her own for a nightcap. I simply invited myself along."

The inspector looked at Angel. "You say you had met Mr. Hargrove in the past."

Angel avoided Max's gaze. "Just briefly. Actually, I'm an acquaintance of his wife's. As I told you before, Mr. Gallagher and I are going to visit Vera Hargrove tomorrow at her villa on Rum Cay. I did wonder if Mr. Hargrove's invitation had something to do with discussing his estrangement from his wife. I had the impression he felt she was behaving . . . vindictively." She hesitated. "I'd even go so far as to say Mr. Hargrove seemed afraid of her."

Max gave Angel a narrow gaze, but she merely looked away. It couldn't hurt to steer the police in the right direction.

"Anyway," Angel went on, "I felt sorry for Mr. Hargrove. He seemed at such loose ends. And he was very tense. I only accepted the invitation because I thought I might be able to cheer him up a little." She gave the inspector an innocent little shrug.

The young police assistant who was squatting on the floor sifting through an array of papers that had been thrown from the desk, looked up and gave Angel an empathetic, white-toothed smile.

The police inspector's face remained bland. "Why didn't you all drive out together? You say you left the bar . . . the supper club . . . nearly an hour after Mr. Hargrove departed."

Angel compressed her lips. "Yes . . . well . . ." She looked to Max for rescue.

"Don't be shy, Angelface. You promised we'd take a moonlight swim and you're a woman who's true to her promise." Max gave the inspector a very cocky smile this time. "I like that in a woman, don't you, Inspector?" Max wasn't surprised when he got no response. He merely shrugged. "I told Hargrove we'd come out for a drink later in the evening."

"Why go at all?" The inspector, whose features afforded no inflection up to now, raised one brow.

"That's a good question," Max said. Now he had to come up with a good answer.

This time Angel came to his rescue. "Don't be shy, Max. Tell the inspector." She, too, arched a brow. "No, I'll tell you, Inspector. Mr. Gallagher wanted to teach me a lesson. He was angry that I'd agreed to have that nightcap with Mr. Hargrove and he wanted to humiliate me by insisting I go and, of course, insisting that he come along. I must admit I was not looking forward to the get-together. You know what they say, Inspector. Two's company, three's a crowd."

The police inspector actually smiled. It was a taut smile, however. "How fortunate, then, that the get-together never happened."

Angel flinched. "Well, I wouldn't say that, considering . . ." She let the sentence trail off, her eyes drifting toward the half-opened bathroom door.

The inspector's eyes followed. He nodded slowly.

"What will you do now, Inspector?" she asked in a low voice.

"We will issue an all-points bulletin for Mr. Hargrove and begin our search for his assailants. There are bound to be some clues right here."

Max moved closer to Angel and put his arm around her. He could feel her trembling. "Can we go now, Inspector? There's really nothing more we can tell you."

The policeman nodded slowly. "If I have further questions, I can reach you in Rum Cay. No doubt I'll see you there regardless, as we will have questions for Mrs. Vera Hargrove."

Max rubbed his jaw. "I don't think we'll be visiting Mrs. Hargrove now."

"Oh?" The inspector queried.

Angel gave Max a puzzled look. Of course they would go out to Vera's.

"Under the circumstances, I think it would be awkward," Max continued, ignoring Angel's questioning glance. "I don't know what Mrs. Hargrove's feelings are for her husband, Inspector. As Ms. Welles said, we are only acquaintances. But I can't imagine she'd want to entertain guests right now considering Mr. Hargrove's . . . disappearance." Max felt Angel tense. "No, we'll skip the visit and head back home."

"I would prefer you remain on Bimini for the next twenty-four hours. Unless you change your mind and do go to Rum Cay where I will have no difficulty reaching you. After that, I hope I will find no further need to detain you, and you will be perfectly free to return to . . ." He flicked through his notes until he got to the first page, "to Boston, Massachusetts."

"Okay, we'll take in some sun at the Buccaneer Creek's beach for another day," Max said casually. "Believe me, Inspector, we'll be happy to help in any way we can. I hope you'll let us know if you do find him."

"I assure you, Mr. Gallagher, we'll most definitely be in touch with you if we find Mr. Hargrove." He paused. "Naturally, you'll let us know if you learn anything yourselves."

Max smiled pleasantly. "Naturally, Inspector."

Twenty minutes later Max swung the rental car into the darkened lot of the Buccaneer Creek Hotel.

"Max," Angel continued the argument that had

217

begun as soon as they'd pulled out from Hargrove's bungalow, "we've got to go to Rum Cay. We're hot on the trail. What if Michael's still alive? What if Vera's got him hidden out there in the villa?"

"Angel, I hate to burst some more of your bubbles, but it's very unlikely that Michael's still alive, at the villa or anywhere else."

"Well, that makes it even more imperative that we go out there. If she killed him, Max, chances are she killed Lou."

Max pulled up the emergency brake. He turned to Angel and gripped her shoulders. "And chances are she could kill us, too."

"That would be too risky. The police are bound to start breathing down her neck now. She couldn't chance axing us, too."

Max shook his head wearily. "Just listen to you, Angel. Axing us? You were the one yelling at me for imitating Bogart. Now you're sounding like some grade-B movie gumshoe. This isn't make-believe, Angel. That was real blood back there. Whatever became of Michael Hargrove, I guarantee you it wasn't very pretty."

"Neither was what happened to Lou," Angel retorted. "If Vera's guilty, Max . . ."

"If Vera's guilty, it's up to the police to handle it. You've certainly led them straight to Vera as the prime suspect."

"But there's no evidence, Max. Without evidence, the police have their hands tied. She's a very clever woman."

"Too clever for us," Max stated firmly.

"Don't turn modest on me now."

"Angel, I'm serious. Neither of us knows what the hell we're doing. We're playing at being detectives. And all we've done so far is . . ."

"Narrowed down the field and found the woman who murdered Lou."

Max shook his head wearily. "You know what a court of law would say about your accusation? Where's your evidence?" He raised his hands up toward the car roof in frustration. "Where's the crime, for godsakes? Lou's death certificate lists his demise as accidental drowning. And we don't have one concrete piece of evidence to contradict that pronouncement. It's all conjecture."

"That pool of blood in Hargrove's bathroom was real enough," Angel protested. "Okay, I grant you that we can't pin Lou's death on Vera . . . yet. So we concentrate on tying her in to her husband's murder."

He looked at her with a mixture of tenderness and frustration. "We have no proof that Michael Hargrove is dead."

"Come on, Max . . ."

"Angel, the police deal in facts, not theories. I know that much from watching cop shows on TV."

"Then we'll get them the facts. They're there, Max. Listen, we'll go out to Vera's place tomorrow as planned and—"

"And what? Get our heads blown off?" His hands slid her hair back from her face. "I happen to have taken a mighty strong liking to that head of yours, Angelface. And I've been fond of mine for years."

"Max, be serious."

"I'm deadly serious." One thick sandy blond brow shot up. "Accent on the deadly. This is way over our heads, Angel."

"So what do we do, Max? Just give up?"

"That's right. We give up."

She stared at him, proud chin tilted up, her eyes glinting with challenge. "I don't give up that easily, Max. I didn't think you did either. I thought you . . ."

"Oh no, Angel. You're not going to pull some guilt trip on me. I've stuck my neck out plenty. And if you stop playing detective, I'm willing to stick it out even more." To prove his point, he leaned closer and kissed her lightly.

Angel's eyes narrowed. "Is that a threat? Are you telling me that if I don't quit . . . we're through?"

His lips moved back to hers. This time the kiss was more emphatic, his tongue teasing the contours of her mouth. He could feel Angel struggle to resist responding. She wasn't a woman who easily suffered being threatened. But he meant it as a threat. He was all for a certain amount of independence in a woman, but he'd made it clear to Angel every step of the way that he intended to do the leading, whatever tune they might be dancing to. If Angel couldn't go along with that, then it was better to resolve it here and now.

He lifted his lips a bare inch. "Don't fight me, Angel." He pulled her to him again with unswerving determination. Skillfully, unrelentingly he began kissing her, savoring the taste and texture of her, slowly but surely stripping away her resistance until her response grew restive and hungry. When his lips slid away to move in a moist, warm trail down the delicate curve of her throat, a whisper of a moan escaped her. Her hands moved around his neck.

"Oh, Max," she murmured, melting into his hold and pressing parted lips to his ear. His seductive assault drained her of the capacity to fight.

When he was certain the argument was over, he reached across her and opened the car door. "Come on. Let's finish this part of the discussion in our hotel suite."

Angel hesitated. Max brushed a kiss over her lips. "No more arguments, Angel. We both agreed we didn't want this . . . thing we've got going for us . . . to end too fast. I'm just trying to see to it that someone else doesn't end it for us." He pushed the door open wider and gave her a provocative smile. "Unless you feel like necking here in the car some more?"

She smiled. There was still an edge of stubbornness there. But then, Angel wouldn't be Angel if there hadn't been. He loved her for it, even though he definitely planned to temper it. And there was no time like now.

He took her in his arms the instant they entered the suite. Angel wasn't sure if the arguing was over or just on hold. She wasn't sure of anything except that she had a yearning for Max Gallagher that seemed to have no limits. Here he was doing just what she'd fought against for years, giving orders and demanding she jump to his tune. What had happened to all those wise lectures she'd given herself about treading carefully in this relationship, not letting it get out of hand? But it was as if she had a switch somewhere deep inside her that no man had found before. Max was able to switch it on at will and instantly her senses were focused solely on the heat that raged deep down inside her. All it needed was Max to set the spark and the fire surged through her, out of control.

He was undressing her as he caressed her, his hands stroking her hips and pulling off her T-shirt at the same time. Then she took off her jeans and there was only a pair of black silk bikini panties to deal with.

Max dropped to his knees, his mouth moist and eager against her stomach as he lowered the panties just below her buttocks, cupping the firm, silky flesh with his hands.

Angel let out a low, primitive moan as his mouth moved lower, his tongue stroking her, probing, thrilling her beyond her wildest dreams. Her fingers dug into his shoulders as she swayed, but his grip was firm. She was quaking against him, gasping as his mouth continued its relentless, hungry assault.

Max was in complete charge and Angel opened herself to him without heed. She clutched at him convulsively, her legs weak and trembling. In a haze, she felt the silk panties being slid lower until they fell to the carpet, Max's hands now moving to her thighs, parting her legs further. She was unable to stand on her own strength anymore. She fell over him like a limp rag doll as he stroked her heated flesh with the tip of his tongue, then enclosed her deeper within his mouth. Small murmuring sounds broke from her throat as her whole being became fully absorbed in blinding streaks of pure feeling.

When he lifted her to the bed, Angel was still suspended on that thin edge, her body pulsating with a yearning for release. But Max had just begun his assault.

He threw off his clothes and fell on top of her. At first they came at each other with a clashing intensity that admitted far more urgency than tenderness. Their movements were like the pounding waves against the cliff, surges of desire crashing between them, their lovemaking almost combative. It was all hunger, all heat. Angel reveled in the feel of Max's hard muscular body pinning her beneath him, his strong fingers tangling in her hair, his mouth moving over hers as his tongue plunged deeply into her.

Wave after fierce wave drove them on, Max's gasps breathing time with hers as he slid into her, her moist warmth enclosing him, contracting against him. Angel felt as though she would drown in the waves, that they would surely consume her, until, at last, the final wave crashed through them both and Max fell panting on her, their shallow breaths rising and falling together, the rhythm changing but still synchronized.

He raised himself up on his elbow then and stared down at her beautiful face, made even more exquisite by the passion they had shared. He kissed her. It was long and sweet.

"You are an incredible lover, Max." She returned a light, teasing kiss. "Very inventive." She stroked his dampened hair, letting her fingers toy with a few strands.

"The second time is going to be even better. I get more creative with practice."

Angel cast him an incredulous look. "You can't mean it, Max. I'm spent, as they say in Victorian novels."

Max's blue eyes sparkled. "Just follow my lead, Angel."

"You've really got to do something about this need you have to always lead, Max. Haven't you ever heard of cooperation?"

He grinned. Then he rolled off her and lay flat on his back beside her. "You're right. I believe in cooperation as much as the next guy."

Angel leaned on one elbow. "Can I quote you on that?"

"Well . . . let me qualify the statement."

Angel grabbed hold of his hair, this time coiling her fingers more tightly around a few strands.

"Ouch." He pulled her down on top of him. "There's a time and a place for cooperation, Angel. This is the time and place. You lead this time around and I promise to follow. I'm yours for the taking, Angel." His voice was husky, mesmerizing.

"You are so damned self-assured, Max Gallagher."

His hand drifted lightly down to her firm, rounded buttocks. "Come on, Angel. Let's ease the pace this time. Let's take it real nice and slow." He trailed his fingers down the backs of her thighs.

"You're leading again." Her voice had a quiver in it.

He nuzzled her neck. "Sorry."

She laughed softly, her mouth pressed against his ear. "Like hell you are."

He let one hand slip between her thighs. "Like hell I am."

It began again, after a few moments neither of them paying attention to who was leading, who was following. They were two parts of a whole, two minds, two bodies, forming one perfect union. They were entwined in an artful tangle of limbs, each eager to welcome the questing search of the other, each finding mutual release.

They continued moving gently together even after they were both sated, neither wanting to break the bond that had grown so strong between them.

"I love you, Angel." His voice was tender and husky, his breath very warm.

She sighed deeply. "I love you, Max." A beguiling smile lit her face. "It doesn't even seem so scary anymore."

He cupped her chin, his gaze meeting hers. Those incredible blue-violet eyes held him spellbound. "Oh, Angel, the only thing that scares me now is losing you."

She eased off him and curled up beside him, letting her fingers idly trail his broad, tanned chest. She didn't speak for a long while, but Max knew the

225

wheels were churning in her head. He could also feel the muscles of his body begin to tighten.

"Max."

"Mmm?"

"I was just thinking . . ."

"Could have fooled me." His tone was wry and more than a touch surly.

Angel's eyes fixed on his profile as he focused on the ceiling.

"What if Michael Hargrove isn't dead?"

Max turned his head very slowly and gave her a rueful look. "Then he's very likely wishing he were."

A shiver ran down Angel's spine and she shut her eyes tightly for a moment to erase a most gruesome image.

Max gently touched her cheek. "I thought we were through arguing."

Angel gave a tiny shrug. "I'm not arguing."

Max cupped her chin, drawing her closer. He lightly kissed her lips. "Good."

"I was discussing."

He groaned deep in his throat.

"What's wrong with discussing the situation?" she persisted.

Max sat up abruptly in bed. "Look, Angel, if you want to have a discussion, let's have it with the police. Maybe we made a mistake about not spilling out the whole story. I mean starting with Lou, the tantalizing trio, right on to Michael Hargrove's accusations about his wife's nefarious dealings. Let's call them and—"

"Spend endless days being interrogated by that imperious Bimini police inspector?" she cut him off. "And then what? We've been over this a hundred times. We need something in the way of proof before we spill out our suspicions. We talk now and I wouldn't be surprised if, on top of everything else, we didn't get slammed with a lawsuit compliments of vivacious Vera for defaming her character. Unless, of course, we came up with something first that would counteract Vera's incredible good fortune to date."

Max grabbed for his trousers from the floor and pulled out a pack of cigarettes. He tapped one out and stuck it in his mouth. Angel knew he was tense even before he struck out with the first three flicks of his lighter. He tossed it noisily on the bedside table and fumbled in his pocket for a book of matches. Not finding any, he muttered a curse.

Angel swung out of bed and switched on the light. With absolutely no self-consciousness, she walked naked across the room to the bureau and picked up a book of matches.

Max couldn't keep from staring as she crossed back to him. She had the most beautiful body he'd ever seen. He was mesmerized by the vision.

She moved with sensuous grace. When she got to the bed, she sat down very close to Max. She lowered her head and struck a match. Then she raised her lids, letting her blue-violet eyes dance over his face. He still had the cigarette dangling seductively from his lips. Angel lifted the burning match.

"Let me light your fire," she murmured tauntingly in that deep, sexy vibrato that Max was utterly unable to resist.

He blew out the match, tossed the cigarette on the end table and pulled her roughly into his arms. Angel didn't offer the least resistance.

CHAPTER THIRTEEN

Angel awoke a little after seven the next morning. Max was still sound asleep beside her. He had one arm slung possessively across her hips and his head was half buried against her right shoulder, his warm breath wafting past her breasts. She smiled to herself as her nipples hardened. Then she twisted her head so that she could get a better view of Max. Her cool fingers lightly threaded through his tousled blond hair. He stirred, his face pressing closer to the side of her breast. She moved a few inches so that his lips lightly touched her skin. In his sleep, his hand tightened around her hip. He inhaled and then breathed out deeply, a contented moan escaping.

The feel of his mouth against her stirred delicious memories in Angel's mind of their lovemaking last night. Her whole body grew warm as she recalled how he'd slowly, deliberately teased and tasted her with his lips and tongue until she'd writhed with longing.

She wanted it to keep going on. Not just the passion that they fired in each other; the tenderness, the excitement, the sharing, even the vulnerability. She had never allowed herself to own up to her vulnerability before. During the lowpoints of her marriage to Lou and after she'd left him, she tried to convince herself that she just wasn't cut out for marriage. She told herself she wanted her freedom. She didn't want to make demands on anyone and she didn't want to have anyone make demands on her. She wanted to be a free agent.

Free to what?

She knew now that she'd been running away from life, trying to flee from her own vulnerability. In the process of toughening up, she'd closed herself off from so many feelings, pushed aside so many longings. Now she could see that she had really felt rootless. For so long she'd been searching in vain for something to grab on to, something to give her life meaning and direction. And that something turned out to be Max Gallagher.

She smiled, tiny tears of joy dotting the corners of her eyes. It was quite wondrous and extraordinary to be in love. Her feelings for Max were a world apart from what she'd felt for Lou. She'd been so young when she'd married Lou, so full of the idea of being in love without the vaguest notion of what it was really all about. Lou had been so cool, so tough and gritty, so sure of himself. If he'd ever felt the slightest hint of vulnerability, it was the best-kept secret in town. And she'd admired him for that, never realizing that his invulnerability was the very reason their marriage had failed almost as soon as it had begun. Lou couldn't really open up to her. He could never make a real commitment to their relationship. And that kept her from making the commitment. She could never risk showing Lou her weaknesses, her fears, her needs. So he played his game and she played hers. And in the end, they both came up losers.

It was different with Max. They'd allowed each other glimpses into their souls. Oh, Max didn't walk around wearing his vulnerability on his sleeve. He had quite a bit of Lou's cool, tough style. With one exception. Max had a tender, compassionate side that he was willing to share with her. He wasn't afraid to be afraid. He wasn't running from himself. At least, not anymore.

That was something else they shared in common. Until now, they'd both been on a treadmill leading nowhere. They'd both tried desperately to erect walls to protect themselves from getting hurt. They were going to keep on the straight and narrow, fighting their instincts, opting for a kind of independence that offered a certain amount of peace and a definite lack of joy.

So, here they were, two people who'd vowed they wouldn't take any more big risks. And now they were contemplating taking the biggest risk of all. Angel tipped her head down and lightly kissed his hair. Taking that risk required that Angel first give up playing detective. She stared down at the top of his head. She could feel the pulse flutter in her throat. *Okay, Max,* she said silently, *we'll play it your way. We'll go have another talk with that Bimini police inspector today, tell him the whole story, let the pros handle the investigation.*

Angel sighed. She couldn't deny a certain disappointment with her decision to give up the case. But Max was right. They were out of their league. Besides, she knew he meant his ultimatum, just as she knew it was his way of finding out how serious a commitment to him she was willing to make.

Max stirred. His mouth found its way to a tender, ripe nipple. Angel laughed softly.

"I thought you were fast asleep." Her voice quivered as his tongue pulled at the nipple.

He mumbled something that Angel couldn't make out. She laughed again. "Don't talk with your mouth full."

He sucked harder, laughing back, the sound low and exciting. Electric charges shot through Angel's veins. Max's hands began roaming her body, seeking out all those special places that drove her to distraction.

His mouth skimmed down her rib cage and moved to her stomach. Her belly made a most immodest gurgle. Then another. Max lifted his head up. He was grinning.

"Are you trying to tell me something? Are you hungry, Angel?" He slid sinuously up her body until they were nose to nose. His mouth descended and he kissed her deeply. Angel wriggled in pleasure, thrilling to the feel of his lean, hard body completely encompassing her.

"I'm famished," she whispered, kissing him again. "Delicious," she murmured, proceeding to kiss his nose, his cheeks, his eyelids. "You taste wonderful." She thrust her hips up against him. "Don't keep a starving woman in agony, Max."

He lifted himself very slightly and looked down at her. "I love you hot and hungry, Angel."

She wrapped her legs around him. "I couldn't be any other way for you." Her lips pressed against his shoulder. She took tiny, nibbling bites. "Oh, Max, I want you. I can't seem to stop wanting you. I've never felt so good. I love you, Max."

He fell hard on top of her, entering her with ease. Their rhythmic movements were as natural as their own breathing. She loved feeling him fill her, loved feeling him key his pace to hers, loved the way he concentrated all his energy on satiating her hungers as well as his own. She gave herself to him with total acceptance, total trust. Slowly, intently, he carried her to the edge and over, until she was floating free of space and time. And Max was sailing with her, drawing out the moment of ecstasy for them both.

"I love you, Angel," he murmured, moving onto his side, his arms still firmly around her. "I never bargained on this happening to me."

She felt a tiny thrill at the fact that he didn't add, "again." She wanted what they felt for each other to be a first for them both.

"What are you smiling at?" His voice was low and raspy. And incredibly sexy.

"I never bargained on it happening, either." She lightly stroked his back. "I was so worried about feeling trapped."

He gripped her more firmly. "And do you?"

She let her hands drift to his hair. She stretched

against him. "No, not trapped. Safe, comforted, loved. I feel happy, Max."

He caught the slight catch in her voice. "And frustrated."

She gave him a teasing smile. "Are you kidding, Gallagher?"

But his expression was subdued. "You know what I mean. The business with Michael Hargrove, and more important, Lou. You can't stand letting it go."

Angel's eyes searched his face. "I can't stand the thought of . . . losing you." She closed her eyes. "I want to give what we have every chance of working."

He kissed her tenderly. "All I'm trying to do, Angel, is keep the odds of it working in our favor." He drew her away from him. "You know I'm right about this. You know we have to let it go. We've gone as far as we can."

Angel didn't look convinced, but she nodded slowly. "I just wish—"

He pressed his hand to her lips, cutting her off. "Drop it, Angel. I want your vow. I mean it."

The stubborn glint in her eyes gave way to a sparkle. "Okay. I promise."

He eyed her warily. "I want one more promise. I want you to promise to tell the preacher you will love, honor and obey me, come hell or high water . . ."

"Whoa. Not so fast," Angel balked.

A flicker of panic flashed across Max's features. He hadn't actually planned on proposing. Not yet, anyway. He wanted to give himself some time, get

Angel firmly away from this mess, see how things developed. But now that he had gone and popped the question, albeit not too smoothly, he was terrified that she was going to turn him down.

He gripped her tightly. "Okay, so neither of us did that great the first time round. This is different, Angel. We've got something that matters, something that's worth holding on to. For keeps."

"Max . . ."

"I know. I know. I told you I didn't want to get hitched again."

"You said it more colorfully than that."

"Can we be serious, Angel?" he said helplessly.

A faint smile crossed her lips. "I wasn't objecting to the proposal, Max."

"You weren't?"

Her smile became more tantalizing. "I want to marry you, Max. I want to have a half-dozen little Maxes."

"Three. The other three will be Angels."

She laughed softly. "Want to bet?"

He laughed, too. "Okay, six little devils. So, what's the problem?"

"I'm willing to tell the preacher I'll love you and honor you, Max. But as for obeying you . . ."

Max let out a long sigh and let her go. "You aren't going to drop it, are you?"

"You didn't let me finish," She said firmly. "I'll go along with you when I think you're right."

"And do you think I'm right now?"

She lifted herself up on her elbow. "Yeah . . .

you're right. This time. But that doesn't mean I plan to let you lead every waltz we dance through life."

"We'd look pretty silly with you leading me in a waltz."

"You know what I mean, Max. This is the eighties. Women have a voice, in case you haven't noticed."

Max scowled. "I've heard your voice loud and clear, Angel." His expression softened. "Okay, listen. I grant you we've got to have give and take in our relationship. Maybe I have come down a little heavy. But that's only because I happen to be in love with you and I don't want anything to happen to you. Besides, you can't say I haven't given plenty in this little escapade of yours. Now it's your turn, Angel. You have to give a little, too."

Angel lifted her hand up to Max's. He took it and she squeezed his fingers. They looked at each other for a long time. Angel turned his hand over and pressed her lips against his palm, their eyes still locked. She slipped one finger after another between her lips. While Angel kept one hand occupied, his other hand drifted down over her flat stomach.

She shivered. "Do you have a particular preacher in mind?"

Pleasure flashed in Max's eyes and spread across his face. He grinned. "We'll track one down as soon as we get back to Boston." He shifted his weight, moving against her. Then he began doing things to her body that made her heart thud, her limbs tremble, her senses reel.

He fell back asleep afterward, a deliciously satisfied smile on his face. But Angel felt energized. And the rumblings in her stomach reminded her she was famished. She glanced over at the alarm clock on the bedside table. It was eight fifteen. She considered phoning Vera Hargrove and making some kind of excuse about not accepting her invitation. But she decided against it. After all, as Max had observed, there had been no RSVP at the end of Vera's note. It was an open invitation and it didn't require a response. So, Angel decided, she'd simply ignore it.

She climbed out of bed, careful not to disturb Max. The poor guy was exhausted. She gave a devilish little smile. She'd plumb worn the man out, she had. Her smile broadened and she stretched languorously as she stood up.

Max snored through her shower and was still asleep when she got dressed. But as she walked to the door, the snoring ceased.

"Where are you going?" His tone was very sleepy, but it didn't affect the sharp wariness.

"Go back to sleep, Max. I'm just going down to the dining room for some breakfast. I'll bring up something."

He rolled over. "You know what I want you to bring me."

Angel grinned. "I know, Max. I know."

"Don't be long."

"Don't worry. Wild horses couldn't keep me away long."

Wild horses couldn't, but a tidily concealed gun dug into her side most definitely could.

Not that she was accosted immediately. It just

237

turned out to be the natural progression of things. She was sitting in a nice, private table near the window of the Buccaneer Creek's dining room, contentedly munching a slightly overtoasted bagel, swallowing it down with a tall glass of refreshing orange juice and checking out the *What's New in Bimini* freebie flyer that she'd picked up at the front desk when a familiar face peered down at her.

Her brow creased. She swallowed bagel and juice in one painful gulp. "Mr. Metcalf. What are you doing here in Bimini?"

He drew up a seat beside her. When a waitress started over, he waved her away. He wasn't here for breakfast.

"Mrs. Hargrove asked me to come pick you up. I'm heading over to her place on Rum Cay as well. Some legal matters she needs to go over with me." He smiled pleasantly. "She's also been kind enough to invite me to be her houseguest for a few days. The launch is waiting at the dock." He glanced down at Angel's half-eaten bagel. "I'm sure Mrs. Hargrove's cook will have a gourmet spread waiting for us when we arrive. I wouldn't bother about finishing." His tone was subtly manipulative. Angel had no doubt he made an effective impact on juries.

She didn't respond immediately, still in the process of digesting that last bite. "How did you know I was staying at the Buccaneer?"

"A few phone calls. It was quite easy to find you. Shall we go?"

He began to rise as if the matter of her going with him to the launch was a fait accompli. When Angel made no move, he dropped back in his seat again. He sat very straight, his hands resting in his lap. He was the picture of composure, but Angel could feel his impatience and irritation despite his flash of white teeth which was Metcalf's excuse for a smile.

"I'm afraid you've wasted your time tracking me down, Mr. Metcalf. I'm not going to Vera's."

His expression was perplexed. "Then what are you doing in Bimini?"

Angel looked at him searchingly. "Just a brief holiday." Her blithe tone belied her gaze. "How long have you been here?"

"How long?" Metcalf squirmed uncomfortably. "Why I arrived this morning on the seven A.M. flight out of Miami. Why do you ask?"

Angel shrugged nonchalantly. "I just wondered."

Metcalf leaned closer to her. "Is there some reason in particular that you've decided to turn down Mrs. Hargrove's invitation?"

"Should I have a particular reason?"

Metcalf pressed his lips together tightly. Angel listened to him breathing. He had a slight wheeze. And he was flushed. He didn't look nearly as debonair and sophisticated as he had when he'd accompanied Vera Hargrove to Lou's funeral. Angel remembered the hint of tension he'd displayed later that day in his office when Max had questioned him about Lou's bank book. That large withdrawal Lou had made just before leaving for Key West was another unanswered question. One of many. She was drowning in them.

Angel sharply reminded herself that she was sup-

239

posed to be fighting her way out of the current, not succumbing to its grasp even more.

Beads of sweat inched across Metcalf's upper lip like a pale, sleezy mustache. He was much tenser now than he had been that day in his office. Maybe it was due to his being out of his element. That was one explanation. Angel could come up with several others.

He broke into her thoughts. "I think it would be to your advantage to accept Mrs. Hargrove's invitation, Ms. Welles. She . . . might have . . . some information . . . that could be of great interest to you." He stared down at the table. It seemed an uncharacteristic gesture. Angel would have thought a successful lawyer like Metcalf would have the art of making eye contact down pat.

"What kind of information?" Her voice was low and even.

He glanced up for a moment and then his eyes skidded quickly off her face. "That's something for Mrs. Hargrove to discuss with you."

Angel plucked a piece of dough from the bagel and popped it in her mouth. "Maybe she ought to save her discussions for the police."

"The police?" Metcalf's eyebrows shot up. The bead of sweat under his nose thickened. He was staring straight at her now.

Angel's smile was downright saccharine. "Tell Mrs. Hargrove that while I was unable to accept her invitation, the Bimini police will be out to pay her a visit. They have some questions to ask her. Tell her, Mr. Metcalf, that she'd do well to answer them.

And if I were you, I'd stick right by her side. Something tells me she's going to want a lawyer close by."

Metcalf stared at her blankly. "What are you talking about?"

"I'm talking about her husband for starters." The words came out before Angel gave them any thought. In hindsight, she realized the less she said to Metcalf the better. Unfortunately she'd started the inexorable ball rolling.

"What about Michael Hargrove?" Metcalf questioned sharply.

Angel didn't answer.

"You . . . haven't seen him? He isn't here? In Bimini?" His eyes watched her face closely. She didn't have to answer. He was a good enough lawyer not to have any trouble reading between her silent lines.

"What did he say?" He gripped her wrist. "What did he do?"

Angel stared at his hand. He released her, let his hand slip into his jacket pocket.

"It isn't what *he* did that you ought to be worrying about, Mr. Metcalf. Or, should I say what Vera Hargrove ought to be worrying about right now." She eyed him narrowly. "Maybe the two of you like to worry together." She tilted her head to the side. "Vera must have something, all right. First Michael, then Lou . . . now you. She does know how to lure her bait in. And something tells me she also knows how to throw a fish overboard that she no longer has any use for. I'd give that some thought if I were you, Mr. Metcalf. Some serious thought."

Metcalf pulled his chair a little closer to her. He was practically shoulder to shoulder, his face drifting toward her ear. For a moment Angel thought she was about to hear a confession. She was wrong.

He cleared his throat lightly. At the same moment Angel felt something being jabbed against the side of her rib cage. Her eyes shot to Metcalf's. He nodded slowly.

"I'm very sorry to have to resort to these measures, Ms. Welles. But it is imperative that I bring you to Mrs. Hargrove's villa." He leaned even closer.

Angel cast her gaze down to Metcalf's jacket pocket. She could make out the shape of the barrel of the gun. His hand shifted slightly as she continued staring in fascinated horror.

"You're crazy . . ." She spoke in a daze. She tried to clear her head. "You can't possibly consider shooting me here in this dining room. You'd never get away with it."

"The point is, Ms. Welles, you won't be around to find out if I get away with it or not. I don't think you want to call my bluff only to discover too late that you were wrong." He looked very solemn. "And there's the matter of your friend, Max Gallagher, to consider. I'm sure you wouldn't want anything to happen to him."

"If I liked you better, I'd be more worried about you than Max. Max is damn good at looking after himself. If you abduct me, Max will be breathing down your neck in no time. And he'll be at your throat just as fast."

Metcalf did not seem particularly distressed about her warning. He merely shrugged. "I can only focus on one problem at a time, Ms. Welles. I'll cope with Mr. Gallagher—if and when the time comes. Please, don't try my patience. I seem to have very little left to spare these days. Once you know the whole story, I'm sure . . ."

"And what is the whole story, Mr. Metcalf?"

He shrugged. "I'm not at liberty to go into that now." With his other hand he fished inside his pants pocket and pulled out a ten-dollar bill. "There," he said, plunking the money on the table, "that should cover your breakfast. Shall we go?"

This time Metcalf rose with assurance, knowing full well that Angel would follow his move. She did.

"You won't get away with this," she muttered as they crossed the dining room.

"Ah, you'd be surprised what one can get away with these days," he said philosophically.

Angel noticed that the perspiration had evaporated from Metcalf's upper lip. She was the one sweating now.

Max woke with a start. His mouth was dry as sawdust and he had a sinking sensation in the pit of his stomach as his eyes squinted toward the clock at the side of the bed. When he read the time, his eyes sprang wide open. It was eleven o'clock in the morning, enough time for Angel to have had a dozen breakfasts. He checked the suite first to make sure she wasn't there, then picked up the phone, dialing down to the dining hall.

The maître d' answered. Max gave him a very accurate description of Angel. The details weren't necessary. Angel was of the unforgettable variety. The maître d' remembered her well.

"I'm sorry, sir. Ms. Welles left nearly two hours ago."

"Did you happen to notice which direction she took?"

"I did happen to notice her walking outdoors while I was ushering some guests to a table on the terrace. Such a glorious morning . . ."

"Toward the harbor?" Max broke in harshly.

The maître d' didn't appreciate the grilling. He contemplated telling the obnoxious man on the phone that Ms. Welles wasn't alone on her walk. In fact, she seemed quite intimate with the gentleman walking along with her. But the maître d' was not a man who liked to make waves. They had a way of sweeping him along with the tide. So instead, he simply replied, "Yes, she was heading in the direction of the harbor. Will that be all?" The only response he received to the question was a sharp click of the phone.

Max lay back in bed. He couldn't believe it. He couldn't believe, after all they'd said, after all she'd promised, that she'd blithely left him sleeping the sleep of the innocent and gone off to Rum Cay.

He got dressed, telling himself he could be jumping to conclusions. Maybe she'd simply gone off for a stroll around Bimini, nothing more. He was going to feel damn foolish for his suspicions when she returned to the suite in a while.

Only he couldn't lie around waiting to find out if he had or hadn't jumped to conclusions. He took a quick shower, threw some clothes on, and headed down to the harbor to do some checking. He knew one thing for sure. If Angel had taken that launch to Rum Cay, his checking days were over. It was all over.

The docks were humming when he arrived. Everyone in Bimini seemed to be bent on taking an excursion around the harbor. Max threaded his way through the crowds, but it only took him a few minutes to track down the information he needed. Once again Angel's incredible, unforgettable looks made his task easy. A young man working in one of the kiosks that sold sightseeing boat ride tickets, had no trouble remembering the stunning young woman who'd boarded *The Royal Dane,* Vera Hargrove's sleek launch, earlier that morning.

Max stood at the dock blindly staring at the bay. She'd promised. Sure.

She'd told him she knew he was right. She told him this time he could do the leading and she'd be a good girl and follow. Of course.

The noise of laughter and good cheer around the harbor rang in his ears. He walked away, ending up at a rundown diner where some of the skippers ate. They were all out to sea now and the place was empty. Max ordered ham and eggs, over easy.

The ham was cold and the eggs were hard as rocks. He ate it all anyway, along with three cups of

245

stale, tepid coffee. As lousy a meal as it was, he felt a little more human after eating.

He tipped his chair back. His outrage tempered slightly by the food, his mood shifted to worry. How could she do it? How could she walk right into the fire like that?

How, indeed. She was a woman who took to fire like a duck to water. Or more aptly, like a lamb to slaughter. He felt an unbidden shiver.

He was through, he told himself. He'd had it. Oh, he was onto her game. She was counting on the fact that after he calmed down, he'd start worrying. And then he'd be hopping the first boat he could get out to Rum Cay.

Well, if she thought she could pull his strings, she had another think coming. If she wanted to risk her neck, that was her business. He'd made it absolutely clear to her that as far as he was concerned he was turning in his badge, or whatever it was amateur gumshoes turned in. He was through.

He wondered if he would get to believe that if he told it to himself often enough. Probably not.

The cold ham and hard eggs repeated on him. But that was the least of the reasons for the sour taste in his mouth. He plunked down a couple of bills, left the diner, and headed toward the harbor.

There was a boat leaving for Rum Cay at noon.

CHAPTER FOURTEEN

Rum Cay was far out in the Bahamas "Out Islands." A sandy little postage-stamp isle, the Rum Cay Club, and a couple of dozen estates were just about all there was to see. Skipping the palm trees and the aquamarine ocean. There was plenty of that, too.

Angel didn't exactly enjoy the trip over to Rum Cay. Not that John Metcalf wasn't a pleasant host. He went out of his way to be charming, even going so far as to let go of his gun and take his hand out of his jacket pocket once they were far enough from the harbor so that he didn't have to worry about her jumping ship and swimming back to shore.

There were no other passengers on the launch, a very nifty forty-foot schooner that was as trim and well groomed as the woman who owned it. If a boat, Angel mused, could be called trim and well groomed. The crew certainly were. Everyone from the captain right down to the lowliest lackey on board was decked out in crisp white uniforms that had a distinct designer flair. The captain was waiting as Angel was escorted, so to speak, onto the launch. He made a formal bow and welcomed her warmly. Maybe he didn't notice the not so subtle bulge in Metcalf's jacket pocket that was sticking into her ribs, or maybe he didn't care. Angel knew where she'd put her money.

"Please relax, Ms. Welles." Metcalf was half-reclining in a lounge chair on the deck. It was one of the expensive, well-padded varieties.

Angel elected to stay on her feet. She stood near the railing, looking out to sea. But her mind shifted from her own predicament to Max, who must have woken up by now and realized she was gone.

Gone, nothing. Deserted. Abandoned him. That's what he would believe. He was probably booking his reservations back to Boston at this very minute. Angel had a feeling when she got back home the apartment next door would be vacant. He'd move out. He'd be on the run again. This time, he'd go all out to stay away from anyone that even hinted of trouble.

Then again, maybe she wouldn't be getting home. Maybe Vera Hargrove had other plans for her. Angel shivered despite the tropical sunshine.

It seemed as clear as day now. Vera had obviously hoped to set Michael up, only he had gotten to tell his story first. Then he had mysteriously vanished. Next, Vera's lawyer had shown up for breakfast dressed to kill. Vera was obviously not about to take any more chances, which didn't warm Angel's heart.

She spun around to face John Metcalf. "The Bimini police will go out to the Hargrove estate today.

248

They might even be there already. They know about Michael Hargrove."

Metcalf's left brow lifted. "What do they know about Michael?"

"Don't play dumb, Metcalf. It doesn't become you."

"Look, Ms. Welles, we are as concerned about Michael Hargrove as the police are. The man is very dangerous."

"Then he's alive?"

Metcalf scowled. "What are you talking about?"

"It's really a very simple question, Mr. Metcalf. Is Michael Hargrove alive? As opposed to dead."

He wrinkled his nose. "Unfortunately, I'm quite certain he is. Alive and ready to destroy . . ."

"The woman who destroyed him?" Angel leveled her gaze at Metcalf. "He's been onto Vera's plan from the start. He even has proof. She's not going to get away with it." Angel took a deep breath. "She's not going to get away with murder."

Metcalf actually smiled. "I'm afraid you've got your facts confused, Ms. Welles. In time, you'll get them straight."

"And then what?" Angel snapped, a clear hint of bravado in her tone. It was totally manufactured. Angel was feeling about as brave as a very yellow chicken.

She didn't get an answer, but then she hadn't really expected one. Nor did she think she'd like the one he could give her if he chose to confide in her.

The launch pulled into Vera's private dock. A young man with brown eyes that matched his tawny skin was waiting for them in a custom designed oversized golf cart. It was a regular Jaguar of carts with plush pale gray leather seats, one up front for the driver and two in the back. Whoever had put it together had even gone so far as to paint it silver. The name, *Tranquility Reef,* was emblazoned in black lettering on the side. Angel assumed that was the name the Hargroves had given the villa. It must have been christened before Vera and Michael started having all their marital problems.

The young man handled the drive up to the estate well. And it was a tricky drive. Lots of curves and some real cliffhanger turns. Angel tried not to notice the precariousness of the ascent. Her situation was precarious enough as it was.

After a few minutes Tranquility Reef came into view. Several words popped into Angel's mind as she cast her gaze up to the hillside Hargrove estate nestled in the tropical gardens above the blue-green sea. Splendorous, opulent, resplendent. They all fit. The villa, done in the Mediterranean style, epitomized the grand tradition. As they drew closer she could see that there were actually several low-slung red-roof-tiled buildings connected by sunswept loggias and arcaded walkways.

The cart pulled around a circular drive of what appeared to be the main house. The swank entrance was feathered in palms and shrubbery. Not ostentatious though. It was very refined, very serene. So was the liveried butler who came out to greet them.

"Welcome, Ms. Welles. Mr. Metcalf." His tone was officious, but some of that might have been the

British accent. He took Metcalf's expensive leather carryall from the cart driver and preceded Angel and the lawyer into the house.

A cool breeze drifted through the circular entrance foyer. Angel and Metcalf were left waiting there while the manservant disappeared down the hall. From where she was standing, Angel got glimpses of some of the lavish rooms, all of which, because of the artful positioning of the villa, offered breathtaking views of the glorious sea as well as broad expanses of lush lawn.

Vera Hargrove made a grand entrance down a spectacular staircase. She was dressed in a bright red lounging outfit. The shirt was open, revealing a matching red bikini bra. With Vera's luxuriant red hair sweeping down loose around her shoulders, she looked like one long burning flame.

In contrast to her hair and the outfit, Vera's flawless skin was quite pale. She obviously avoided the fantastic island sunshine as much as possible. A regular hothouse flower, Angel thought. A pale, delicate orchid. Beautiful but very fragile. Angel had to remind herself that looks were deceiving.

Vera managed a bright smile, but Angel could see it took a lot of effort. And it disappeared real fast. If the mood of the house was tranquil and dazzling, Vera Hargrove was anything but. She appeared to be sprung as tight as a coiled wire.

Vera led them silently through the hall into an enormous living room, one whole wall of which was a huge open expanse showcasing the ocean and island panorama. The breeze was stronger in this room, the bright sun shaded by a generous overhang of roof. The furnishings were done in sparkling white against a blue marble floor.

"I'm so pleased you came," Vera said, sitting down on one of the sofas that Angel realized on closer inspection was upholstered in the softest white Italian leather she'd ever seen. Angel noticed that Vera tried to plaster the smile back on her face as she greeted her, but she couldn't quite manage it.

"I didn't have much choice," Angel said coolly, casting a narrow glance at John Metcalf who had joined Vera on the sofa.

Vera turned to the lawyer with a questioning gaze.

He shrugged. "Ms. Welles needed some encouragement."

"Oh, John," Vera said in a strained voice.

He put a hand on her shoulder. "She's seen Michael."

Vera's pale complexion turned paler. "I knew it. I knew he'd come down here." She clutched John's hand. "He means to do it, John. He means to kill me."

It was a bravura performance, Angel thought, but a wasted one. "I doubt Michael's in any condition to light a cigarette much less commit murder," Angel said ruefully. "But then you know his condition better than I do. So why don't we get to the point of this . . . command invitation?"

Vera frowned. "You're here because you're in danger. I'm doing this for Lou. He would have wanted me to do whatever I could to protect you."

She managed a faint smile. "He was very fond of you. I was always a little jealous."

"Jealousy wasn't what made you arrange to have him thrown overboard though, was it?" Angel knew she was doing it again, talking too much, asking too many pointed questions. But she couldn't seem to stop herself. Maybe if Max were here, he would have been able to get her to control herself. *Oh, Max*, she thought balefully, *I should have listened to you right from the start. We could have been back in Boston now finding that preacher. We almost made it.*

But "almost" wasn't good enough.

"You're right about Lou's death not being an accident, Ms. Welles. But I had nothing to do with it. I was in love with Lou." Tears glistened in Vera's green eyes. "Oh, I knew what Lou was like. I knew he wasn't the kind of man a woman could really tie down. But I was willing to settle for what he had to offer."

John Metcalf sat very quietly during Vera's dramatic little speech. His face was expressionless. Angel thought he ought to spruce up his performance if he and Vera were going to play out this scene for other audiences.

He felt Angel's eyes on him and met her gaze. His blank expression turned rueful. "If only you had dropped this whole affair, Ms. Welles, you wouldn't be in this predicament."

"But I didn't drop it," she snapped. "And I'm not the only one who knows the truth about what's been going on. Max Gallagher is probably at the Bimini police station right now." She stared harshly at Vera. "We both know you tried to set Michael up as the patsy in the embezzlement scheme you hatched up with the syndicate. When Lou wised up to the truth you had to get rid of him fast. Then, thanks to Rick Seidman's assistance, Michael got exonerated of those embezzlement charges. With him walking around free as a bird, not to mention being bent on bringing your nefarious crimes to light, you had to contend with him, too. We saw your handiwork back at Michael's cottage. So did the police. They know you attacked him. Or at least that you were behind it. I'm sure their guess is that you had him killed and dragged him off into the woods."

"What are you talking about? I didn't even know Michael was in Bimini," Vera said, a stunned expression on her pale face. "Oh, I expected him to show up. But, at least while I'm on Rum Cay he can't get at me as easily. That's his plan, you know. Another accident. Just like Lou's. So much less complicated than trying to frame me for his crimes. I wouldn't be surprised if he were thinking of making my death look like a suicide. I'm sure he'd compose a great note in which I confessed to embezzlement as well as Lou's murder. Ever since you began nosing around into Lou's death, I'm sure Michael's been up in arms. If you kept at it, the Key West police might decide to reopen the investigation. My written confession would take care of that possibility."

Vera ran her tongue across her dry lips. "But Michael knows that you are a very clever woman. He won't take the chance of letting you stick around after he's taken care of me. You might start asking embarrassing questions. You might begin checking them out. Just like Lou did. Michael means to silence you for good, Ms. Welles. You must understand that. You may be clever, but Michael is more than clever. He's quite ingenious. For years he was diverting money into his own pockets after convincing investors to buy into some of his grand schemes for the company, schemes that existed only in Michael's imagination. He might not have gotten away with it for so long if he hadn't joined forces with the syndicate professionals who make crooked deals look legitimate."

"Still Lou managed to pin Michael," Metcalf broke in. "But Lou felt compelled to track down Michael's syndicate backers. Michael was a clam on that subject, and his buddies in the mob rewarded him with the scheme to get him released from prison. Which they did. Lou went undercover as a rich investor with money to launder. He almost had a couple of syndicate organizers caught in his web."

Vera dabbed at her eyes with the tips of her fingers. "Only Michael got to him first."

Angel studied Vera and John thoughtfully. They were better rehearsed than she gave them credit for. In fact, she might almost have believed them, if she hadn't heard a very different tale from Michael Hargrove and then seen that ravaged bungalow and the blood-stained floor.

"I suppose that's the story you intend to give to the police when they come calling," Angel said.

Metcalf gave her a sneering glance then turned to Vera. "We're only wasting our breath. Apparently, Ms. Welles is not nearly as clever as we thought."

Angel was thinking of a good comeback line when the butler appeared at the entryway.

"Two policemen from Bimini are here," he announced solemnly.

"Take them into the sitting room," Metcalf said authoritatively.

Vera looked too troubled to say much of anything.

Before Angel had a chance to react, Metcalf's hand went back into his pocket. This time it only stayed there an instant before it reappeared, gun in hand. He pointed it at Angel, but addressed Vera.

"I'll take Ms. Welles out this way to the guest house. Then I'll come back and join you. Make small talk with the police until I arrive."

Angel glowered as Metcalf motioned her over to the exit with his gun. "Just when I was starting to think there might be something to your story, too," she muttered.

Metcalf gave her a skeptical look. "Something tells me, Ms. Welles, that's not what you'd say to the police. I'm afraid you've complicated matters quite enough as it is. You can make yourself at home for a time while Mrs. Hargrove and I try to straighten things out."

The guest cottage that sat just to the north of the main house was charmingly decorated and came well equipped; everything from fresh tropical fruits and a good French champagne in the fridge to body-guards at the front and rear of the cottage.

After Metcalf hurried off to buoy up Vera, Angel sat down on the edge of a white sofa. This one wasn't leather, but it was a good design. She leaned back after a few minutes and tried to make herself as comfortable as possible. She wasn't thinking of going anywhere, not with those two bruisers standing at their posts.

She checked her watch. It was eleven fifteen. She thought about Max, imagining what went through his mind when he realized she was gone. Her spirits did lift a little thinking that the Bimini police chief might have already contacted Max this morning before coming out to Vera's. As angry at her as he'd be, she knew Max would warn the police that she'd headed out here and could be in danger.

Could be? At least she hadn't lost her sense of humor.

Of course, Vera and Metcalf could simply deny she'd come to Rum Cay. Max, after all, didn't have actual proof of where she'd gone. Not unless he went down to the harbor and someone had remembered seeing her get on Vera's launch. Otherwise, it would be Max's word against Vera's. Angel had a feeling that the local police wouldn't want to offend one of their wealthy residents without plenty of cause. And they'd need a search warrant to go looking for her. Not to mention looking for poor Michael Hargrove. If he really was still alive. By the time the police had enough just cause to get a warrant issued, Angel had a sickening feeling that it would be too late for them to rescue Michael or her.

Vera and Metcalf did tell a good story though. They even supplied the answer to her unasked question about why Lou had withdrawn all that cash from his account. That much was probably true. It was always smart to put in as much truth as possible when you were fabricating a tale. The twist was that Michael Hargrove wasn't the one involved with the mob. If Vera was juggling the books, then she had to be the one with the mob connections. And Metcalf. Angel didn't want to forget him. He obviously was playing a lead role.

Angel guessed she'd been privy to the dress rehearsal. Now that they'd run through it with flying colors once, Vera and Metcalf were probably giving the performance of a lifetime to the police.

As the minutes ticked away, Angel's nerves started to get the best of her. She began pacing. She even opened the bottle of champagne, but one taste of the bubbly made her feel ill. It also brought back memories of the time she and Max had drank champagne and made love throughout the night. Her forehead creased in a pained frown.

"Oh, Max," she whispered, "don't desert me now." She dropped down weakly into the couch. The silence made her feel worse. Despair, helplessness, bleak awareness of her predicament washed over her. The worst part was, Max would never know that she had done everything in her power to keep her word to him. He'd never believe that she desperately loved him.

* * *

The excursion boat docked at the Rum Cay Club at noon. Max disembarked with a half-dozen other tourists, all of whom were heading to the club for lunch. He melted in with the group, worried that Vera Hargrove might have some goons stationed at the dock to keep an eye out for him.

Rum Cay Club was an exclusive spot, one of those members-only kind of places, but they let their standards slip a little in the off-season, allowing nonmember holiday goers to dine on the seaside terrace during the afternoon hours. At night, the club resorted to its members-only policy.

There was an air of sleek elegance about the place, but it was very understated. No doubt a lot of the tourists were disappointed not to find gold-leaf moldings, crystal chandeliers, silk wall coverings. There weren't even any cascading fountains.

Guests were greeted in a skylit solarium and then led out to tables, reservation only, on a trellis-roofed terrace. Ceiling fans helped move the sea breeze around. As for the casino, that remained members-only, day and night.

Without membership or even a reservation, Max wasn't going to get far. But he didn't have all that far to go. Just off to the left of the solarium were discreet signs to the restrooms. Max strolled in that direction, glimpsing back over his shoulder to see if anyone was following him.

No one was behind him, which greatly helped still his paranoia. There were a couple of men in the restroom. Once they left, Max opened the bathroom window, hoisted himself out, and cut across the club's gardens to the main road.

At the one combination gas station/general store on the tiny island, Max got directions to Tranquility Reef. It was less than a mile from the store.

Max kept off the main road as much as possible. Whenever a car came by, he ducked into the shrubs. It didn't happen very often. There couldn't have been more than a dozen cars on the island. Rum Cay would have sunk if there were many more.

Max was still feeling mad as hell, and he was still plenty worried. What made matters worse was that his worries were so nebulous. Was Angel really in any danger? Was Vera Hargrove really the villainess Michael Hargrove made her out to be? Okay, so someone had obviously gotten to Michael. Max had no proof who that somebody was, any more than he could prove that anything had actually happened to the man.

Something didn't sit right with Max. No matter how hard he tried putting the facts into focus the edges kept being blurry. What really had him thrown was Angel taking off like that. It didn't make sense. She might be stubborn, impulsive, even intrepid, but she wasn't a liar. She wasn't the type to feed him a line. If she was determined to go see Vera Hargrove, Max found it difficult to believe she wouldn't have just told him she was going to do it, come hell or high water.

He shook his head slowly. No, it didn't make any sense. Maybe, he sighed deeply, he just had her wrong. One thing he was certain about. She was definitely trouble. More trouble than even he'd guessed possible.

If Angel had figured he'd follow her here, she'd been right. If she figured he would forgive her . . . well, she was wrong there. Or, at least, that was something he was working hard to convince himself of. Just like he was determined to convince himself that it was over between them.

He found the Hargrove villa without any difficulty. The problem was getting in. Max was worried about what reception he'd get if he went strolling up to the main gate so he began circling the property, quite a task considering the estate had to cover a good ten acres or more. Half the property jutted out on a peninsula. The landbound half was protected by ten-foot-high walls. Max figured his best entry would be to swim in. He headed for the beach that bordered the property, chucked his shoes and shirt into the bushes, and rolled up his trousers to the knee, glad that he had his gun in his pocket.

The water was deliciously cool, but Max didn't find it particularly refreshing. His mind was on more serious matters. He cut effortlessly through the shimmering aqua sea. When he got close enough to Tranquility Reef to be spotted if anyone was watching, he dove under and made for a far corner of the sandy beach. He lay flat in shallow water with just his head breaking through the surface, for several minutes. When he was fairly certain there was no activity, he made his way to shore. Keeping out of sight as much as possible, he began cutting across the tropical foliage to the main house.

A couple of hundred yards from the villa Max came to an abrupt halt as he spotted a familiar figure cutting across the lawn to a smaller replica of the main house.

Max ducked behind a tree as he watched John Metcalf stop for a moment to have a word with a man sitting on a lounge chair outside the house. The man wandered off as Metcalf entered the cottage.

Max waited until he lost sight of the man who was strolling off. Then he dashed across the lawn to the house. As he got close to an open window he heard Angel's voice, but he still wasn't close enough to make out her words. When he got to the window, she'd stopped talking. He peered in cautiously.

A sharp frown etched his features as he saw Angel sitting on the couch sipping a glass of champagne while Metcalf poured one for himself. Max was livid. Here he'd been fighting off one gruesome possibility after another, and the whole time Angel was sitting pretty, drinking champagne and shooting the breeze with Lou Chapman's lawyer. The two of them looked real chummy. But then Angel never did waste much time in getting down to the preliminaries, Max thought spitefully.

He threw open the front door, the very picture of the irate lover. When Angel's lapis lazuli eyes shot up in shock, it merely confirmed his worst suspicions.

"I guess I made the trip for nothing," Max said coolly. "You seem to be doing just fine on your own."

"Max . . ." Angel went to leap up from the

couch, but Metcalf's hand gripped her shoulder. That left one hand free. Angel knew just where it was heading.

She shouted a warning to Max, but it was too late. Not only did Metcalf's hand pull his trusty gun from his pocket, but the goon minding the back of the house had come around to see what the commotion was all about. The bodyguard was the type to act first, ask questions later.

Max tried to dodge the attack, but his reflexes were slowed by his surprise at the sudden turn of events. The bruiser, on the other hand, was as fast as a cat. And as strong as an ox. He swung his fist with one short but well-placed jab on the side of Max's jaw. There was a lot of weight behind that punch. A good two hundred and fifty pounds. Max felt all of it. He went numb fast, tiny lights dancing before his unfocused eyes.

Max thought he heard Angel scream as another blow landed just below the first one. The lights stopped dancing. They were a steady white now. And then he went down and the lights switched off. There was just darkness. And a long, drawn-out scream that got trapped in the night.

CHAPTER FIFTEEN

Max slowly lifted his heavy lids and looked fuzzily at the most exquisite pair of blue-violet eyes he'd ever seen. His vision cleared a little more. The face that went with the eyes was equally exquisite.

"Are we in heaven, Angel?" He sat up, pressing his hands into what turned out to be very thick piled carpeting. His balance was woozy.

Angel's smile was beautiful, but rueful. "We're definitely not in heaven, Max."

He lifted his head a little. John Metcalf was standing just behind Angel. "Here, let me help you up," he said, coming forward and extending a hand. Metcalf looked apologetic, but Max wasn't in the mood to take any chances. He glanced back over his shoulder to see if the ox who'd plowed into him was around. He wasn't.

Metcalf's arm was still extended. "I'm sorry, Mr. Gallagher. Believe me, this whole business has gotten entirely out of hand." His arm dropped to his side heavily. "I'm afraid Arnold is very much like a protective pup where Mrs. Hargrove is concerned."

"If Arnold is a pup, I'd hate to meet the dog

who's his father," Max muttered, helping himself up with Angel's assistance. He wasn't too steady on his feet. Angel led him to the couch, then poured him a glass of champagne.

Max drank it down even though his jaw hurt to swallow. He rubbed it gingerly.

"I am sorry for Arnold's overzealous attack," Metcalf said soothingly.

"Overzealous?" Max lifted an eyebrow. That hurt, too.

"Vera will be very upset," Metcalf said, sinking into a chair, the gun he was still holding in one hand resting across his thigh. "If only Michael—"

"Hadn't wised up?" Angel snapped. Now that Max was here and reasonably intact some of her terror gave way to cold fury. "You aren't going to get away with this, Metcalf. You and Vera have been too sloppy, made too many mistakes."

While Angel raged, Max's attention was drawn fully to the gun in Metcalf's limp hand. Metcalf was sitting across from them, a low wood and wicker coffee table between them. Max's head was still too fuzzy to figure out everything that was going on. But his mind was clear enough to know one thing. He and Angel would be a hell of a lot better off if that gun was in his possession instead of Metcalf's. Especially as the gun he'd brought along had been lifted after he'd been knocked cold.

"The Bimini police are no fools," Angel went on. "They know that you had Michael beaten up at his cottage. The poor man must have been practically bleeding to death when you dragged him off."

Angel had Metcalf's undivided attention. Max leaned forward, as if to pour himself another drink. Instead, he took hold of the edge of the table and gripped it tightly. Metcalf looked over at him for an instant, apparently thinking Max was simply trying to regain his equilibrium. As soon as Metcalf's eyes shifted back to Angel, Max shoved the table forward with all his strength.

Metcalf let out a sharp cry as the table edge rammed into his shins. Then, before the attorney could piece together what was happening, Max leapt over the table and wrested the gun from Metcalf's hand.

That tricky maneuver had taken all the strength Max possessed and he slid back to the couch with a heavy sigh. But the gun had changed hands and Max managed to point it at the stunned attorney, who was rubbing his bruised shinbones.

Angel couldn't contain her relief. She flung her arms around Max's neck, careful, however, not to upset his aim. "Oh, darling, you're wonderful . . . incredible . . . so brave." She laughed softly. "And insane to take such a dangerous risk."

Max shot her a dry look. "I'm insane? I don't hold a candle to you, Angel. You really had me going there for a while. I was actually dumb enough to believe you really meant it when you said you'd give up the chase."

"I did mean it."

But Max wasn't listening. His eyes were focused on Metcalf, who sat wearily in his chair, looking as if all the air had been let out of him.

"Max, you've got to believe me," Angel said earnestly. "I wasn't lying to you. I didn't come here of my own free choice."

Max's gaze narrowed as he gave her a sidelong glance. "You didn't?" He didn't sound convinced.

It was Metcalf who responded. "She's telling you the truth, Mr. Gallagher. I . . . insisted . . . Ms. Welles come out to the island." His eyes dropped to the gun in Max's hand. "It was too dangerous for her to stay in Bimini."

There was a rustle of silk behind Max. He turned sharply. Vera Hargrove had taken a few steps into the cottage. Max waved the gun, motioning her to take a few more. "Well now, the gang's all here. Have a seat, Vera, and join the party." Max pointed his chin toward the chair next to Metcalf's. "You look like you ought to be sitting down . . . before you fall down."

Angel watched Vera move on shaky legs toward Metcalf. She wasn't sure the woman would make it. Metcalf rose and helped her with the last few steps. He eased Vera down to the seat, then pulled his own chair closer, clasping Vera's trembling hand tightly.

Vera Hargrove seemed oblivious to the gun in Max's hand or even to his presence. The frightened look on her face seemed to be related to some other fear. Her eyes were tense and restless. She stared at the attorney. "They'll never find him," she said grimly. "Not until it's . . . too late. I know Michael." Tears misted her eyes. "I know him too well."

"Is that why you had him half beaten to a pulp last night?" Max asked sharply.

"I did no such thing," Vera said, gathering a bit of strength as she acknowledged Max's presence with a fiery look. "Until Ms. Welles arrived here, I didn't know Michael was in Bimini. But I've been expecting him here. Maybe if I'd known he was in Bimini I would have sent someone to . . . to try to frighten him off. Not that it would have been successful. Michael is one of those men who don't experience fear. He's an egomaniac, absolutely confident in coming out the winner . . . in the end." Vera's voice held such conviction that for a minute Angel was thrown.

"If you didn't have him beaten up, who did?" Angel asked, a touch of hesitancy in her voice. "Who else would want to rough him up so brutally?"

Vera didn't answer Angel right away. She took a few long breaths to try to quell the shakes. It seemed to work a little. "At first I suppose I thought that Rick Seidman might have been the one to get to Michael," she said finally.

"Rick?" Angel shook her head. "You can make a better guess than that. Rick was working for your husband. And getting paid quite well."

"Rick was blackmailing Michael," Vera said emptily. "I don't have the proof if that's your next question. But it doesn't matter whether or not you believe me. Rick has had ties with the syndicate from the start. When Michael was sent to prison, Rick acted as the middle man. The syndicate supplied the trumped-up evidence that made it seem as though Michael had been set up and Rick pretended to uncover that information in his investigation. He supplied the phony evidence to the police and . . . Well, you know the rest. Michael was released from prison. I'm sure you're right when you say that Rick was paid well for his services. But I'm equally certain that Rick felt Michael owed him even more. And since Rick could easily prove that the evidence exonerating Michael had been rigged by the mob, I have no doubt Michael would pay a great deal for Rick's silence. When you told me about the attack at Michael's cottage, my immediate thought was that he'd refused to give Rick any more money. He might have decided Rick was bluffing. After all, if Rick went to the police, he'd be incriminated as well. So Rick might have decided to give Michael a harsh taste of what would happen to Michael if he stopped cooperating. But now I don't know. Michael is so clever. He'd kill Rick to keep him quiet before Rick could hurt him."

"It sounds like you changed your mind about Rick being the one who roughed up Michael," Max said. There was a note of curiosity in his tone that Angel found confusing. Surely he wasn't buying Vera's innocence.

"No one attacked Michael, Mr. Gallagher," Vera said in a low, low voice. "I just spoke to the police."

"Now, you really disappoint me, Vera," Angel said dryly. "We were at the cottage, remember? We saw . . ."

269

"What did you see, Ms. Welles?" Metcalf cut in sharply.

"Skipping the shambles the place itself was left in, we happened to see a pool of Michael's blood on the bathroom floor. How do you explain that if Michael wasn't attacked?"

"It's quite simple, Ms. Welles," Metcalf said calmly. "It was Michael's blood." He paused. "However, according to the police lab, it wasn't fresh blood."

Angel and Max shared a stunned glance. "I don't understand," Angel said.

"It is puzzling, isn't it, Ms. Welles?" Metcalf said pointedly. "The police are equally puzzled. And suspicious about the entire situation."

Metcalf leveled his gaze at Max. "We tried all along to explain the situation to Ms. Welles, but she didn't believe us. Not that I altogether blame her. I doubt I'd be very receptive to explanations with a gun pointed in my ribs either."

Max gripped Angel's hand tighter. It was first sinking in how much danger Angel had really been in. He had a driving urge to sweep her in his arms and ask her to forgive him for ever doubting her. However, this wasn't the time for asking forgiveness. It was the time for getting some straight answers from Vera Hargrove and John Metcalf.

"Well now, Metcalf, since the gun's in the other hand," he said with a clear touch of threat in his tone, "how about trying your explanation out on me."

Metcalf hesitated. He glanced over at Vera. "It's

really very simple, Mr. Gallagher. Mrs. Hargrove has explained most of it. Michael was guilty all along. He used Vera's business as a front for all sorts of dirty deals. When Vera got suspicious she hired Lou. Lou nailed him. Michael went to prison."

"I hoped that would be the end of it," Vera said glumly. "Only Lou was nervous some people in the syndicate might . . . bother me. He wouldn't let it go." She smiled wanly at Angel. "You know Lou."

Angel nodded. Yeah, she knew Lou, all right.

"I was afraid . . . so afraid. Not for myself. For Lou." Vera had to stop talking because she was trembling badly. Angel thought she might pass out. She went and got her a glass of water. Vera had trouble holding the glass. Angel had to help her get it to her lips.

Vera nodded gratefully to Angel after taking a few swallows. "I was desperately in love with Lou. He was . . . an extraordinary man."

"Why bring Angel here at gunpoint?" Max asked sharply. He was less sympathetic to Vera's distress than to the distress Angel had been under.

Metcalf frowned. "I convinced Vera that she should invite her here. I had promised Lou I would . . . look after Ms. Welles if she was in any serious danger. I believe she is, indeed, in danger."

"And I believe Chapman knew damn well she would be in danger, too," Max said acidly. "When he sent her those files he knew she'd start snooping around if anything happened to him. And once she started snooping, she'd be in very serious danger all right."

271

A faint smile was visible on Angel's lips. "I guess Lou knew me pretty well."

Max felt a sharp flash of jealousy. He didn't smile back.

"Please, Mr. Gallagher, you've got to believe us," Vera said, intruding abruptly into Max's thoughts. "Michael is very dangerous."

Max pulled his gaze from Angel. "Hargrove didn't look dangerous when we ran into him at the hotel supper club last night. He looked scared. Scared of you, Mrs. Hargrove. He had a similar tale to tell, only in his version you were cast as the bad guy."

Vera gave him an impatient look. "Don't be a fool, Mr. Gallagher. Michael would do anything to point the finger at me. If you don't think I'm telling you the truth about the blood . . . call the Bimini police. Ask them." She paused, and glanced at Angel. "I know you're wondering why we hid you from the policemen before. I couldn't let you speak to them before I had a chance to talk to you myself. As it turns out, the police proved very enlightening."

Angel hesitated and then stood up.

"Where are you going?" Max asked.

"To call the Bimini police. Maybe Vera's telling the truth. Which means we've been played for fools by Michael. He set us up."

She walked around the couch to the small table behind it and lifted the receiver.

"That won't be necessary," came a low masculine voice from the door.

CHAPTER SIXTEEN

Vera's breath caught as she saw her husband, Michael Hargrove, step into the cottage. He had a gun in his hand. It was pointed at Angel, first at her back and now at her chest, as she'd whirled around at the sound of his voice.

Max, too, had pivoted around. He was half off the couch, his gun pointed at Michael Hargrove.

"I'd drop the gun, Mr. Gallagher. Unless you want to chance seeing your girlfriend blown away. I guarantee any blood that's shed in this room will be very fresh." Michael smiled sadistically.

Angel was too numb to be scared. She stood frozen, the telephone receiver still clutched in her hand, a droning dial tone the only sound to be heard in the room other than the group's heavy breathing.

Max set the gun on the table behind the couch. It was close enough to Angel's reach for her to get her hands on it. Michael realized that too.

"I wouldn't advise it, Angel." Michael motioned her to step away from the table. She hesitated, but then took a few steps when she saw that Michael had shifted his aim toward Max.

Vera's gaze was drawn to the door. Michael laughed. "If you're waiting for Arnold and that new ape you hired to protect you, Vera honey, you can forget about them. They won't be coming to your rescue. I've already seen to that." He smoothed back his ruffled hair.

"You don't look any the worse for wear," Max said glibly. "Pretty clever scheme you worked up, Hargrove. I hate to admit it, but you did have us going in circles for a long time."

"I did think it was a clever plan," Hargrove gloated, a demonic glint in his eyes.

"But you figured wrong with the blood trick," Max observed in a cool voice. "The police are on to you, Mike. I'll give you odds they nab you for Lou's murder, after all."

"There was nothing in Lou's files to incriminate me."

"You were the one who broke into my apartment," Angel said sharply.

Michael continued to grin. "A real waste of time and effort. Once I saw that you were going around in circles, I realized Lou hadn't stuck anything into his files that could be . . . awkward for me."

Angel shook her head ruefully, feeling utterly deflated. She was so annoyed at her failure to figure out the real culprit, she forgot for a moment just how much trouble she, Max, Vera, and Metcalf were in right now.

Max reminded her abruptly with his next words. "What are you going to do now, Hargrove?"

A flicker of rage blended with his diabolic grin.

"You've all interfered with me for the last time. You've caused me nothing but problems since I got out of prison." His eyes seethed as he stared at Vera. "You should never have messed with my operations in the first place, you little fool. Well, at least now you know that I'll end up with the last laugh. It's going to be just about the last thing you ever do know."

"You're going to make Vera's death look like an accident, too?" Max smiled derisively. "Just how many accidents do you think you can get away with?"

"As many as I need to," Hargrove said heatedly. "I'm not going back to prison, Gallagher. Never again. I'm in nice and tight with the syndicate. They're going to be even more pleased with me when I get rid of all the loose ends. That means all of you in this room as well as that cipher, Seidman."

"With everyone else out of the picture, Hargrove, when the cops reopen the investigation into Chapman's death, which they plan to do, that doesn't leave anyone to blame but you, Mike old boy," Max pointed out.

"I'll worry about that, Max. As for Lou . . . I was very careful. Lou wasn't as smart as he thought he was. That meeting he was planning to have with the syndicate boys was a ruse. They set him up." Hargrove paused, smiling broadly. "And I finished him off. I am confident the Key West police will never be able to tie me to Lou's murder. And as for Vera . . . before my lovely wife departs for a better world, she's going to write a suicide note, admitting all her crimes, including the murder of her lover, Lou Chapman, and my kidnapping. Then, filled with remorse, she's going to take her own life by setting fire to this cottage. Of course, she will have locked herself in the bedroom, unaware that the three of you were resting here in the living room at the time, all a bit out of it from drinking too much champagne. The fire will get out of control before any of you can escape."

Hargrove laughed, but there was no humor in the sound. It had a quality of madness to it. "This will be the biggest tragedy to ever befall the sleepy island of Rum Cay. I'm sure it will make the headlines in their little weekly newspaper." He clapped his hands together. "And then, just imagine, when I reappear a few days from now and recount my horrible ordeal and harrowing escape. The natives will love reading about that, too. Everyone adores a story with a happy ending."

Hargrove stepped back closer to the door, his gun still pointed at the group. "I hope you don't mind, Vera. I borrowed some gasoline from the garage. But then, since our final divorce decree won't come through for another eight days, I suppose half the gasoline is mine. As well as half of everything else. And when you're gone, it will all be mine. Which is only just. And fortunate, since that cipher, Seidman, has just about drained me dry. But I'll take care of Seidman soon. That will tidy everything up."

"Yeah," Max said coolly. "Seidman talks to the cops and your mob friends are going to drop you like a hot potato, Mike old boy." He paused, giving a low laugh. "More likely, they'll drop you like a cement block."

Hargrove looked amused. "Don't worry, pal. Seidman won't be quick to talk to the cops. His own neck would be in a sling."

Hargrove was just about at the door, although his back was still to it. He leaned slightly, reaching his hand down outside for the gasoline can he'd brought up from the garage. Only it wasn't there.

A man stepped behind him, holding the metal can up for inspection . . . along with a Colt .45 he was holding out with his other hand.

"Is this what you're looking for, Michael?"

The new arrival produced utter chaos in the room. Vera Hargrove fainted dead away. Angel let out a low gasp, all the color draining from her face. Michael Hargrove fell back into the room, the gun falling from his hand, a grotesque mask of shock and terror on his face. In sharp contrast, John Metcalf was smiling broadly, a clear look of relief written across his features.

Max merely stared at the man as he stepped into the room and punched the shaken Michael Hargrove square in the jaw. Michael went down like a log. Max knew just how he'd feel when he came to.

"That's one I owe you," the man behind the punch said in a low, gruff voice to the slumped figure.

Metcalf was wiping his brow with a laundered linen hanky. "You had me scared for a while there, Lou. You certainly made one hell of an entrance,"

277

he said, the smile fainter now as he attended to the prone Vera Hargrove, who was still in a dead faint.

"Lou Chapman, I presume." Max said the line as if he were in a parody of a Sherlock Holmes movie. His gaze shifted to Angel for confirmation.

Angel didn't hear Max. She was staring with dazed eyes at her ex-husband. "You're supposed to be dead."

Lou grinned. "Don't sound disappointed, Angel."

"Damn you, Lou," she said hotly. "What kind of a stunt was that to pull?" She didn't give him a chance to answer. "You faked your death to trap Hargrove, didn't you? I should have known. Lou Chapman . . . the man who never says . . . die."

"Take it easy, Angel," Lou said soothingly. "It was the only way I could flush Hargrove out. Anyway, he damn near did kill me. Guess I just have a hard head."

"You can say that again," Angel snapped. "To think, I actually shed a few tears for you at your funeral." She gave him a bemused look. "Whose funeral was it, anyway?"

Lou's smile turned sheepish. "While I was keeping a low profile and letting my head mend from the beating Michael gave it before he tossed me overboard, I read in the Key West paper that an unidentified body had washed up on shore. Some poor guy who nobody knew. I did some digging, found out that the guy was a drifter who was staying at one of the local dockside hotels. I was quicker than the police in tracking the info down. When they finally did get around to tracking down the drifter's hotel room, they found my wallet and a few of my personal belongings there. They also found a note with my attorney's address on it and sent for John to identify my body." He grinned at Metcalf, then walked over to Angel.

"I'm sorry, babe," Lou said softly, brushing his hand across Angel's cheek. "I didn't intend to drag you into this at first. When I sent you those files I had every intention of retrieving them when I got back from the Keys. I just didn't want them left around while I was gone. A few people seemed interested in getting their hands on them. I wasn't really sure who they all were. There'd been a few breaks into my office."

"I don't think there'll be any more," Angel said with a slow grin that she shared with Max. Max wasn't in the mood for sharing smiles. More to the point . . . he wasn't in the mood for sharing Angel. Lou Chapman's hand had drifted from his ex-wife's cheek to her shoulder. What was more upsetting to Max, Angel's hand had drifted to Lou's chest. They looked to be having a very happy reunion.

"Once I let Hargrove think he'd killed me, I figured you might get suspicious and start asking questions."

"And you figured that could work to your advantage," Angel said with a wry grin.

"You sure made Hargrove nervous. I knew he'd zero in on Vera at some point. I planned to be there when he did, of course. You sped up the action.

Which I greatly appreciate." He walked over to Vera who was slowly coming to. He took her hand.

"That was crummy not to tell Vera the truth. Do you have any idea what you've put that poor woman through?" Angel scolded.

"I needed Vera to be convincing or Mike would have seen right through her. The only one who knew the truth was my trusty attorney."

Angel nodded sagely. "So that's why you acted so skittish the day we went to your office after the funeral?"

John Metcalf was still wiping his brow. "Yes. Believe me, I had my hands full keeping my eye out for you, Ms. Welles, and Vera." He gave Lou a rueful stare. "This is the last time I get involved in one of your harebrained schemes."

Lou grinned. "It worked, didn't it? I bet Michael here will be more in the mood to name names now. And so will my old pal, Rick, who the police should be paying a visit to right about now," he added, glancing at his watch. "I do believe that wraps this case up very tidily, as Hargrove would say. No more loose ends."

"What about Ross Allen? He and Janine still have a few loose ends hanging. Like that warrant dangling over Ross's head," Angel said, arching a lovely brow.

Lou grinned. "Don't worry your pretty head about Ross, Angel. Now that I've returned to the land of the living, I'm back in business again. I'll look after my client." He gave her a jaunty wink.

By the time the Bimini police arrived on the scene

a few minutes later, thanks to a call Lou had put into them earlier, Vera Hargrove was weeping with joy, her arms flung around Lou. Michael Hargrove was weeping, too, but for less gleeful reasons. Max was still stewing. He didn't much care for the way Lou kept shooting Angel these little intimate smiles, or the way Angel smiled back.

Lou handed over a tape from the miniature recorder he'd kept running in his breast pocket during Michael Hargrove's confession. Although it might not be admissible evidence in a court of law, Lou was sure it would start the ball rolling. He could usually tell a man's cracking point, and he was confident Hargrove had reached it. The Michael Hargrove the police dragged off was a defeated man.

The Bimini police inspector and two of his staff stayed behind to gather statements from the group, each of them escorted off into different rooms in the main house to give their accounts. Angel's statement was long and complex. By the time she got through, Max was gone. Angel glanced over at the inspector as he walked into the living room. He saw the wan look in her eyes and gave her a sympathetic smile. "Your friend asked permission to leave. He seemed very anxious to return to the States. There was no reason for me to detain him any further."

Angel nodded glumly. Lou came up behind her and put his hand lightly on her shoulder. "The boyfriend took off."

Angel compressed her lips. "Like a bat out of hell. I can't really blame Max. I caused him nothing but trouble from start to finish." The word "finish"

had a painfully hollow sound to it. "I guess he decided . . . he got more than he ever bargained
for."

"Now what?" Lou asked softly.

Angel stared bleakly into space. "That's a good
question."

Max returned to his room from the Truro beach on
Cape Cod around six P.M. He'd been back from
Rum Cay for three days, having stopped in Boston
only to pack a suitcase. He didn't want to be home
when Angel came back. He wasn't ready for that
encounter yet. Maybe he never would be.

Max was working real hard at convincing himself
he was smart to have gotten out clean. It was the
best way. He kept reminding himself he'd planned
to end the relationship with Angel even before Lou
Chapman "rose from the dead" to reclaim his ex-
wife. Angel was more trouble than he could handle.

He poured himself a drink, but after one swallow
he set down the glass. It only made him feel worse.
It only made him think about Angel more. It only
made the missing harder. And the longing more intense.

He walked into the bathroom, stripped quickly
out of his bathing trunks and stepped into the
shower.

The hot spray stung his skin. That old tune about
devils and angels kept running through his head. He
couldn't remember ever feeling more rotten.

His back was to the shower curtain when it
opened. He whirled around in shock. The shock was

even greater when he saw Angel standing there. Standing there in all her naked glory.

Max's mouth fell open.

Angel held up a small Swiss Army knife. "Even a kid of five could have pried open that lock on your motel door, Gallagher. If you're trying to protect yourself, you're doing a lousy job of it." She stepped into the shower.

Her hands moved slowly up Max's broad chest. She looked into his eyes. Drops of water darkened his lashes. She thought he'd never looked more compelling. "Are you trying to protect yourself from me, Max?"

He smiled, faintly at first, and then wider as she nuzzled up against him. He reached behind her and turned off the shower faucet.

"How'd you find me?" he asked as she let her fingers drift up to his wet hair. She brushed some strands from his face.

"Lou helped me track you down. I told you he was a great detective."

Max's muscles tightened. "You told me a lot of things about Lou. And how you felt about him. You looked mighty happy to see him back at Rum Cay."

Angel tilted her head and gave Max a rueful smile. "Of course I was happy. I was happy for Vera, too. She's been through hell and back. I haven't stopped giving Lou a piece of my mind for doing that to the poor woman. He should have trusted her." She placed her hands on the sides of Max's face and felt the rough stubble of his three-day-old growth of beard. He looked incredibly rugged, incredibly sexy. "You should have trusted me, Max. What kind of relationship do we have if we can't trust each other?" Her blue-violet eyes devoured him and then she pulled his head down to hers, claiming his mouth. She felt an intense thrill as Max responded fully to her seduction. When she tilted her head back, she asked, "Is that why you ran out on me, Max? Because you were jealous of Lou?" She grinned. "I thought you'd finally gotten fed up with all the trouble I'd caused you and just wanted me out of your hair."

"I kept trying to tell myself that was why. But, the truth is, I was scared. Scared you and Lou might want to rekindle an old flame."

Angel wrapped her arms around Max. It felt so good to lean into his firm, familiar body. She felt utterly content, knowing this was exactly where she belonged . . . where she meant to stay. "There never was a flame, Max. The most it ever was was a brief spark. There's nothing to rekindle. Maybe it will be different for Vera. She really is in love with Lou. And even though he's fighting it mightily, I think Lou is in love with her." Angel's lips curved in an enthralling smile that made her eyes shimmer like rare jewels. "And I happen to be in love with you, Max. I've got this flame inside me . . . one of those eternal flames. Nothing can ever put it out. I've been on fire from the day I dumped those boxes into your arms in the elevator. You make me so hot, Max. Hot and hungry."

Max pulled her tightly to him. "I love you hot and hungry. I love you, Angel."

She gave him a deliciously wanton smile. "I was hoping you'd say that."

He kissed her greedily.

When she got her breath back, she asked huskily, "Do you still want to find that preacher?"

His hands moved over the slant of her shoulders to the curve of her back. "First thing in the morning, Angelface." He brought his lips very close to her ear. "Meanwhile, I'll have to keep you good and busy so that you stay out of trouble."

Angel's heart filled with joy as Max lifted her in his strong arms. "Mmm. That sounds like a very good idea."

Max smiled lovingly at her. "I was hoping you'd say that."

Jennifer Heath Trilogy

If you enjoy Alison Tyler romances, you'll fall in love with her romantic adventure novels, the Jennifer Heath trilogy. Starting with CHASE THE WIND her daring new heroine, Jennifer Heath teams up with CIA Agent Alex Perry in a series of adventures starting from Rome in CHASE THE WIND to France in CHASE THE STORM (October) to the Orient in CHASE THE SUN (November).

☐ CHASE THE WIND   11006-8 $2.95

**Watch for CHASE THE STORM in October and
CHASE THE SUN in November**

 At your local bookstore or use this handy coupon for ordering:

**DELL READERS SERVICE, DEPT. DAT
P.O. Box 5057, Des Plaines, IL 60017-5057**

Please send me the above title(s). I am enclosing $_____ (Please add $1.50 per order to cover shipping and handling.) Send check or money order—no cash or C.O.D.s please.

Ms./Mrs./Mr._____

Address_____

City/State_____ Zip_____

DAT-9/87

Prices and availability subject to change without notice. Please allow four to six weeks for delivery. This offer expires 3/88.